D1602327

# The Girls from Hush Cabin

# The Girls from Hush Cabin

## MARIE HOY-KENNY

BLACK
STONE
PUBLISHING

Printed in the United States of America

First edition: 2023
ISBN 979-8-200-87775-1
Young Adult Fiction / Mysteries & Detective Stories

Version 2

Blackstone Publishing
31 Mistletoe Rd.
Ashland, OR 97520

www.BlackstonePublishing.com

*For my mum, Dianne, and dad, James.*

# 1
# Zoe

As far as fake IDs go, mine couldn't look much *less* like me.

But here I am, swiveling around on a sticky imitation-leather barstool, and there Britney is, outside on the front step in the snow, waving her hands around at the bouncer, who's crossing his arms and shaking his head. Yeah, there's no way she's getting in. I can't believe he bought my lie about having some work done.

Everyone knows Maverick Inn's bouncers are usually the easiest to fool in Birchbrook, which is why when my slightly older internet date suggested meeting me for the first time in person here, I figured the little lie about my age wouldn't be a problem. Plus, Britney and I were dying to try out the IDs we bought. The plan was that she'd inconspicuously sit at a nearby table and rescue me if I gave her the secret signal: two tugs on my hoop earring.

But I guess I'm on my own now.

I turn away from the window to face the bar, decorated with a string of mangled gold tinsel that doesn't exactly scream *Merry Christmas*. More impressive is the enormous line of bottles, the longest I've seen since Frank Dalton's homecoming after-party. A bartender with a shaved head and long goatee walks up to me and raises his eyebrows like he knows I literally *just* turned eighteen but is too jaded to care enough to do something about it. "What would you like?"

I used to stick to beer after, let's say, some "bad experiences" with liquor, but I've been expanding my horizons lately. "A Tom Collins, please." It's my dad's girlfriend Jill's favorite drink, and although she's not the nicest person in the world, she seems to know her alcohol.

My phone buzzes and I tug it out of the back pocket of my jeans. A text from Britney:

Mine didn't work. You coming?

No. Staying.

It's 8:50, and I've got ten minutes until Rick arrives. As I put my phone down on the bar, my hand trembles slightly. This had better go well. The last three guys I met on the internet were nothing like their online personas and it was more than a little disappointing. At the rate I'm going, I may make it all the way through high school without falling in love, or even *in like*, once.

Goatee Man sets a tall clear drink with two lime wedges in front of me and heads back to the other end of the bar. I grab the straw and take a deep breath. Liquid courage coming my way. I suck back a huge gulp, shudder at the bitter taste, and struggle to get my neutral expression back. The biggest underage giveaway is acting like you can't hack your booze. This is like a mix between lemonade and nail polish remover. I can't believe Jill drinks these for fun.

A tall man who smells like he sprayed himself with an entire bottle of Chanel Allure climbs on the barstool beside me. He opens a newspaper to the crossword puzzle page and taps a pencil against his chin. "Hey, what's a meat you eat for breakfast?"

I shrug. "I don't know? Bacon?" Is this some weird way of picking up girls that I haven't heard of before?

"Whoa." He writes it in the squares in block letters, looks up to survey me from head to toe, and gives me a creepy wink that reminds me of my dad's super inappropriate work friends. "Gorgeous and smart. What's a girl like you doing alone in a place like this?"

"Meeting my date." I shudder and roll my eyes, spinning my stool around to face a little Christmas tree decorated with beer cans.

"He's not here yet," the guy says, but I don't bother turning around or answering. He sighs loudly, gets up, and heads over to a curly-haired woman in a velvet dress and knee-high boots. Good luck, buddy.

I check the time. 8:55. Online, Rick and I talk about where we'd go if we had the money to travel anywhere, which dead celebrity we'd like to have dinner with, why college is an overly expensive waste of time. What if we have nothing to talk about in person? I take a small sip of nail polish remover and bite my lip.

"Mic check, check," the karaoke MC says into the

microphone, and the next thing I know, I'm listening to Taylor Swift's "Love Story" sung by someone who sounds as much like Taylor Swift as I would if I had the guts to get up there. Which is nothing like her at all.

I grab my compact from my purse and check my reflection. The shine serum I put on my chin-length black hair seems to have worked, and for once, I really nailed the cat eyeliner trick. Rick says he likes my look, that I remind him of Uma Thurman in some old movie. I reapply my pineapple-scented lip gloss. Why didn't I order a drink that tastes like this? 9:00. I glance over at the people waiting outside the front door. No sign of a muscular twenty-two-year-old with a perfectly groomed chin strap.

A few minutes later, my phone buzzes again, and I check my screen.

> I'm coming in now. Where are you sitting?

I glance at the door. A guy who's easily thirty-five with longish hair, a tight white shirt, and faded blue jeans steps inside. *That's* Rick? My heart plummets into my Converse high-tops. It's painfully obvious that his profile picture was from at least ten years ago. His forehead furrows and his eyes dart around the room, but he doesn't spot me. He types something on his phone, and mine buzzes.

> Where are you?

So much for meeting the love of my life. There's no way I want to spend the evening with someone who's old enough to be my dad. Even if we both picked Australia as our most desired vacation spot. I text back:

Sorry, something big came up.

Rick stares at his screen, and his face gets stop-sign red. He shakes his head and storms out of the bar.

Bullet dodged, I guess. Which really sucks because none of the guys at my high school talk about the stuff Rick and I talked about. All they care about is parties, getting into college, and cars. Yawn. I'm due for some attention, considering my dad only gives me between 5 to 10 percent of his. I want to be someone's number one. I text Britney:

Total bust. Pick me up?

Be there in ten.

I wave over the bartender and pay my tab. Then I hold my breath and take another sip of my drink. Might as well get my money's worth, I guess.

A man with gray hair and a Buffalo Bills jersey paces back and forth across the stage singing a Queen song. It's one my dad listens to on repeat. Maybe I should tell him to come here sometime, only without Jill, because she'd call this place a dive.

The newspaper that Crossword Guy left behind is still on the bar. I slide it toward me and spot the first clue on the crossword. Greek cheese.

Obviously feta. I feel around in my purse for a pen to write it in but nada. Why the hell am I doing crosswords anyway?

This is nothing like the hot date night I was expecting, that's for sure.

I flip the page, and something catches my eye. It's a black-and-white photo of a beautiful smiling girl with long wavy hair, and my heart jumps. I know her. I glance above to see the name. *Violet Williams. Rest in Peace.* I suck in a sharp breath, and a cold feeling courses through me, chilling me to the bone. Violet Williams, my favorite camp counselor and childhood role model, is dead. I scour through the rest of the words, trying to make sense of them, but they blur together. The off-key karaoke and loud conversations blend into a garble as if I'm underwater. I blink quickly, whisper, "Keep it together, Zoe."

*Violet died suddenly, leaving behind her mother, Tina, and grandparents, Albert and Claire. She is predeceased by her father, Benjamin. Violet was studying law and lived life to the fullest. She will be greatly missed.*

I sit, frozen, my fist pressed up against my mouth.

Scenes from my camp days roll through my mind like a movie. Violet's the main character, always the star we orbited. We had so much fun.

Until things got dark, and the regrets got real.

Can this really be true? Could she really be dead? What could have happened?

I grab my phone, scroll through my contacts, and click on the name of a person I haven't spoken to in four years. I need to tell someone about this. Someone who will care as much as I do.

# 2
# Calista

SUNDAY, DECEMBER 26

It's 9:12.

My phone's ringing.

Way to ruin my concentration.

I told Javier that I'd be busy working on my cover letter for Mr. Molina tonight. The number on the screen isn't one I recognize, and my finger hovers over the Reject icon.

But what if it's Javier, calling from his brother's phone?

It's got to be something important because he knows I hate being interrupted when I'm in the zone, even by my boyfriend. I press Answer and lean my head back against my plush office chair.

This had better be dire.

Seriously.

"Hello?"

"Callie? Is that you?" a vaguely familiar female voice responds. I feel like I should know who this is, but it's not coming to me.

"It's Calista," I correct. No one calls me Callie anymore. "Who is this, please?"

"Zoe. Remember? From camp?"

I blink. Zoe? Why would someone I haven't talked to since middle school be calling me out of the blue so late at night? "Of course. Sorry, I didn't expect to hear from you. How have you been?"

Zoe clears her throat. There's a long pause on the line, and I can make out someone singing, badly, in the background. What the heck is this about? "Good," she finally says. "I'm good. It's just that . . . remember Violet?"

"Yes. Why?" Of course I remember Violet. She's unforgettable. Her pep talks made me realize it was never too early to start accomplishing things that would make me stand out on college applications.

She's also extremely good at covering for people.

Zoe clears her throat again. I hear loud applause in the background. Wow, where is she? A bad concert? "I . . ." She exhales loudly. "I just read her obituary. Callie, she's gone."

My body stiffens, and I grip the phone tightly against my ear. It's so loud on her end, and maybe I heard her wrong. She can't possibly mean what I think she means. There's no way. "Gone as in dead?"

Zoe lets out a long breath. "Yes."

I'm suddenly light-headed, and my hand flies to my mouth. "Did . . . did it say how she died?"

"No. It said suddenly. You don't think she killed herself, do you?" Zoe asks.

"I highly doubt it." My voice shakes and I exhale slowly to

calm my jittery nerves. "She was always so bubbly and happy and confident. Plus, she had big dreams for herself. I can't see her doing something like that." Violet is . . . or rather *was* the definition of confidence. She'd walk into a room, and everyone would just stop what they were doing and look at her, hanging off every word she said.

"Yeah, you're probably right," Zoe says. "Do you think we should go to the funeral?"

Wow, a funeral. This is becoming more real by the second.

I fumble through my desk drawer and pull out a pen and paper. "Of course we should. What are the details?"

"I'll text you a picture of the obituary," Zoe says. "Hey, I just thought of something. Are you still living in Shawdale?"

"Yes," I answer. I want to add that I'll be out of here as soon as I get into NYU, but I remember her family didn't have much money to spare, so I hold back.

"You could come by tomorrow for dinner and sleep over here since the funeral starts early Tuesday morning and it's close to where I'm at. The house will be empty except for me anyway. My dad and his girlfriend are going on a trip."

"That could work. The only plans I have for the rest of the break is my family's Nochevieja party on the thirty-first. I'm sure I could spend a day or two with you," I say in the calmest, most composed voice I can muster, the words sounding strange to my ears. My charm bracelet slides down my wrist and clinks against my desk. Is this actually happening?

We're arranging our plans for *Violet's funeral*.

She made promises to me. What happens now?

A tingling feeling runs up and down my spine, and suddenly I just want to end the call so I can process this. "Thanks for calling. Can we go over the details tomorrow?" I can make out someone screeching a Madonna song in the background. If I were in better spirits, I'd definitely be asking questions.

"Wait," Zoe cries. "We should probably tell everyone else."

"How about you let Holly know and I'll contact Denise and then we'll talk again tomorrow morning?" I write Denise's name down on my notepad and underline it twice.

"Okay," Zoe says softly. "Well, good night."

I end the call and stare at my screen, shaking my head.

I glance up at my bulletin board, and a pang of sadness hits me as I study a photo of the four of us—Zoe, Holly, Denise, and me—holding paddles in the summer sunshine, which starkly contrasts with the snow falling heavily outside my bedroom window now. To our left, beside a red canoe, stands Violet, her bright smile taking over her entire face.

How could someone so amazing, so young, be dead?

The door creaks as my twin brother, David, opens it and peeks his head in. "Who were you on the phone with? It didn't sound like you were talking to Javier."

"Were you listening outside of my door?"

"Nah. I have more of a life than that. Your voice is just so loud and these walls are thin." David taps my gray-striped wallpaper. "See, I practically made a hole just by touching it." He brushes his mop of brown curls out of his eyes.

The absolute last thing I want to do right now is shoot the breeze with my brother. "Can I help you with something?"

"I'm heading over to Eddie's. You sure you don't want to come?"

I sigh. David just doesn't quit sometimes. "I told you no already and I haven't changed my mind."

David shakes his head. "Would it kill you to hang out with some friends once in a while?"

"I don't need friends. I need to get this letter done."

David steps closer to me. "Wait. Are you sad or something?" He squints at me with concern in his eyes. "*¿Estás bien?*" he asks softly.

David only talks to me in Spanish when he's worried or upset, which isn't very often; he's usually upbeat and clowning around, without a care in the world. I pat his arm lightly. "I'm fine. Honestly. I just really need to focus." I thought I had a total poker face, but then again, we do have twin intuition.

"Okay, if you're sure. See you later." David shoots me a suspicious look but steps out of my room, shutting the door behind him.

Back to work.

The cover letter on my computer screen stares back at me, and I'm drawing a blank. Dad invited his lawyer, Mr. Molina, to our Nochevieja party and told me that it'll be my big chance to land the internship I've always wanted—the firm has one spot available. I only have a few days to write the perfect letter to convince Mr. Molina that he must choose me. I completely had it. I knew what I was going to write. The ideas were percolating in my head all day long. Earlier today, I could picture my engraved nameplate on one of the doors in Molina & Herrera LLP's downtown office, but now the only thing I'm picturing is Violet's wide blue eyes in the canoe photo.

Instead of my chance at success, all that's in my head is Violet.

Violet showing me what tackle to use to catch the biggest fish.

Violet giving me tips about how to win at card games like Blackjack and Snap.

Violet, by the campfire, showing me dance moves to use in the lip-synching contest.

Violet was the one who helped me after I made The Mistake, and if it wasn't for her, who knows what would have happened?

All I *do* know is that it wouldn't have been good.

She told me she'd bring my secret to the grave. I didn't think she'd be heading there this soon.

# 3
# Holly

*This is me: thirteen years old, sitting on the bench in the camp's shower building with Violet next to me, applying my lip liner. "The trick is to extend the lips by drawing just slightly over them . . . like this." She leans back to admire her work, then fills in the rest with pink lipstick. There's a glint of excitement in her blue eyes as she tucks her wavy blond hair behind her ears, one corner of her mouth turning up in a smirk. "Like that. Perfect. Very kissable."*

*I frown as I fidget with my thumb ring, and my cheeks heat up. "Yeah . . . I don't know about that."*

*Violet stands and pulls me to my feet. She leads me to the mirror and stands behind me, resting her sharp chin on my shoulder. "Look at yourself," she murmurs. "You're beautiful. He's going to pass out when he sees you. You look at least fifteen."*

*I take in my lashes, curled so they look even longer than usual. The eyeliner Violet applied extends at the ends, and the carefully blended shades of eye shadow accentuate my eyes. My lips look plump, like I'm making the pouting face that usually works when I want Mom to take a night off work to have a movie night with me. I'd much prefer to have a movie night tonight. With Mom. Or the other girls. Or Violet. Anything but hanging out with him. "He likes you better . . ." I begin. "Seriously. I don't know about this . . ."*

*"You haven't dated anyone before," Violet snaps. She shakes her head and glares at my reflection. "How do you expect to be good at dating if you don't practice? It's not like I'm trying to convince you to do something terrible. Get a grip, Holly."*

*"Okay," I whisper. Violet's the nicest person ever until she gets annoyed. And right now? She's acting like I'm a whiny, immature baby who doesn't appreciate her time and advice. "I guess you're right."*

*Violet grabs my hand and spins me around to face her. "Look: the thing is you're pretty. I'm trying to help you realize the power you have. One day you'll thank me. So come on, let's go."*

*Violet leads me out of the shower building. We step outside into the humid night air. The high-pitched screech of the cicadas is loud and urgent, making my heart pound even faster. Violet squeezes my hand as she brings me through the forest, toward his house. "You're going to have such a great time," she whispers.*

*"Yeah," I say, but my squeaky voice comes out sounding like I'm a little girl. I channel an alter ego that's a little less me and a little more Violet. "Yeah," I say again. "I know."*

MONDAY, DECEMBER 27

The truth is, I think this whole thing is pretty fucked up. Violet, dead? That girl seemed invincible.

Also: if I had known I'd be attending a funeral, I would have bought a dress with a longer hemline.

"Is that what you're going to wear?" Alex sputters as I step out of my closet holding a short black dress with a plunging V-neck. "Seriously, Holly? Are you planning on seducing the pastor?" His face is cinnamon-heart red, and he's blinking at me incredulously. He strides past me and pulls a black cardigan off its hanger. "You can wear this on top, buttoned up."

What I want to reply: *Why don't you wear that? The shade would match nicely with your soul.*

What I do reply: "Good idea. I forgot I had that sweater."

"Pack it," he says firmly and watches as I place it in my suitcase.

"Look at you, my personal wardrobe adviser." I punch him in the side playfully, and he wraps one of his sculpted arms around my waist and pulls me in, his breath coming out in warm bursts against my neck. The alluring scent of musky after-shave sends my head swirling, but I don't have time for a make-out session. Believe me, it's hard to resist. The only thing stopping me: I should have left for Zoe's an hour ago. The girls and I have dinner plans.

Alex doesn't seem to be worried about how late I'll be. He leans in and kisses me firmly, his tongue slipping its way into my mouth. "We've been together almost every day since we met," he whispers when he pulls away. "It's going to suck with you gone."

Alex and I met at a party last summer. I went there with a guy I was seeing but not really all that into, and I ended up leaving with Alex. We've hardly let go of each other since that day, to be honest. He's definitely a winner with my mom, who says she feels A LOT more comfortable working double shifts at the hospital knowing there's someone around who cares about me almost as much as she does.

I press my lips softly against Alex's and trace a finger along his jawline. "I'll be back in two days, tops." A tingle runs up and down my spine, followed by a surge of fresh guilt. As much as I'm eager for a road trip, the reason for it is someone's death. Someone I used to idolize.

Alex's eyebrows draw together. "Last time you left to go somewhere you never answered your phone. I wrote back to your mom's texts saying you were great when I had no idea if you were okay or not."

Truthfully? I didn't know if I was going to be okay or not either. Sometimes I get pulled into some pretty strange situations.

Also: I knew Alex was going to bring it up again. He just doesn't quit, does he? I shake my head and give him a reassuring smile, draping my arms over his broad shoulders. "I told you, I accidentally left my phone in the car. I won't forget to keep it on me this time. Don't worry."

He shifts his weight from one foot to the other and gives me puppy-dog eyes. Honestly? I'm torn on whether I find it endearing or annoying. "I can come with you, you know. I'll call in sick at the shop. I haven't taken a sick day in a year, so it's not like they'll care."

I shake my head. "That's sweet but I'm staying at Zoe's. It'll be only girls there . . ."

"It had better be only girls." Alex runs a hand through his dark hair and frowns. Oops. It seems like this isn't something that was on his radar yet. "I don't want to have to worry about someone trying to get with you. I knew I should have got you a promise ring for Christmas instead of the necklace so everyone would know you're taken." He lightly tugs the diamond heart pendant he gave me.

"It's *me* you have to trust and I'm all yours." I cup his chin with one hand and press a finger against his lips with the other. God, he has the best lips; they're so soft and full. I head back to my closet, scoop up an armful of bodysuits, jeans, leggings, dresses, bras, and underwear, and toss them in my shiny purple suitcase. I snap it closed and fasten the latch. "There. All packed."

Alex gives me a longing look. "Why don't we say goodbye to each other properly?" He grabs my hand, leads me to my bed, and pulls me into his lap. "Why rush?" he whispers and slips his hand up the back of my shirt, brushing it against my bra.

"Easy there, mister." I pull away and wink at him. "I'm supposed to be there in time for our dinner reservation."

"And?"

"Which means I have to leave now. Zoe's is two hours away." I stand and walk toward my suitcase, pausing in front of the mirror to check out my reflection. My blond hair falls across my shoulders in loose waves. My dark jeans and white bodysuit are form fitting, but I still look like the girl-next-door type I used to be the last time I saw the girls. Exactly the image I was going for.

I grab Alex's hand and give it a squeeze. "Come on."

He sighs. I go to pick up my suitcase, but he grabs it first and slings it over his shoulder. No one would know how heavy it is with all the clothes and shoes I jammed in there, because he carries it so effortlessly. We head downstairs and out the front door into a picture-perfect winter wonderland. Snow falls gently on my red 2010 Camaro, and the late-afternoon sky is gray with a tinge of pretty pink.

"Snow's coming down hard," Alex says, lifting a hand to point upward. "I don't think it's safe for you to drive in this."

Is this guy kidding? I laugh and pop the trunk. "It's me you're talking to. Driving's my number one skill. I've driven in way worse weather than this. You worry about me too much."

Alex sets my suitcase inside and shakes his head slowly like he knows he's out of tactics to convince me not to leave.

I wrap my arms around his neck. "So, I suppose this is see you later?" I ask, resting my nose gently against his.

"Promise you'll be good?"

"Promise," I say, and before I can say more, Alex is kissing me. I gently pull away. "Now I really have to go."

Alex slowly lets go of my hand. "Drive safe, baby."

I get into the car and turn the ignition, backing slowly out of the driveway. The fluffy white pair of dice that hang from my rearview mirror wave back and forth like pendulums. I sit in silence as I drive out of my subdivision and pull onto Main.

The first thing I do with my newfound freedom? I reach into my center console and pull out two sticks of strawberry gum. Alex hates when I chew gum, says it's a bad habit. But Alex isn't here right now, so I snap a small bubble and then immediately feel guilty.

The next thing I do is switch on the radio, and as if it's my lucky day, the new Lila Leveck song's playing. "He's got the smile I love," I sing along, quietly at first, then louder, until I'm shouting the lyrics at the top of my lungs. At a red light, I glance at the driver who pulls up beside me, but I'm not going to stop even though I have an audience now. He's laughing and gives me a thumbs-up. I'm sort of proud that my pipes are big enough to be heard through two closed windows. I'd be much happier if I sang like this more often. Like I used to.

A shiver of excitement courses through me. I love driving on my own like this. I'm always with Alex. The last time I went anywhere without him I was following someone else's instructions. Not this time.

This time I'm free.

# 4
# Denise

I zip up my bag and let out a long sigh. I can't believe she's actually gone. I called her about a week ago, and we talked for a few minutes before she had to let me go. It kills me that that was our last conversation.

I've never told anyone something like this, but I think I was someone really special to her. Now I'll never know *how* special. I don't want to go to the funeral. It will be too hard. Plus, it's in Birchbrook. I promised myself I'd never go back there again.

Mom steps into the room, points at my navy-blue duffel bag, and raises her eyebrows at me quizzically. "This little bag? This is all you're taking, Denise? You'll be at Zoe's for two days. You'll be going to the funeral, maybe a reception, out for meals. You need to bring enough outfits for all of that." She sweeps my hair into a ponytail and pins up my long bangs. "And also, you're a pretty girl, you don't want to hide behind all that hair."

I sigh. "I'm far from pretty and I have all the outfits I need." I sit on my floral bedspread with slumped shoulders. "I still don't think it's a good idea for me to go." My head's been reeling since Calista messaged me yesterday.

Mom settles down next to me and drapes her arm across my back. "Of course you should go. You had the best time at camp. You were so carefree back then before the stuff with your dad happened. Maybe seeing the girls will be good for you. They might remind you of the way you used to be. You were my little flower child."

I shake my head. *She doesn't know the half of what's been traumatizing me.* "I was a little kid. I had no idea how shitty life could be."

Mom narrows her eyes and runs her hands through her short black curls. I know that look. She's going to bring up wanting me to see that grief counselor again, and that's the absolute last thing I want to talk about now. She bites her lip like she's holding back the words.

"I can call and tell them something came up," I say. "You might need me at the restaurant. Will you guys be okay without me?"

Mom's dark eyes widen. She grabs me by both shoulders and smiles, but it's kind of a sad smile. "Your brother and I will be fine. You're going. It'll be good for you. That's final." She opens my closet and fills my duffel bag with dresses and a pair of heels I've never worn. Then she steps out of my bedroom and into the hallway. "I'll be waiting in the car."

*Well, it seems like that's decided.*

I head downstairs and out the door, trekking through the snow on the driveway to get into Mom's burgundy minivan.

Katy Perry bursts through the speakers, and Mom smiles brightly as I step inside and plop down on one of her tacky reindeer seat covers. She's obviously hoping her peppy mood will rub off on me.

"Here we go," she says and pulls out of the driveway. She slowly drives along Spruce Avenue toward the bus station. As usual, the driver in the car behind her lays on the horn.

"What's the rush? I'm going the speed limit," Mom mutters, glancing in the rearview mirror.

I check out her speedometer. Ten miles an hour below.

The car zips around her, and Mom laughs. "I don't get why people are in such a hurry all the time."

Holy moly. This is exactly why I refused to let Mom drive me to Zoe's. Driving cautiously is one thing, but driving turtle-slow can be almost as dangerous as driving fast. The last thing I need is for someone else in my life to get hurt, or worse.

I stare out the window as we pass the grocery store, the gas station, my school, the doctor's office. I know it's coming, and part of me wants to squeeze my eyes shut, but a bigger part of me wants to check if anything new has been placed there since Mom finally took all the gifts away. I take a deep, shaky breath as we pass it. The place where the wreaths for Dad were laid. Candles. Teddy bears. Photos of him cooking in the restaurant or smiling beside his piano students. I glance at the empty patch of grass. No more gifts. No one new to town would know that a year ago, this was where Dad's life just stopped. To them it would be a regular field with overgrown weeds.

I glance at Mom, who taps her hands against the steering wheel to the rhythm of "Roar." It could just be the streetlight's reflection flashing in her eyes, but they do look a little glossy.

Mom pulls up in front of the bus station. "This is it," she says and leans across the center console to plant a kiss on my cheek. "Now, go and pay your respects to Violet and please offer my condolences to her family. Don't be worried, honey. It'll be fine."

We climb out of the van, and Mom takes the backpack and duffel bag out of the back and hands them to me. She pulls me toward her in a tight hug. "I'll be here to pick you up on Wednesday morning."

I nod. I know if I say even one word, my wavering voice will give me away and Mom will know that I'm not okay. My eyes prickle and I blink quickly. *Think happy thoughts*, I tell myself. *The last thing you want to do is cry.*

I pull the ticket Mom bought me out of the front pocket of my jeans and climb the steps onto the number 25 bus.

A woman with a long braid draped over her shoulder smiles at me from the driver's seat. "Hello," she says with a warm smile. "Happy holidays."

I force a smile back and slide my ticket into the machine.

The musty-smelling bus is empty except for an older couple who sit near the front, holding hands and laughing about something. I head toward the back and sit on a torn vinyl seat on the side facing Mom's van. She's too far away for me to see her face through the window, but if I could guess, I'd say she's probably smiling, confident that I'm finally making progress.

But the truth is, I'm not.

Things are only getting worse. I used to think what happened to Dad was karma for what I did that day in the woods. But the karma keeps on coming around to destroy me.

# 5
# Zoe

The doorbell rings, and I'm 99.9 percent certain I know who'll be outside, first to arrive. I peer through the peephole, and sure enough, I'm right. With her petite frame, perfect spiral curls, and warm complexion, she looks almost exactly the same. I scoop up my yipping poodle and fling open the door. "Callie . . . I mean Calista! I'm so glad you're here."

She nods stiffly. "Hello, Zoe. Good to see you again."

"You too. Come on in." I gesture inside with my free hand.

She stomps her shiny black boots against the welcome mat and puts her suitcase down. "Well, it's been a while." She crosses her arms over her chest and shoots me a forced smile.

"It sure has," I agree, hoping I can think of something to talk about that isn't dull like the amount of snow we've been getting lately or what gifts we got for Christmas. Calista was always kind of proper, but now she's giving off an uptight 2.0 vibe. I hope the others show up soon.

"Cute dog, what's her name?" she finally asks.

"He's a boy. His name is Bark because, well . . ." I point at him, yapping and squirming in my arms, and shrug.

Calista raises an eyebrow. "Clever." She hangs her long white coat on the rack and settles on my patched-up corduroy couch.

I put Bark down, and he rushes straight for her, standing on his back paws and resting his fluffy head by her thigh. Calista pats the top of his head awkwardly and turns to me. "You look great, by the way. I like your haircut."

I run a hand along the back of my bob cut. "Thanks. I got sick of the long hair." I dart into the kitchen and open a cupboard. "Hey, do you want a snack? How about some . . ." I trail off. All that's in here are a few cans of chili, some beans, and a bag of an extremely unappetizing invention called pork rinds. Jill's got herself and Dad on the keto diet, and apparently this is an approved snack when one's craving chips. I cringe and wave the bag so Calista can see. "Would you like some of these delicious treats?"

Calista's nose twitches. "No, thank you."

I open the fridge to the sad sight of yellowish broccoli and wilted celery stalks. It's a good thing we're going out for dinner tonight. Dad and Jill didn't leave me with enough food for myself, let alone three other people. I return with a bottle of water that I place on the coffee table in front of Calista.

She examines her French-manicured nails. "Where did your dad go on his trip?"

"Niagara Falls for the week. Jill wanted to go somewhere romantic for New Year's, so he rented some cheesy room with a heart-shaped Jacuzzi. She was hoping for a fancy trip to NYC, but it was out of his price range." I leave out the part about Jill throwing a tantrum when he told her what he'd arranged. It was a big one with slammed doors and plenty of shouting about Dad being a cheapskate loser. She calmed down shortly before they left and even whispered to me that I could help myself to a bottle of wine from the cellar while they were gone.

I plop down beside Calista and pull my knees to my chest. "What's new with you?"

"I've been busy. Trying to land an internship." She scooches closer and tilts her head. "So, what do you think happened?"

"What do you mean?" Is she still talking about Jill and my dad?

Calista rolls her eyes slightly. "I mean, how do you think Violet died?"

My heart skips a beat. So she's going straight to that subject. "I've been thinking about it nonstop since I found out." I bite my lip and shake my head. "I honestly have no idea. I wanted to call the funeral home to see if they'd give me some details, but I chickened out. Maybe we'll find out tomorrow?"

"Maybe," Calista says, a faraway look in her eyes.

I glance at the clock above my kitchen table. "It's seven forty. The reservation's for eight. Do you think I should change it?"

She nods. "If they don't get here in a few minutes, I would."

Just as she finishes speaking, the doorbell rings and Bark runs to the foyer. I spring to my feet and rush over to check through the peephole to see a tall girl with a ponytail. "It's Denise," I call and pick up Bark with one hand, opening the door with the other. "You're here," I cry.

Denise stares back at me, her face red and her eyes wide.

"Yeah, hi," she answers, struggling to catch her breath. She bends forward and rests her hands on her thighs. "Sorry."

She's acting like she ran here all the way from Shawdale. "Are you okay? What's wrong?"

"I'm okay," Denise breathes. She stands up straight and turns to look behind her. "I walked from the bus station but ended up running the last two blocks. There are some sketchy-looking people around here. Holy moly."

"Welcome to Birchbrook," I say with a laugh.

Calista comes up behind me. "Why did you walk? I would have driven you if I had known you don't have your own car. I'm still in Shawdale too. For now."

"I didn't want to bother anyone."

Calista shrugs. "I wouldn't have been bothered. Next time."

Holly's not here yet, but the way things are going so far, I doubt there will be a next time.

Calista grabs Denise's backpack and bag from the front step and carries them inside. Denise steps inside nervously, and I close the door and let Bark go. He rushes toward her, and she crouches down on the floor beside him. "Hey there," she coos. "You're such a cute pup, aren't you?" Bark flips onto his back, and Denise scratches his tummy. Her breathing slows and her tense expression transforms into a smile.

I blink. "He doesn't usually warm up to people so fast."

"He knows I'm a dog lover," Denise says with a giggle.

"What's the name of the restaurant?" Calista interrupts, cell phone in hand. "Holly's late and I'm going to change our time."

"Mood," I answer. "On Maple Manor." It's definitely on the pricey end, which is why I usually order a burger or a plate of fries and a soda. I picked it because the waiters are absolute eye candy, especially in their cute little uniforms. One way to get over the Rick disappointment from last night is a fresh new distraction in a bow tie.

"Mood?" Calista repeats, scrolling through the Google listings on her phone. "Okay, I'm on it." She turns on her heel and disappears into the kitchen.

I sit cross-legged on the floor in front of Denise, who now has Bark curled up in her lap, a fluffy ball of apricot fur with a tongue hanging out. "So, how are things going with you?" I ask.

"Pretty shit," Denise answers, still talking in the baby voice she was using on Bark.

Finally, some realness. "Why shit?" I ask. "Girlfriend troubles? Tired of school?"

"My dad died," Denise answers.

My mouth drops open. "What? I didn't know that. I'm so sorry."

"It happened a while ago," she says. "A year ago. But the last thing I want to do is go to the funeral tomorrow." Her forehead furrows and her cheeks flush. "It's going to bring back so many memories I don't want. My mom forced me to come this weekend. I'd rather be doing anything else."

"That's really tough," I say, and I can't think of anything else to add to that. Thankfully, there's a knock on the door.

Denise cradles Bark, who's so comfortable that he doesn't bother barking or try to get up, and Calista goes to get it.

Holly steps into the foyer like a beam of sunshine, flipping her wavy blond hair over her shoulders and grinning at us with a dazzling toothpaste-commercial smile. "Girls, it's been way too long. I missed you," she cries, flinging her arms around Calista and then leaning down to hug Denise and me. She stands and begins unzipping her coat.

Calista narrows her eyes. "Stop. We need to leave for dinner now before we miss our new reservation time. Why are you late?"

"Oh, sorry," Holly says with a laugh. "Well, it's a two-hour drive here from Devonville, and I also stopped for a walk by the river on my way over here."

Calista makes a face. "Why would you do that?"

"It's been a while since I've been on my own. It felt kind of good," Holly answers. She wraps an arm around Calista, who pulls away slightly. "Anyway, sorry again for being late. Let's go have some fun."

"We're here for a funeral," Calista mutters. "Not a party."

"Tomorrow's the funeral," Holly corrects. "Today we can catch up. Let's go. I'll drive." She gestures out the window to a cool-looking red sports car.

Calista sighs and bends down to zip her boots.

I start getting up, but Denise grips my forearm and gives me a wide-eyed look. "She's way too cheerful . . . It's so weird," she whispers.

She has a point. Something about Holly is screaming "red flag" to me too. "Maybe a little," I whisper back. "But don't worry." I pat Denise on the arm and stretch out a hand to help her to her feet.

She stands there frozen and looks at me uncertainly. "I . . . I don't want to go."

"Dinner will be fine," I say, but I shiver as the words leave my mouth. It feels like I'm jinxing something.

# 6
# Calista

I'm sitting on the large rock down the path from the shower building—waiting. I peek into my backpack at the small pink bag. A rush of adrenaline charges through thirteen-year-old me, and I shiver.

All of the other campers are in their cabins, and apart from the buzz of crickets, the forest is silent. I glance at my watch. 10:11 p.m. She's late.

Crunch. Crunch. Twigs crunch louder. Louder. A person—or an animal—is approaching. My body stiffens, and I clutch my backpack strap tightly between my fingers.

Then, silence. I spin my head around in a panic, looking to my left, to my right, then behind me. Nothing.

A figure in a dark hoodie jumps out from behind a tree. I spring to my feet and start running toward my cabin. It's Violet, I tell myself. It has to be Violet. But part of me wonders, what if it's not? Why would she want to scare me like this? The figure sprints behind me and hooks an arm around my abdomen, roughly pulling me to a halt. "Boo."

I yelp and thrash around, trying to free myself. My blood runs ice cold.

The hood comes off. It's definitely Violet. She tousles her long blond hair and smirks at me.

I take several clumsy steps backward and grip my chest. "What the heck, Violet? Why'd you do that to me?"

"Relax." Violet makes a face and rolls her eyes. "You need to get over being so jumpy. I'll scare it out of you."

I force a laugh. "I think you already did. You don't need to do it again."

Violet grabs my hand and leads me back to sit on the rock with her. "What did you want to show me?" she whispers.

My body's buzzing, and it feels like my hands are vibrating as I unzip my backpack and reach inside for the small pink snakeskin bag.

Violet lets out a low whistle. "You did it? Really?" She takes a flashlight out of her hoodie pocket and switches it on, and her eyes gleam in its light. "I didn't want to doubt you, Calista, but I just didn't think you had it in you."

I open the bag's clasp and take out a small bottle of Chanel Chance perfume and a MAC eye shadow palette.

Violet's grin slowly widens. "That will show Farrah not to brag. When did you take it?"

"I went into her cabin during dinner. You were right. She doesn't lock her door." When I think of Farrah's reaction to returning to her room to discover her aunt's gift to her gone, a pang of guilt pinches my chest, and I take deep breaths to ease it away. Violet hates Farrah. There has to be a good reason for that.

*Violet drapes her arm over my shoulder and pulls me into her chest. "Thank you. She's been so awful to me. Always bringing up Grayson being gone. She kept eyeing him up when he was around. Right in front of my face." Violet takes the items off my lap, lays them on the rock, and examines them under the beam of the flashlight. She runs her finger along the snakeskin bag, then the palette. She picks up the bottle of perfume, sprays it in the air, and inhales deeply as she breathes it in. "Do you know what that smells like?"*

*"Flowers?" I suggest.*

*"No." Violet shakes her head firmly. "Trouble. Every time Farrah pisses me off, I'm going to wear it, and one hundred percent she'll notice and it will make her blood boil. She'll search my room but she won't find it." Violet's words come out bitter and singsong, like a recess taunt. "Because you'll have it."*

*"I don't think I like that idea," I whisper.*

*"Farrah's horrible. This is harmless revenge. No one gets hurt." Violet puts one hand on each of my shoulders and leans into me, so close that I can feel her warm breath on my cheek. Her cascade of blond hair brushes against my collarbone. "You're good at this," she says. "Now I know how slick you are, I'll keep you in mind for other opportunities."*

*Violet, with her intelligence, great advice, and incredible charisma, is the role model I need in my life. If she wants something, she goes after it, and she gets it.*

*She holds the perfume bottle out, nods at me, and winks.*

*I flip my arm over, my palm facing up, and she spritzes my wrist. I lean down to breathe in the scent. Not quite floral now that I'm smelling it for the second time. It really is much more complex.*

---

MONDAY, DECEMBER 27

Wow. How the heck did Holly get her license?

After a nail-biting drive through Birchbrook, we arrive at Mood. I had my hand against the roof the entire way, bracing for impact. I breathe a sigh of relief.

"How was *that*?" Holly says proudly as she parks in the center of two spots.

"I like your driving style. That was exciting," Zoe gushes.

*I have other words for it, such as "dangerous,"* I almost say, but I hold my tongue. I can tell by the looks passing between the others that they already find me annoying. A few months ago, when my brother was on a Dr. Phil kick, he tried to psychoanalyze me. He told me I get snippy and overbearing when I don't feel in control.

It seems like today is one of those times.

I glance at Denise, who looks absolutely rattled, the poor girl. I'm not the only one who didn't enjoy the Mario Andretti impersonation.

We get out of the car and trudge through the snow. Holly holds the door, and we step inside into the warmth. With the candlelit interior, the decor definitely matches the restaurant's name. Abstract paintings are artfully placed on the brick walls, and a white Christmas tree adorned with gold balls and crystal snowflakes stands beside a blazing fireplace. It's busy for a Monday, and judging by the delicious scents of steak and garlic that waft in the air, the food might be the reason for that. The conversations from the tables in front of us blend into a low hum.

I check my watch: 8:14 p.m. Thank goodness I changed our time.

A guy with auburn hair and a white collared shirt and bow tie grins at us from the host stand. "Hi, ladies. Looking for a table?"

Zoe nudges me and whispers, "I've had my eye on him for months. He's cute, isn't he?"

I give her a halfhearted nod, step toward the counter, and lean my arms on it. "We've got a reservation. I called to make it a few minutes later. It's Calista Diaz."

The guy looks at his computer screen and nods, glancing back at us with a cheeky half smile that probably has Zoe giddy. "Sure, right this way."

He gestures to a booth in the back corner and places the menus down on the table. "How's this?"

"It's perfect," Zoe says, eyeing him like he's what she'd *really* like to order. "Are you going to be our waiter? We'd like some sodas, please."

"No, that will be Felix," the guy says, pointing at an equally attractive man polishing glasses behind the bar. "I'll let him know you'd like your drinks right away. What would you like?"

"Coke, please," Holly says.

"Same," I say.

Denise nods. "Me too."

"I'd like a Sprite, thanks." Zoe twirls a strand of her short black hair around her finger. "I'm very thirsty."

"You certainly are," Holly says when he's out of earshot.

Zoe swats her arm playfully. "Well, look at all the hotness surrounding us. Aren't you?"

Holly shrugs. "I'm more excited about the food. This place smells *amazing*."

Felix approaches our table holding a tray of drinks and puts them down on our coasters. "I'm your waiter for the evening. Can I tell you about our specials?"

Felix lists off several fancy-sounding dishes, but I'm barely listening. I look across the table at Denise, who's fidgeting with a locket that hangs from a chain around her neck and chewing on her lower lip. I reach out and touch her arm. "Are you okay?" I whisper.

She nods but her shiny eyes say otherwise. Wow, what happened to her? Zoe filled us in about her father passing and how the approaching funeral is bringing back some emotions, but her entire demeanor is completely different. She used to be carefree and easygoing.

After Felix takes our orders and disappears through the swinging door into the kitchen, Zoe pulls a vintage-looking brass flask out of her purse. "Who's up for something extra in their soda?" she whispers and grins mischievously.

"No, thanks. I'm driving," Holly answers. She sits with perfect posture, as though there's a string at the very top of her head that someone's tugging on, and her phony smile reminds me of a collectible Barbie posing in her display box.

I don't know who she's trying to fool with this smug persona she's putting on, but it's not me.

There's certainly something off about her. Mark my words.

"You can have some and I'll drive your car back," I offer. I'm partly suggesting this because she might be more real when she's tipsy, but mostly it's because I drive much more cautiously than she does and I've had too much excitement, as Zoe would call it, for one day.

Holly shakes her head firmly. "Thanks, but no. I'm the only one who drives her."

"Her? Don't tell me you named your car." I blink quickly to stop myself from rolling my eyes.

Holly nods. "Yes. Red."

I laugh, but her unamused frown suggests she's actually serious. "You and Zoe have some very literal name choices. Bark and Red."

Zoe reaches across the table to grab Holly's hand and squeeze it. "I love both names. We rock."

"I'll take some," Denise whispers, pointing at the flask. I definitely didn't see that coming.

Zoe's eyes widen, and a slow smile spreads across her face. "Sure." She makes sure the coast is clear, then takes off the cap and pours some unknown liquid into Denise's cup, then hers.

"Where do you get all the alcohol from?" I ask.

"What do you mean *all the alcohol*? It's just one little flask," Zoe says indignantly.

I raise my eyebrows. "I mean, remember when you brought that bottle of vodka to camp the last summer we went?"

Zoe takes a sip of her drink and shudders slightly. For someone who likes drinking as much as she does, she doesn't seem to enjoy the way it tastes. "My dad and Jill have a healthy collection," she says. "We all had some that day, remember?"

I nod. "How could I forget?" Everything about that night was wrong. Us sneaking out of our cabin, then going into the forest to drink Zoe's smuggled bottle, not to mention all the strange things we saw while we were out there. I shiver and wonder if that night's still a disturbing memory for them too. My gaze darts around the table, and I study each of their expressions. Zoe's eyes shift from the table to her lap, and Holly turns her thumb ring with a faraway look in her eyes. Denise's face is flaming red, and she wrings her hands.

"Remember—" Holly begins.

Denise scowls at her. "Stop talking about it."

"Whoa, relax," Holly says and holds her hands up in mock surrender. "You don't even know what I was going to say."

Denise turns to glare at each of us. "Violet told us never to mention it. The last thing I want is to go against something she said, now that she's gone."

"Do you think Camp Bellwood Lake is cursed?" Holly continues. "First Grayson goes missing, then Farrah has that accident and dies, and now Violet? Who's going to be next?"

"I told you, that's enough!" Denise shouts. She pounds her fist against the table, and her lip quivers.

My mouth drops open. I haven't heard Denise talk in anything above a whisper since she arrived. I didn't know her voice could get that loud.

Denise blinks quickly like she's equally surprised by her outburst. "I'm sorry," she says softly. "I don't want to talk about other tragedies right now. I'm having a hard enough time coming to grips with the fact Violet's gone."

Zoe nods. "That's understandable."

Holly's got a point, though—a point I'd be up for discussing.

Holly grins and I think she's going to keep yapping, but instead she waves a hand dismissively. "Fine. Let's catch up. But let's do it true to our camp style by playing Truth or Dare. That's always an exciting time, right?" She smirks. "Zoe, you're up first."

Zoe laughs and takes another sip of her drink. "Truth. But go easy on me."

Holly looks up at the ceiling as if the perfect question will come to her that way. "Is it true," she begins, "that you want to get with our waiter?"

"I prefer the guy that brought us to our table," Zoe says. "I'd get with him any day of the week."

Holly steps out of the booth to take another peek. "Yeah, he's pretty hot. I see what you mean." She plops back down on her seat and tucks her shiny hair behind her ears. I can't get a good read on her anymore. She used to be what-you-see-is-what-you-get. Now she's more mysterious, like she's holding something back. She bats her impossibly long eyelashes at me. "Callie, what will it be? Truth or dare?"

"It's Calista," I correct. Violet once told me that Callie didn't suit me. "*You're much too sophisticated for a name like that,*" she said.

Holly taps her fingers against the table. "Okay, *Calista*. What's your choice?"

This game is highly juvenile, but I want to show them I can be fun too. "I choose dare."

"I dare you . . ." Holly looks around. "To take a shot from Zoe's flask."

Wow, creative. I reach my hand out and Zoe gives it to me. I shoot back a gulp of bitter-tasting alcohol, but instead of shuddering, I smile. "Done."

"Still a pro after all these years," Zoe says with a laugh.

My chuckle comes out more like a snort. "Hardly."

Felix comes back with our meals. He places a steak and a Caesar salad in front of me. I cut a small square of meat and pop it in my mouth. It's so tender it practically dissolves. This place is certainly a lot better than the restaurants we have in Shawdale.

Denise takes a long drink and waves to Felix, who lingers behind the bar. "Another?" she calls, holding up her glass. She shifts her french fries around on her plate.

"Your turn," Holly says, taking a small bite of her salad. "What do you choose, Denise?"

Denise pushes her plate forward as if two fries were all she needed for dinner. "Truth."

Holly eyes her like she's trying to assess whether the question that popped into her mind is the right one. "Is it true that you think Violet liked you the best?" she says sweetly.

That's a bizarre thing to ask, so I shoot her a look.

Denise just gazes down at the table. After a while, she looks up. "Yes," she says. "I know for a fact that she did."

Zoe tilts her head. "What does that mean?"

Felix comes back with Denise's drink, and she stares into her glass and sighs.

"Enough with this silly game," I interrupt. There's no way this conversation is going to end any way but badly. "We should go over the plan for the morning. The funeral's at ten a.m. so we need to decide what time we'll be leaving." I turn to Zoe. "Do you have stuff we could make for breakfast?"

Zoe shakes her head. "Not unless you like canned chili first thing in the morning."

I make a face. Really? Not even a box of cornflakes? "Okay, so we'll head out at nine then, and grab some food on the way?"

"Sure," Zoe says. "Sounds good to me."

I look at the others for their opinions. Denise is staring at Holly, unblinking.

"You never had your turn," she says to her.

"Truth," Holly says and leans forward.

Denise frowns. "Is it true that you hated Violet?"

"No," Holly says. "I didn't hate her. We had an argument, and I didn't exactly love her after that, but I didn't hate her."

What is up with these two? What the heck is Holly even talking about? I didn't come here for drama. I clear my throat. "So, we probably shouldn't stay up too late tonight, since we have to be up early."

Denise is still scowling at Holly, but Holly just smiles, her eyes twinkling. Denise turns to Zoe. "You were wrong when you told me that dinner would be fine. It's not. Can I have another drink?"

Zoe nods and drips her flask into Denise's cup. Denise takes a long gulp.

"Come on," Holly says. "This night will be so much fun if you all lightened up a little. We used to be best friends."

We really were best friends. For five summers. Every July we shared a cabin and became family for the weeks we spent together. We settled into a comfortable groove with each other, year after year, as if no time had passed at all. The first four years were the best. Violet was happy and energetic. Every day was an adventure. The last year was tense, to put it mildly. Violet's boyfriend, Grayson, went missing, and Violet started acting less like the fun counselor we'd grown to love.

A good word to describe her that year might be *unhinged*.

I'd hoped that it was just a rough patch. Grayson would return, and the following summer would be the best yet. Then, I made a terrible mistake that affected Mrs. Felmont more than I realized it would. After that, her daughter Farrah had the horrible accident and died, and that was the end of it. The camp closed down. The girls and I vowed that we'd get together the next summer anyway, but we never did.

"We haven't spoken in four years," Denise says. "That was a long time ago."

"Not really," Holly says. "We were really close. We just need to remember the things we had in common and it'll be like it was before."

The biggest thing we all had in common was Violet. Maybe she was the glue that held our cabin together because I'm realizing more than ever that me and these girls are nothing alike. Violet's in all my camp memories. She crossed my mind about a week before Zoe called me. I was thinking that I'd contact her to make sure she was still keeping my secret.

Now, I'll never get to.

"We should do a toast, to Violet," I say, holding up my soda.

The girls lift their glasses and Denise beams at me.

"To my role model. Thanks for all the advice you gave me. I miss you already," I say, and there's an ache in my chest as I realize I mean it. I really do. "Anyone else?"

"I always looked up to you and I'm so sad you're gone," Zoe adds.

"You were so special to me," Denise says, her eyes welling up with tears. She lets out a short sob and presses her fist against her mouth. Zoe puts her arm around her.

Holly's gaze roves across the ceiling before it rests on us. "You were so beautiful, and I can't believe you're gone."

"To Violet," I say and lightly clink my glass against theirs.

Denise sighs and dabs her eyes with the back of her hand. "I wonder what happened to her."

"We'll learn that tomorrow," I say firmly.

One way or another, I'm going to find out.

# 7

# Holly

TUESDAY, DECEMBER 28

When we arrive at the funeral home, we sit in my car in stunned silence. I trace Violet's name across the bare stretch of thigh below the fringe of my short dress and glance around at the others. None of us budge.

Honestly? This is SUPER weird. For one: the parking lot is absolutely rammed with cars. It's so busy that I had to park illegally in front of a dumpster. Secondly: none of us have been to a funeral before, besides Denise, but she's not going to fill us in about what to expect since she's barely spoken all morning.

My phone buzzes in my purse, breaking the silence. I pull it out and notice Zoe glancing at it curiously from the passenger seat. I tilt the screen away from her to read yet another text from Alex:

I haven't heard from you. You said
you wouldn't do this again.

I clutch the heart charm on my necklace, then type my reply.

I can't talk now. At funeral. Love
you.

His response comes fast.

Call me as soon as it's over.

"We should probably head in," Calista finally says from the back seat. She slowly opens her door, climbs out of the car, and smooths her long coat over her hips.

What I want to do: Run. Run as far as I can in any direction, I'm not picky.

What I actually do: I join the others standing in an awkward line facing the entrance, wrap my arms around myself, and shiver. In my thin waist-length jacket, short dress, and black heels, I'm not exactly dressed for the weather. The snow's a few inches deep, and some has gotten into my shoes. Ugh. I eye the other girls' cozy-looking boots. I don't want to admit this, but MAYBE I should have listened to Alex and packed different stuff after all.

"I don't know if I can do this," Denise whispers. I turn to give her a sympathetic look, but she frowns back at me. God, what is with this girl?

"You can absolutely do this." Zoe drapes an arm around Denise's shoulder. "We're here for you."

"Yeah," I say, forcing my best shot at a friendly smile. "We're in this together."

We step forward, past a group of people smoking cigarettes in front of a cluster of pine trees. A woman takes a long drag, then uses her free hand to dab her eyes with a Kleenex. The man beside her whispers something into her ear.

We hesitate in front of the large wooden doors. Calista takes a visibly deep breath and tugs on the metal handle. We follow her inside, stepping onto a plush burgundy carpet in the wide foyer. The scents of incense and lilies practically smack me in the face. Small tables topped with lamps and floral arrangements stand on either end of couches lined with people with sad expressions, shaking their heads and talking quietly. Out of nowhere this heavy feeling hits me, like there's something in the air. Death. This got too real, too fast.

"Over there," Zoe whispers, pointing to a huge photograph of Violet propped up on an easel outside of a room that's brimming over with people. Violet looks so happy and animated in the picture just like she did four years ago, and I can't even get over how strange it is that I won't be able to see her in person again. I take a shaky breath. No matter what we argued about, there's no way I wanted her to end up here. My eyes sting and I bite my lip hard, hoping *that* will distract me from becoming a blubbering mess already.

Calista strides toward the open door and gestures for us to follow her into the crowded room. My eyes go straight to the casket at the front, where several people hover, one of whom I recognize as Violet's mother. My heart skips a beat.

"Good morning," a guy with slicked-back hair says. I note his dress shirt has the funeral home's logo on it. "Thank you for coming. Could you please sign the guest book?" After I sign my name, I pick up one of the cards that are piled high in the basket beside it. It's got the same picture of Violet on it that's displayed outside of the door. I open it, hoping that some information about what happened to her will be inside, but instead it's just a prayer. I fold my hand around it.

A group of guys who look about twenty enter behind us. Zoe's face brightens slightly, and she eyes them with interest. They move toward the center aisle and stand in a circle with their arms crossed. A guy with a thick beard, who looks vaguely familiar, turns to look in each corner of the room as if he's assessing every person in attendance, and he's not exactly subtle about it. His eyes finally settle on us. His thick eyebrows knit together, and he leans over to say something to the shorter muscular guy beside him, who turns to look at us with narrowed eyes.

"Why are they looking at us like that?" Denise whispers. "Is this funeral for family only?"

"No," Zoe says, patting her shoulder. "The details were published in the newspaper. All are welcome. Maybe they're trying to figure out who we are to Violet? The ripped one's pretty hot, don't you think?"

"Nope." Denise sighs and sits on a folding chair in the back row, the only spot where there are seats left next to each other. "Why are there so many sketchy people in Birchbrook?"

Zoe perches on the edge of the seat beside her. "You get used to it," she says with a wink.

I start moving toward a chair, but Calista grabs my arm and raises her eyebrows at me. "We should all pay our respects to the family before the service begins."

Denise shakes her head. "I can't."

Zoe gives us a small smile. "I'll stay here with Denise. You two go."

"All right," I say and link arms with Calista. She turns to glance at me like she's considering pulling away, but instead she strides forward, weaving around the people huddled together in the aisles.

"Don't worry," she whispers, and I wonder if she said that because she can feel me trembling. Honestly? Trembling might be an understatement. I'm shaking like a leaf.

"That's her mom," I say, pointing at the pretty woman who looks about forty-five. She's got noticeably puffy eyes, and she's leaning on the shoulder of a man with gray hair who stands beside her. I'm probably the only one of the girls who met Mrs. Williams. Violet and I hung out a few times after the camp shut down, and I've been to her house.

I stop a few feet in front of her and clear my throat. "Um. Hello, Mrs. Williams. I'm very sorry for your loss."

Mrs. Williams breaks away from the man and stares at me as if she's trying to place me. "Are you one of the girls from the camp Violet worked at? You've come by my house a few times."

I nod. "Yes, I'm Holly and this is Calista."

"Violet was our counselor since we were little kids," Calista adds. "We were so deeply sad to hear about this devastating news."

Mrs. Williams blinks quickly, her whole body begins shaking, and she starts sobbing loudly. "I'm sorry," she says. "It happened so suddenly. It's hard to keep my composure."

The gray-haired man beside her rubs her back. "I'm Albert, Tina's father, Violet's grandfather." His eyes well up with fresh tears. "This is a big shock to our family. Thank you for coming today to remember our girl."

Tears flow down Mrs. Williams's face, and she doesn't wipe them away. "Thank . . . thank you," she stammers.

Violet's grandfather takes her gently by the hand and leads her to the first row, where she crumples into her seat.

A guy with striking blue eyes and dark hair who was lingering close to them steps forward. "My aunt's having a very hard time," he says. "She and Violet were very close." He extends his hand to us, and I reach out to shake it. "I'm Hector, Violet's cousin," he says. "On behalf of our family, thank you for coming today."

"You're welcome," Calista says and shakes Hector's hand. "We're so sorry."

Hector nods solemnly. "What happened to her . . . it's so sad."

"Very sad," I murmur.

We step away, and he greets the guests who've lined up behind us.

Calista cringes and her brow furrows. "I was going to ask what happened, but it wasn't the right time."

"Yeah," I agree and peer at Mrs. Williams, her back heaving as she cries. "I feel so bad for her. I don't think we should ask her about it. Maybe we can find out from another guest?" I swivel around the room to face the group of guys Denise called sketchy. "Maybe an unintimidating guest?"

"After the service," Calista agrees. "But before it starts, we should also pay our respects to her." Calista tilts her head in the direction of the casket.

"Her, as in Violet?" I ask. Oof. I don't know about that. I'd rather go back to where the others are. I'd rather remember Violet as she was before. Alive.

Calista grips my hand and pulls me toward the kneelers,

surrounded by tall floral arrangements, at the foot of the casket. She kneels and I stand behind her, looking at my shoes. I can't bring myself to look at Violet's face.

Calista gasps. "Oh my God," she murmurs in a panicked tone.

I slowly look up at the dark-haired girl lying against the white satin pillow. Her skin has a yellow tone, making her resemble a wax figure. They've clothed her in a navy-blue dress, its three-quarter sleeves high enough to reveal most of the dolphin tattoo on her left arm and the wolf tattoo on the other. It's strange to see her like this. So still. So dead. I try to widen my eyes so I look surprised too.

"That's not Violet," Calista whispers urgently. "This. This is Violet." She lifts the prayer card we got at the entrance and jabs at the picture of the curvy blond girl we used to know, who looks nothing like the thin girl with angular features who lies in front of us. "She'd never dye her hair black, and she'd never get tattoos."

Violet really did use to hate tattoos. She lectured Zoe every time she said that she wanted one. "*They're hard to remove once you get one,*" she would say. "*You have to be absolutely sure it's something you want on your skin forever.*"

Violet's eyes are closed but it seems they could open at any second, and she could sit right up and say, "Ha, fooled you," like she used to do at camp. She was always pranking everyone.

"Is that even her?" Calista hisses. She nibbles her thumbnail and glances at me with wide eyes. It's unusual to see her looking so untethered.

"It's her," I whisper. "But I have a feeling that the Violet who just died is nothing like the Violet we knew at camp."

# 8
# Denise

*I'm thirteen years old. Violet hands me a tiny model sailboat, and I pass it from one hand to the other before handing it back to her. "Pretty," I whisper. We sit together on the grass, leaning up against our cabin. The others are inside, getting ready for the campfire.*

*"You're the only one I show these things to," Violet whispers and slips the little boat back into the pocket of her cutoff jean shorts. She brushes my hair back with her hand and looks into my eyes like she's studying them, trying to figure out what I'm feeling.*

*Part of me wants to stay guarded, but a bigger part of me wants her to know. I want her to know how special I think she is. I tilt my head so my face is closer to hers.*

*"Thank you," I murmur.*

*"When Grayson comes back and we get our house, I'm going to*

*put this on the mantel. Above the fireplace," she says, and my heart clenches like a fist. I let her see that pain in my eyes. I hope she sees it.*

*She leans closer, her lips grazing against my cheek. "You can visit, Denise. Whenever you like." She slips her hand in mine, our fingers interlocking.*

*We sit there for a long time, our backs resting against the wooden cabin, staring out at the still, dark forest.*

*"What do you think happened to Grayson?" Violet sighs and stifles a sob.*

*"I don't know," I say, squeezing her hand.*

*"You don't think . . . you don't think someone hurt him, do you?" She presses her face up against mine and inhales deeply.*

*"I don't know," I say again.*

*Her grip on my hand tightens, and I flinch. "You're supposed to reassure me," she snaps.*

*My body stiffens. "Sorry," I whisper. "I think he's fine. Don't worry, Violet."*

---

## TUESDAY, DECEMBER 28

My pounding head feels as heavy as a cement truck. I should have known better than to drown my sorrows in whatever Zoe had in her flask because it's definitely taking its toll on me now. The others don't know that besides the drinks at the restaurant, I had two more after they fell asleep. I was hoping it would take the edge off, but I've never felt as edgy as I do right now in this stifling room full of sadness. I'm struck by the fact that when someone dies, the urge to have at least one last conversation with them is overwhelming. If I could talk to Violet right now, I'd ask her if she meant everything she said to me. If she said yes, all of this would feel even harder. We went through so much together. Things no one else knows about.

"Are you sure you don't want to go up there with them, say goodbye?" Zoe says softly and fiddles with a gold button on her silk blouse.

I glance at the front of the room where Calista kneels by Violet's casket and Holly stands behind her. I turn back to Zoe and shake my head. The day of Dad's funeral I felt like I could keep it all together until the moment I saw him lying there, and that's when it all hit me in one swoop and I collapsed onto the floor in a fit of sobs. I've never felt so out of control in my life. I don't want to get up there and have the same thing happen in front of a bunch of people I don't know. "You can go if you want. I'm fine by myself."

Zoe's pinched expression reveals how little she does want to do that. Then she dashes to join the girls before she loses her nerve. She stands beside Holly and immediately swivels around to face me, her eyebrows raised and mouth hanging open. *Weird. She looks more confused than devastated.*

A middle-aged woman wearing a black pantsuit slides into a seat two rows ahead of me. Her long brown ponytail looks familiar, but it can't be her. My eyes must be playing tricks on me. My heart revs up. *Don't worry, Denise. It's just the guilt again*, I repeat in my head. But this time I don't think it is. As if she can tell I'm staring at the back of her head, the woman turns around. It's her. It's Mrs. Felmont. She narrows her eyes and glares in my direction like she knows. As if my legs are mechanical, I

rise and bolt toward the doorway. I squeeze through the clus-
ters of people talking near the entrance and crash through the
ladies' room door and into a stall. I lean with my back against
the door, my breath coming out in bursts. *Why is she here? Why
is she here after what happened to Farrah? Violet hated both of
them. She must know that. Everyone did.*

———————

When I cautiously return to the doorway, the girls are back at
their chairs, and Zoe's craning her neck to look at me curiously.
Mrs. Felmont isn't sitting two rows ahead of our seats anymore.
I can't see her anywhere, and suddenly I'm doubting myself,
questioning if she was even here to begin with. I concentrate
on keeping my breaths long and even. I can't make any more
of a scene; running out of the room was suspicious enough.

The pastor approaches the podium and begins shuffling a
stack of paper. "Hello, everyone. May I have your attention,
please?" he says into the microphone and waits a few seconds
until the room falls silent. "We will begin the service in five
minutes," he continues, then steps away and begins talking to
the organist.

I settle on the empty seat beside Zoe. Holly and Calista sit
on the other side of her.

"Where did you go?" Zoe asks. "I saw you rush out."

"I freaked out for a minute," I whisper, and the desire to
confide in her is suddenly overwhelming to the point that I
have to bite my lip to remind myself that if I do, things will get
much, much worse for me.

Zoe nods. "I get it. It must be tough being here after what

happened to your dad." She shifts in her seat, drumming her red fingernails against her dress pants.

I glance at the others. Calista's eyes are round and she's tugging at her hair, and Holly spins her thumb ring and stares at her lap.

Either they're nervous about being at a funeral, or something else is going on. Maybe they saw Mrs. Felmont too. Maybe they know more than I think they do. "Did you . . . did you see anyone you recognize?" I stammer.

"No." Zoe frowns and rubs her temples. "That's the problem. I didn't even recognize Violet."

"I felt that way too," I say, bristling at the memory. "When I saw my dad, he looked so different. It was a facial expression I'd never seen before and the way they folded his hands together against his chest. It was strange."

"No," Zoe whispers urgently. "It wasn't like that. She looked completely different. Like a totally different person. Her hair was super dark, and she was so thin, and she had tattoos. Remember all the times she lectured me about them?"

Holy moly, do I ever. I used to think Zoe only brought up the tattoo thing to get Violet's attention. Every time she said she wanted one, Violet would go on a tangent about how an image someone may like at twenty might not be one they still would like at thirty because people change their minds. I guess Violet changed hers. "Four years is a long time. We're all different now," I say softly.

Zoe starts talking to Holly and Calista, and I face forward. This will probably last about forty minutes. It kills me to say goodbye to Violet, but I can't wait for this to be over so I can go home, where there is zero chance of running into Mrs. Felmont and there are far fewer reminders of a night I need to forget.

A pretty woman who looks about twenty-five sits in the empty chair to the right of me. She's got pin-straight brown hair and smells like expensive perfume. She catches me peering at her, gives a half smile, then turns to wave at someone behind her. "It's so crowded here," she murmurs. "My friends couldn't even find a seat."

I look behind me at the group of women standing in the doorway. They're wearing dark eyeshadow and fake eyelashes and look like they've been heavily spray-tanned. "It seems like Violet knew a lot of people," I say.

She tucks a strand of hair behind her ear and tilts her head. "How did you know V?"

"She was my counselor at summer camp." *That and so much more.*

"V used to work at a camp?" she says with a smirk. "That's so strange. I can't picture that at all. Hey, I'm April by the way."

"Denise," I answer. "How did you know Violet?"

April hesitates for a minute and looks at the ceiling, which I know people often do when they're about to lie about something. "We worked together," she finally answers. "But not at a summer camp." A vaguely amused expression dances across her face.

The pastor approaches the podium, and the slow classical music on the speaker system fades to silent. The chatter in the room subsides, and the people lingering in the aisles move swiftly to their seats.

"On behalf of the family, I would like to welcome you here today. We are gathered together to remember the life of Violet Williams, who left this world too soon," the pastor begins, his voice crackling in the microphone. "Violet will be missed. She was a loving daughter, granddaughter, niece, cousin, and a friend to many."

His speech continues, and I'm struck by how similar it is to the words spoken at my father's wake. The organist plays "Amazing Grace," and I quickly swipe away the tears that have snuck out of the corners of my eyes.

An attractive middle-aged woman approaches the podium, accompanied by an elderly man. "Violet's death came as a shock to us all," she begins. "She was a wonderful daughter. She cared so much about her family and would have been a great lawyer one day."

"Too much school," April whispers, and I raise my eyebrows at her.

"I can't believe she's really gone," Violet's mother says, her voice catching. "I'm sorry. I can't . . ." The elderly man guides her back to her seat, and she rests her head against his shoulder. I dab my eyes and press my hand against my mouth to stifle a sob. My mom couldn't finish her speech either.

The pastor begins saying some shit he thinks will comfort people, like how Violet will be a star in the heavens looking down on us all, and my eyes travel around the room to examine everyone's reactions. Some people cry openly, not bothering to wipe away the tears that drip down their chins. Others look at their laps and shake their heads like they still can't believe this is real life. I spot the sketchy-looking guys, scattered in various spots around the room as if strategically placed. The tall one with the beard, who I thought was the creepiest, sits a few rows in front of me on the left side of the room. While most people shift in their seats, cross and uncross their arms, he sits perfectly still, staring ahead like a mannequin, with no emotion at all.

When the service ends, the pastor announces that only close family will be going to the cemetery, and people begin streaming toward the exit. April nods at me and joins her friends, who linger beside a tall vase of lilies near the door.

Calista stands and drapes her purse over her shoulder, her eyes scanning the room. "If we want to find out what happened, who do we ask?"

"It's hard to get closure if we don't know what happened," Holly agrees and tugs on the bottom of her dress. "I definitely don't want to ask her mother though."

Zoe steps around them into the aisle. "People are gathered in groups in every corner of this room. Maybe we can join one of their conversations?"

For outgoing girls, they sure are pretty helpless sometimes.

"I can ask," I pipe up. If someone doesn't offer, we'll never leave. Outside is calling my name. I can't breathe in this place, and I can't risk the chance of Mrs. Felmont showing back up and giving me that knowing look again.

The others gawk at me with round eyes.

"You'll ask them?" Holly says, resting her perfectly manicured hand on my shoulder. "Really?"

"Why not?" I answer.

"That doesn't seem like you, to go out of your way to talk to people," Holly says. "Wait. Are you still buzzing from last night?"

I scoff. "Don't be ridiculous. It's not like it's a horrible question. We just want to know. I'll ask the woman who was sitting next to me." I make my way toward her with the others trailing behind.

When I hesitate in front of her, April stops talking to her

friends and smiles at me. "I was just telling my friends that V used to work at the summer camp you went to," she says, flipping her hair over her shoulder. The other women exchange amused glances.

"I couldn't believe it," a woman with short bangs and high cheekbones says. "She didn't seem like the type of person who'd want to look after kids."

April laughs. "The one funny moment in a sad day." She turns to me. "Are you going to the celebration-of-life reception tomorrow?"

My stomach flip-flops. *Another event?* "I hadn't heard about it."

"V's aunt was passing out invite info earlier. You can have mine." April hands me a slip of paper. "We're probably going to stop by."

"We might make it," I say, looking down at the pink paper covered with flowery calligraphy. "But first, I need to know something. I don't know who else to ask."

"Shoot," April says, crossing her arms over her chest and jutting one foot forward.

"I need to know how she died."

April glances at her friends, then spins back to face me with a dark expression. "She drowned."

My heart jolts. There's no way this can be true. No way at all. "She drowned?"

"Yeah." April cringes. "In her mom's indoor swimming pool. Isn't that the saddest thing?"

Calista steps forward. "Are you sure?"

April gives her a surprised look. "Of course I'm sure."

Calista squints at her. "Was she alone when it happened?"

"Yeah, she was alone. I heard there was a ripped-up picture

of one of her exes on top of her towel. Heard he up and left town years ago and broke her heart. Maybe she was thinking about him and drowned because of the stress?"

"Was this ex a person named Grayson?" Calista asks.

"Yeah," April raises an eyebrow. "Why?"

"No reason," I answer, then look at the girls and subtly nod my head toward the door. "Okay, thanks. Maybe we'll see you tomorrow."

"Yeah. See you then," April says and continues her conversation with the other women.

I follow Calista as she weaves through the people slowly moving toward the exit. When we're outside, we rush to Holly's car, lumber inside, and shut the doors.

Holly spins around in her seat and her mouth drops. "What the fuck?"

"Yeah, exactly," Zoe agrees.

I run a hand across my face, which is warm even though the temperature outside is colder now than when we arrived. "She was one of the strongest swimmers I've ever seen. There's no way she drowned. Something messed up is going on."

Calista cradles her head in her hands, her elbows resting on her knees. "And she ripped up a picture of Grayson? Highly unlikely. She loved him more than anything. Someone else had to have done that."

Zoe's frown deepens and the color drains from her face. "This is really odd, there's no question about that. We have to go to that reception. We'll find out more there."

# 9

# Zoe

"Through here," Violet whispers, shining her flashlight into a cluster of pine trees with low branches. "You'll need to crawl."

"I . . . I don't know about this," I stammer, but Violet's got the only flashlight and she's already on her hands and knees, beneath the underbrush. My thirteen-year-old self follows her, pushing the branches aside, my bare legs scraping against the twigs and rocks.

Violet sits cross-legged and shines the flashlight on her chin, making her face look skull-like and distorted.

I suck in a shuddery breath. I want her to be proud of me. She can't know how scary I find this. She'll never pick me for anything again.

"This is the perfect hiding place," Violet whispers, her eyes gleaming. "Don't you think?"

"Yep," I say. "It's great."

Violet points her hand through the branches to a clearing. "See *through there? That's where the other counselors come to smoke weed and drink. And this . . . this is the perfect place to watch from. If you don't make a sound, no one will know you're here."*

*Violet's grin widens, and she shuts off the flashlight. It's pitch black. There's rustling in the bushes, and I can't stop my breath from coming out quick and ragged. I feel a hand clench around my ankle, and I yelp.*

*"Just me," Violet calls in a singsong voice. "I'm testing you."*

*"Can you turn the light back on?" I plead.*

*"If you're going to help me, Zoe, you're going to need to get braver. Can you do that for me?"*

*"Yeah," I splutter. Violet's doing this for my own good.*

*"I don't want to hear you breathing. I want to know that you're calm. That you can handle this, okay?"*

*"Okay," I whisper.*

*What feels like a finger strokes my cheek. It's just Violet's, I tell myself. She's testing me. I press my lips together hard, trying to hold back the pent-up breaths that gather painfully in my throat. I sit for what feels like an hour, ignoring the scurrying of God knows what animals through the bushes around me. I want to ask her if this can be over now, if we can return to the cabin, but I hold back the words. This is a test. For my own good.*

*"Better," Violet says. "You might be cut out for this job after all."*

---

## WEDNESDAY, DECEMBER 29

Mrs. Williams opens the front door, her face as red as the droplets sloshing out of her wine glass onto the hardwood floor.

"Come in, campers," she says, patting each of us on the shoulder sort of roughly as we step inside and take our boots—or in Holly's case, stilettos—off on the welcome mat.

At least she remembers who we are, I guess.

"Violet used to talk so fondly about you back when she worked at the camp," Mrs. Williams says with a glazed-over expression on her face. "Everyone's in the living room looking at photos of . . . her," she stammers. "Can I get you a drink? Wine maybe?"

"No, thanks," Calista says, just as I'm about to say, "Sure." She gives me a look and shakes her head. I like adults who are liberal about underage drinking. Calista's a bit of a killjoy.

"Oh well, more for me," Mrs. Williams says with a strained laugh. Then her face clouds over as if she's struck by a memory, and she leads the way down the wide hallway lined with paintings in gold frames. She staggers slightly and steadies herself against the wall.

"Are you sure we should be here?" Denise whispers, her hands balled up in fists against her sides. "It's going to be all the people Violet's been around the last few years. No one's going to know who we are."

"Don't worry. We're not staying long." I touch her forearm lightly, and she flinches.

Denise was the toughest to convince about extending her stay at my place. She kept going on about her plans for her mom to meet her at the bus station until Holly grabbed her cell and called Denise's mom on speakerphone. She sounded delighted that we wanted Denise to stay longer. "Of course you should stay for a few more days," she said. "It'll be good for you." Denise used to be so much fun, always so carefree and easygoing. Maybe her mom misses that side of her too.

"This place wasn't always as fancy," Holly says as we step into a beautifully furnished living room where about fifty people have gathered, sitting on white leather couches, standing around a marble table, or clustered in circles beneath a crystal chandelier. "I think they came into some money."

Must be nice. Maybe Dad will win big at the slots in Niagara and we'll have the same good fortune. Our shabby furniture could definitely use an upgrade.

Mrs. Williams stumbles onto the couch beside a tanned, dark-haired, gorgeous specimen of a man. He looks about twenty-five, which means he probably is, since my age-guessing skills are usually on point. His hand flies up to save her wine from spilling onto the white shag rug. What quick reflexes. My kind of hero.

"Who is *that*?" I whisper to Holly, who's got her eye on him as well.

"Your future boyfriend?" Holly says, wiggling her eyebrows suggestively.

Denise bites her lip and shakes her head as if she'd like to lecture me that this is a celebration of life and not a meat market. I'm pretty sure she stopped herself because I'm the only one who's nice to her lately. Calista sits down on one of the chairs lined against the wall opposite Mrs. Williams, and the rest of us do the same.

Calista and Holly whisper to each other and glance in every direction around the room. I prefer to check out the guy. His muscular physique is obvious, even though he's got on a blue long-sleeved dress shirt. Every movement of his body, as he leans to point out photos in an album Mrs. Williams flips through, shows a line of definition beneath his shirt. Who is this guy?

THE GIRLS FROM HUSH CABIN

Her neighbor? A classmate? A brother she never mentioned? It doesn't matter to me. I am down for it.

"I said, it's the woman from the funeral," Denise says. "April." She's frowning, probably because it isn't the first time she's spoken.

"Sorry," I answer. "I was a little distracted there." I look across the room at April, dressed in a red bodycon dress. She holds a glass of wine and stands by the windows beside a guy with bright blue eyes and slicked-back hair. Holly pointed him out at the funeral as Violet's cousin, Hector. "That's nice. Are you going to say hello?"

Denise looks down at her navy-blue linen pants. "Maybe later." Someone needs to get Denise a glass of wine too. She could use a bit of loosening up.

Mrs. Williams closes the photo album, and the beautiful man takes it from her and places it on the solid-wood coffee table in front of them. He rises, holding out a hand to pull Mrs. Williams to her feet.

He clears his throat loudly several times. "Excuse me," he almost shouts. The room falls into a hush, and all eyes are on him, instead of just *my* ogling pair. "Tina would like to say a few words," he continues in a deep husky voice, which is exactly the way I expected him to sound.

"Thank you, Damien," Mrs. Williams says, swaying slightly. "Thank you all for coming today to remember my daughter." Her voice cracks, and she presses a hand against her lips. "She would have loved to be with all of you today." She squints as she swivels around to peer at each guest. "Some old friends," she says, gazing right at me. "Some new," she says, looking beside her at Damien. So, Damien is Violet's new friend? What kind of *friends* were they? "It's so nice to be with so many of you who treasured my dear daughter. I'm looking forward to having conversations with each of you tonight. Damien, would you like to say something as well?" Mrs. Williams turns to him, admiration, and maybe it's just me projecting, but perhaps also desire in her eyes.

"Yes," Damien says. He clears his throat again, and his eyes roam around the room like he's suddenly uncomfortable being put on the spot. "Violet was my beautiful girlfriend and I'm devastated that she's no longer here with me." He stares at the floor, his face expressionless. "She was a fascinating person and it's very odd not having her around."

So that's how he knew her. My crush fades away as quickly as it formed. I'm not going to try and date my deceased camp counselor's grieving boyfriend. I could never do that to Violet.

Calista inhales sharply. I guess she was surprised to hear it too. I never expected Violet to give up on Grayson coming back; she was always googling him, writing posts on social media asking if anyone knew any information about his whereabouts. But it seems like she did move on in the end. Understandable, since this guy's cute enough to get anyone over their past love.

"Sorry," Holly whispers and squeezes my hand. "There's plenty of fish in the sea," she says with a wink. "And men in this room." She tilts her head to the group of mysterious-looking men we saw at the funeral. The ripped one with the eyebrow ring grins when I look their way. Nothing wrong with keeping my options open.

"Thank you," Mrs. Williams says. "Damien was with Violet all of the time, up until the day she died. If only he'd been there when . . ." She trails off.

Damien's face reddens, and he puts his arm around Mrs.

Williams's waist, gently lowering her back onto the couch. He hands her the glass of wine, and she finishes the rest of it in one gulp. He strides to the kitchen, returning with a bottle in hand to top her off.

The room begins bustling with conversation again.

"That's weird," Calista says.

"That he's keeping his mother-in-law comfortably intoxicated?" Holly asks. She cracks a smile and tucks a blond wave behind her ear.

"No," Denise answers, her brown eyes blazing. "It's suspicious that he doesn't seem like he cares. That was one of the worst speeches for a deceased person I've ever heard, and I've heard a lot."

"Exactly," Calista says. "His face was blank. He didn't know what to say. *¡Dios mío!* If my boyfriend died, God forbid, I'd have a lot better things to say about him than that he was *fascinating*. What does that even mean?"

"What are you trying to say?" I ask. "You think he didn't like her?"

Calista shoots me a look like she thinks I'm kind of dense, but then her expression changes, like the wheels in her head are turning at an even faster pace than usual. "Do you really think Violet would drown in her own mother's pool?"

"It's definitely not the cause of death I was expecting," I answer. I thought we went over this yesterday. "Why?"

"I'm sure it's crossed your mind, too," she murmurs. "Maybe someone drowned her." Calista turns away from us and glowers at Damien, her lips set in a thin line. I'm surprised he doesn't feel her boring holes through him with her death stare.

# 10
# Calista

It's 5:30 p.m. We've been here for thirty minutes, and we've already found our number one suspect.

As the law case studies I've been reading suggest, it's almost always the husband, or in this circumstance, the boyfriend.

Damien doesn't look like someone whose girlfriend just died. He looks nervous and edgy, not sad. If Javier acted this way at my memorial, I'd come back to haunt him.

Damien turns to whisper something in Mrs. Williams's ear, and she nods, taking long blinks that make it seem like she'll pass out at any moment. The poor woman looks completely plastered, which is probably a common way people handle grief. Violet's cousin Hector sits down on the other side of her, looking even more heartbroken than he did at the funeral yesterday. He cradles his face in his hands and shakes his head as if he still can't believe this is reality. I watch him turn and narrow his eyes at Damien, and I instantly realize, he probably suspects him too.

Even though Damien's gaze is on his very shiny black shoes, he must feel people staring at him, because he stands and begins to weave his way around the other guests. My eyes are glued to him as he bounds up the stairs. I'm tempted to follow him but that would be crossing major lines.

I turn back to check out Mrs. Williams, who runs a hand along her blond hair, which is smoothed into an elegant chignon that contrasts with her untucked shirt and wrinkled skirt. She whispers something to Hector, who nods like a bobblehead and stands. He leaves the room and comes back with a stand and the large portrait of Violet that was displayed at the funeral home. He sets it up and stands in front of it for a few minutes, frowning as he slowly sways back and forth to the Bruno Mars music that's playing quietly in the background.

A man with a black beanie and dark glasses and another man with a ponytail walk up behind him. The guy with the ponytail taps him on the shoulder, and Hector whips around, looking annoyed. They huddle together talking, and then Hector marches out of the room again, the two men following behind.

"The one with the beanie looks familiar. I wish he'd take the glasses off so I could figure out where I know him from," Holly says, craning her neck to watch them step outside. "Maybe they're security or something."

I nod. "Maybe. But why would a celebration-of-life reception need security guards? Unless the hosts are scared of unwanted guests showing up."

Mrs. Williams squints as she swivels her head to study the

room until her bleary eyes rest on me. She pats a space beside her on the couch and mouths, *Come.*

"Is it just me, or is Mrs. Williams trying to get you to sit beside her?" Holly asks in that perpetually amused tone that's starting to irk me.

"It looks like it." I stand and brush the creases off my dress. "I'm going over there." Before Holly comes up with a smart reply, I beeline across the room to take a seat next to Mrs. Williams on the smooth white leather couch.

It's time to get some information from the best source here.

She reaches out and strokes my cheek with her cold hand. "You're one of the campers," she slurs. "Violet used to love her job at Bellwood Lake before that awful tragedy happened there. I think those may have been some of the best years of her life."

That seems odd. I thought Violet's life would only get better after her stint working at camp. She went to NYU. *Those* would have been the best years of my life, not the time spent at a minimum-wage summer camp job.

"It was fun," I agree. "Violet taught me a lot there."

"Like what?" Mrs. Williams asks. She shifts even closer to me so that our thighs rest together and leans her head toward me so it's inches away from mine, and I can smell the sour scent of wine on her breath.

"She taught me to swim," I answer, instantly wishing I could take it back as soon as the words leave my mouth. I could have mentioned the card games or the dance moves instead of something that's still so raw.

"Oh." Her face clouds over, and she arches her head back, then takes a long sip of wine. It's stained her chapped lips a purplish color. "She used to be a very good swimmer."

I consider asking her about it. Getting her take on what caused Violet to drown and whether she suspects something else happened, but it suddenly feels all wrong. I push my limits with people sometimes, but I'm not cruel enough to suggest someone's daughter was murdered and announce that at her celebration-of-life reception of all places.

I glance across the room at the girls. Holly twists a strand of hair around her finger and grins at me. Denise sits with her arms crossed tightly across her polka-dotted blouse. Zoe's not even looking my way. She's got her gaze fixed on the angry-looking group of guys we saw at the funeral. They lean against the wall by the bookshelf in the back corner of the room.

Mrs. Williams reaches out to grab my hand with ice-cold fingers that twitch like she's a bundle of nerves. "Violet moved into her own place years ago, but she came back several days before our family Christmas party. She used to love to swim in my pool. It's salt water and it's heated . . . who wouldn't like that? It was the most dreadful thing. Finding her like that." Her grip on my hand tightens, and her long red fingernails dig into my skin.

"I'm very sorry. It's tragic," I murmur, gently removing her fingers from their death grip on me and folding my hands in my lap.

She turns to me with a weary look. "You and your friends should go up to her room to see the photos she had from her camp days. They're all over the walls."

I sit up straight. If Violet really was murdered, this might be the way to find out. "You'd let us go into her room?"

Mrs. Williams shrugs. "Why not? You and your friends would like to see them, wouldn't you? It would be nice for you girls. I'll show you the way." She struggles to stand, falters, and lands back on the couch. I offer her a hand to help her to her feet and then follow her out of the living room, gesturing for the other girls, who are eyeing us curiously, to come with us.

"Where are we going?" Zoe whispers, falling in line beside me.

"To Violet's room," I whisper back. "Mrs. Williams wants to show us some photos."

Zoe grimaces. "Really? Okay."

Mrs. Williams stumbles past the staircase I expected her to step onto and heads toward the sliding door leading to the snow-covered backyard. She points to a door to the right of it and gives me a grave look. "That's the pool I told you about." Her shaking hands hover in front of her mouth, and she lets out a noise that sounds like a yelp and sinks to her knees.

Denise swoops to her side and crouches on the floor beside her. "I'm so sorry," she says, and Mrs. Williams's head crumples against her shoulder.

I peer through the window on the pool room's door, but I can't make anything out because the lights are off. It's like staring into a dark abyss. "May I?" I ask, opening the door an inch.

Mrs. Williams looks up from Denise's shoulder and nods slightly.

I push the metal bar, and the door swings open. It creaks closed behind me as I step inside. I feel along the wall for the light switch and flick it. The room has floor-to-ceiling blue-and-white tiles, and the rectangular pool stretches a good forty feet from deep end to shallow. Impressive. I can't make out any of the sounds of the party. Besides the hum of the fluorescent lights, the room's eerily quiet. I picture Violet coming in here for a swim, maybe a romantic swim with Damien, and then him holding her head under the water and leaving before Mrs. Williams even knew he was there. Why did he want her dead, though? What don't we know?

The door creaks again, and I can make out the sound of the guests' conversations blending into a low buzz. I jolt and spin around to see Holly behind me, her face screwed up like she's bit into a lemon. "This is so fucked up," she whispers. "Why does her mom want us in here?"

I shake my head. "No idea but now I'm in here and I hear how soundproof it is with the door shut, I feel like it's the perfect place to drown someone. And drowning is the perfect way to kill someone. Make it look like an accident."

"I think something else could be going on too." Holly walks along the edge of the pool, her forehead furrowed as though she's playing out the day Violet died in her head. "If Violet liked drinking half as much as her mother does, maybe that could explain how she drowned. She might have come in here for some drinks and passed out in the water. Anyway, this place gives me the creeps. Let's go see the pictures."

I take one final look at the still water and follow Holly back out to the others.

Mrs. Williams seems to have partially recovered from her fit of grief. She leans against the wall with Hector and Denise standing on either side of her.

Hector looks at us with his blazing blue eyes. "Thinking about going for a swim?" he asks curiously.

Mrs. Williams sniffs. "Of course not. They wanted to see . . . where it happened."

"Tragic," Hector whispers. He shakes his head sadly and heads back to the living room.

"He and Violet were very close," Mrs. Williams murmurs. "They had a special bond ever since they were kids. He was there for her when her father passed away. The last few years they were always talking on the phone or going out places together. He would have done anything to protect her. No one could mess with her when he was around. It kills him that he wasn't there to save . . . to save her that night."

"He seems devastated," Denise says, pointing to where Hector stands again, in front of Violet's picture, slowly rocking back and forth on the balls of his feet.

"The whole family is," Mrs. Williams says with a deep sigh that makes her shoulders slump. "Ready to see the pictures in her room now?"

I nod. "Sure."

Mrs. Williams labors up the winding staircase, gripping the banister as she trudges slowly stair by stair. We follow behind.

The door at the top of the staircase swings open, and Damien steps out, his face contorted in anxiety. I glance inside the room before he shuts the door and see a king-sized bed and floral prints on the wall. He stops in his tracks, startled, and frowns at Mrs. Williams. "Where are you going?"

The corners of her mouth turn up in a small smile, and she steadies herself by leaning her hand against the wall. "To Violet's room. I want to show her old friends something."

Damien's right eye twitches. Is that a tic, or his guilt coming through? "I'll come," he says.

"I thought Violet's room was the one he was coming out of," Zoe whispers. "Was that Mrs. Williams's room that he was in then? That's strange, isn't it?"

"Extremely," I whisper back.

"Her room's there," Holly says, pointing to the door that's open a crack at the end of the hall. "I remember."

Mrs. Williams takes a few steps down the hall and heads through the doorway of the room Holly pointed at. She switches on the light, but the chandelier only has one working bulb so it's still very dim.

The first thing I see is the huge bulletin board with photos pinned to it. I step across the plush cream-colored carpet so I'm close enough to get a better look. Mrs. Williams wasn't kidding about the number of photos Violet had. My eyes rest on a shot of the four of us, holding up little fish, beaming like we're proud of ourselves. Then my gaze moves to another picture of us sitting on the rocks near the forest. Violet stands behind us, her arms stretching across all our shoulders like wings, as if she's the mother bird and we're all her babies.

"Holy moly," Denise breathes. "I forgot about some of these times. These are great."

Mrs. Williams nudges Damien in the side. "Let's leave them alone for a bit so they can reminisce."

"You're going to leave them in here on their own?" Damien says, folding his arms and turning to us with a scowl. "Are you sure about that?"

Mrs. Williams raises her eyebrows and rests a hand on her hip. "It's not like they're going to steal anything."

Damien stares at me grimly. Did Violet point me out in one of the photos? Maybe he heard about The Mistake, and that's why he's suspicious. She told me she'd never breathe a word, but maybe she changed more than just physically.

"They're just going to look at the pictures and talk. Let's go. I should chat with the other guests," Mrs. Williams continues, taking a step backward and nearly losing her footing.

Damien sighs and links arms with her.

I watch them walk down the hall and descend the staircase. They pause on the landing, and he runs his hand across her waist and kisses her on the cheek. They continue walking, and I close the door once they reach the bottom. "Did you catch how suspicious he was acting?"

Holly makes a face. "Yep. Definitely questionable."

Zoe sits on Violet's bed and steeples her fingers beneath her chin. "It's still so hard to believe that she drowned. Do you think we'll find anything in here that could be like a clue or something?"

Holly plops down on Violet's chair and drums her hand against the desk dramatically. "Twenty dollars says that Mrs. Williams and Damien are boning. Who wants to bet?"

I cross my arms. "He just kissed her cheek on the stairs. They do have romantic energy. Would she really do that to her daughter?"

"Enough!" Denise says. "Let's just look at the photos and give our condolences again and go. I think it's bizarre that she drowned too, but if the police thought anything was suspicious, they probably would have investigated, right?" She's trembling like a cornered animal. Her father's death must have caused some deep trauma.

I spot a suitcase lying on the floor near Violet's closet. She was staying with her mom for a few days for Christmas, and this must be what she brought with her. I unzip it and rifle through the dresses and leggings. "I wonder where her purse is?"

A slow smile spreads across Holly's face. "Violet would never leave her purse unattended. She'd hide it." She wheels the chair she was sitting on across the room and past me into Violet's walk-in closet. Then she climbs up on it and grips the top shelf.

"What are you doing?" Denise cries. "What if Mrs. Williams and Damien come back and see you doing that?"

Holly just grins, carefully lifting the ceiling tile above her head and pulling out a wooden box and a small black purse decorated with silver studs. "We came here to investigate, right? Well, that's what I'm doing." She climbs off the chair, opens the box, and sighs. "This is her Grayson box. It's got pictures of the dream house she wanted to live in with him, movie ticket stubs, and newspaper clippings back from when he went missing." She puts the box on Violet's desk, and I walk over to read the article I've read so many times before, always searching for answers, but only finding more questions.

> The Birchbrook Police Service is requesting the public's assistance in locating Grayson DANTE, 18. Grayson was reported missing on August 9th.
>
> Grayson is believed to have been last seen in the area of Main Street and Hillcrest Road, near his family home.
>
> He is described as 5'11", medium build, with brown shaved hair and brown eyes. He was wearing a hunter-green hoodie and cargo shorts at the time of his disappearance.
>
> Anyone with information on Grayson's whereabouts is asked to contact the Birchbrook Police Service at 555-2100.

Holly comes up behind me and rests her sharp chin on my shoulder. "Why would that boy just up and leave her, not to mention his dad and sister?"

"I don't know," I say, nudging her off me. "And there's a few other things I don't know about either. Like how *you know* where Violet hides her stuff. When was the last time you saw her?" Holly shrugs and hands me the purse. "Two years ago, why?" I frown. "How did you know about her hiding spot?"

"I guess she didn't have a reason to change it," Holly answers. "You're just jealous you didn't find this yourself."

Denise crosses her arms and scowls. "How come she asked you to come to her house and not us?"

Holly shrugs again. "I don't know. Whatever."

I look down at the purse in my hand and unzip it before I have second thoughts. I'm not doing this for bad reasons, I remind myself. I'm doing this to find out the truth. For Violet. I pull out her wallet and peer at the other contents. A lipstick, some tampons, a pocketknife, her keys, a cell phone. I click on the side button. It's dead. At the bottom of the purse are two pieces of folded paper. I unfold one, and in thick block letters, it reads, "I TOLD YOU ALREADY TO WATCH OUT. YOU'RE FUCKING WITH THE WRONG CREW." My blood runs cold. I *knew* it.

I put Violet's wallet and purse on her desk and hold the slip of paper up triumphantly. "Anyone want to quit saying that her death was an accident now?"

Zoe's eyes widen. "What? We need to show that to someone. Like the police."

"That could be about something else," Denise whispers, biting her lip. "Maybe."

"If someone who killed Violet wrote that, don't you think going to the police might make them want to get back at us?" Holly says, squinting at the ceiling and twisting the chair she's sitting in again from side to side. "We need to be careful. We have to think all of this through."

I unfold the second piece of paper, expecting to find something equally ominous, but instead it's got Violet's name, hours, and wage typed on it. "This is a pay stub dated a month ago," I announce. "So I guess we know where she worked with April."

"Where?" Zoe asks.

I glance down at the slip of paper. "Some place called Bennington's."

Zoe's eyebrows shoot up. "Are you sure?"

"Yes," I say, holding it up for her to see. "Is that some type of country club?"

Zoe shakes her head slowly. "No. It's a bar in downtown Birchbrook that has a terrible reputation. Criminals hang out there."

"Criminals?" Denise repeats, her face growing more flushed by the second.

"Look," I say. "My family's Nochevieja party's Friday night. I need to get home tomorrow to get ready. We might as well check this place out while we're still here." I slip Violet's phone and pocketknife into my purse and head toward the door. "If Violet really was murdered, maybe we can find out some information there. Mrs. Williams looked at Damien when she referred to Violet's new friends. Maybe they worked together there. He looks like a bouncer type."

Holly raises her eyebrows. "Good thinking, Sherlock, but did you forget that we're underage? How the hell are we going to get in?"

"We can get April to bring us there," I say, my hand already on the doorknob. "I bet she'd be able to get us in." As eager as

I am to get to the bottom of this, a sick feeling hits me right in the gut as I think about the words in the note. *You're fucking with the wrong crew.* Are we going to get to the bar and come face-to-face with them?

# 11
# *Holly*

Who knew that during my visit for a funeral, I'd be cruising through downtown Birchbrook with the girls, on our way to a bar that criminals chill at? Alex would freak out if he knew about this. Except, news flash: he's ALREADY losing his shit. Has been since I told him I was staying an extra day. But this latest update would make it THAT much worse.

I switch on the radio for some driving jams. A Rihanna song that I love is playing, and I sing along quietly.

Zoe nudges me. "Sing louder. You've always had such a nice voice. I remember at the lip-synching contests at camp you always sang."

"And you always won. Even though the point was to lip-synch, not sing," Calista says with a hint of bitterness in her voice.

Honestly? There's nothing like a compliment to boost some-one's confidence. I sing louder even when I catch Calista in my rearview mirror rolling her eyes. Then I pull out of Mrs. Williams's neighborhood onto Richmond and abruptly stop singing. There's the cemetery again. I take in the long field of headstones and shiver.

"Violet's probably buried there. It's the only cemetery in town," Zoe says quietly.

"I hate that we pass it every time we go anywhere," I add. "It's kind of creepy actually."

There's a long silence until finally Calista clears her throat. "How far away is Bennington's?"

"Five minutes," Zoe answers. "Not far."

"What did you mean when you said criminals hang out there?" Denise asks. "Are we putting ourselves in danger?"

"Oh, that . . ." Zoe trails off. And I just know: this is going to be golden. I smile at her, and she chews on her lip like she's holding back a smile of her own. "The SWAT team kind of raided it a few times."

"The SWAT team?" Denise's voice rises. "Why?" I peer at her in the rearview mirror. Her mouth is set in a hard line, and she rubs her temples as though this day just got a few notches more eventful than she can handle. I'd bet money that she'll suggest waiting in the car.

Zoe shrugs. "Might have been drugs. Or taking down a crime ring. I heard a few different versions of the story."

"Why would Violet work there when she could work at a normal bar or restaurant?" Denise says, frowning.

"She probably thought she'd make more money at Benning-ton's," I reply. "For sure it was about the money. That's all she cared about after Grayson left."

"She had goals to get her dream house and there's nothing wrong with that," Denise says gruffly. Typical. Despite her disappointment in Violet's career choice, she never fails to come to her defense like a loyal puppy.

I stay silent. Whatever. These girls don't know Violet the way that I did. Basically, they saw a hint of another side every time a "joke" seemed mean or a "prank" seemed wrong. I saw a whole lot more than that. Some people unknowingly end up entangled with the wrong crowd. Violet seemed to handpick them. Maybe we'll meet some of that crowd tonight.

I tap my fingers against the steering wheel in time with the Justin Bieber song that just started playing and wonder what kind of music is generally played in dens of danger. I hope stuff with a good beat. And that we're allowed inside in the first place.

When Calista asked April to help us get into the bar, her eyes twinkled, and she told us we were in luck because that's where the after-party was at. Before she left for her shift, she gave us her number and added us all to Instagram. "Do you think April will really be able to get us in tonight?" I ask.

Calista shrugs. "Possibly. She's our best shot."

"Make a left at the light," Zoe says, and I turn, coasting along Main Street past a line of brightly lit stores and lampposts decorated with garlands and white Christmas lights that illuminate the dark streets.

Zoe points. "It's there. Across from the gas station." I spot a small dark building with the name Bennington's written on the window in small white letters. If I wasn't looking for this place, I'd miss it. Maybe that's the point. I pull into the lot, and we step out of the car.

"Hey, bad guys, are you ready? We're coming in," I say,

blow a little bubble with my gum, and turn to look at the girls. Denise is pacing along the parking blocks, staring at her boots, and chewing on her bottom lip. Calista's eyes are darting around, sizing everything up, and she may as well have brought a spy kit. Zoe's stealing a sip from her flask and looking at the front doors eagerly as if this place is an amusement park she's always wanted to go to but was too afraid to try. Extra underage-looking. All of them.

I sigh. "Look, even though April is going to try to get us in, you still need to appear at least twenty-one, or someone's going to kick us out. You've got to act confident."

"Yeah," Zoe echoes. "I've got into a few bars before with my fake ID and I agree with Holly. Act confident and you'll be fine. This place is going to be great."

Calista sniffs. "You have a fake ID?"

Zoe nods proudly.

Denise looks upward as if she's hoping Wonder Woman will fly down to rescue her. "I'll text April and tell her we're here."

Surprise, surprise, I guess she'll be coming in with us after all.

"I hope she responds fast, it's way too cold out here," Calista complains. She pulls her cashmere scarf up around her neck and stands rigid against the building's dark windows.

Zoe fiddles with one of her dangle earrings, then reaches back in her purse for her flask.

Calista blinks quickly. "Again?"

"You're telling me you don't need liquid courage in a place like this?" Zoe says and takes another sip.

Calista scrunches up her face and shakes her head firmly. "No, actually." Too bad. I'd pay good money to see Calista have a drink or two and become a little less like a tiger ready to pounce. She taps her foot and turns to Denise. "Please tell me she's written back."

Denise shakes her head. "Not yet."

"Great," Calista mutters. "Looks like we'll be hanging out in the parking lot freezing to death then."

Zoe opens the door a crack and peeks inside. "Why don't we try getting in without her? There's a bouncer in there but I've got my ID. Maybe you guys could say you're friends of Violet's and you were so upset and distracted you left your IDs at home by accident."

Denise looks back down at her phone screen. "Nothing from April yet. I think we should wait for her. None of us really look twenty-one."

"I'll DM her on Instagram too," Zoe says. She types something and turns her phone toward us. A picture of April in a yellow bikini fills the screen. "Look at her in this shot. Talk about *Sports Illustrated* worthy. I'd kill for legs like hers."

"Come on, Zoe, your legs are hot too." I bounce in place and shiver. I'm not dressed right for hanging out in North Pole weather. "Okay, enough waiting in the cold. I'm game to try. Let's do this." I channel my inner diva, open the door, and walk in.

That's all the invitation Zoe needs. She's behind me as I lead the way through a dark foyer toward a burly bouncer with a shaved head. He stands in front of a second door that has metal floor lamps on either side of it. I stop in front of him and whirl around to see Calista and Denise have joined us. The bouncer eyes us up and down with a lopsided grin. "Good evening. Can I see your IDs, please?"

I rifle around in my purse and muster my best flirtatious

smile. "Oh darn," I say softly, batting my eyelashes as subtly as I can. "I'm here for my friend's memorial party and I was so flustered and upset I must have forgotten my card at home."

The bouncer's forehead furrows. "Sorry, I'm afraid I can't let you in."

The look I gave him always works on everyone I use it for. This guy gave me laid-back vibes. I didn't peg him as a rule follower. "Please," I say. "Can't you make an exception for us?"

Zoe takes out her wallet and flashes an ID of a plump brunette woman who looks nothing like her. "Here's mine," she says proudly. "My friends and I are the same age."

The bouncer looks at her card and laughs loudly. "That's not you, sweetheart. I wasn't born yesterday."

"It's me," Zoe says indignantly. "It's a sensitive subject for me but I lost weight since then and got a nose job."

He points at the exit. "I gotta ask you to leave." The door he's standing in front of swings open, and April steps out. Her makeup is flawless, and she's wearing a short pink sequined dress with spaghetti straps. Interesting waitressing uniform.

"Sorry," she says in a singsong voice. "I was serving a table and just got the messages. Come on in."

The bouncer shakes his head firmly. "I can't let that happen, April. They don't have ID."

April juts her hip forward and shoots him a cheeky grin. "They're friends of Violet's from college."

The bouncer points at Zoe. "Then why did this one have a fake ID?"

April snatches the card out of Zoe's hand and studies it. "That's her," she says and winks at me. "I know her from back then. Doesn't she look so much better now?"

The bouncer sighs. "Fine," he says wearily and pushes on the door, holding it open for us as we step inside the dim room, illuminated by warm orange lamplight. The customers are mainly men, most of them wearing black, and they sit huddled in leather booths or around a dark oak bar, sipping amber-colored drinks out of crystal tumblers. Trip hop music reverberates from the speakers, and several people sway to the slow beat with their eyes closed, like they're in a world of their own. The other waitresses are dressed like April, in red, pink, or purple sequined dresses. They hold trays lined with drinks and glide gracefully around the room looking sultry. Whoever owns this place seems to have a type he likes to hire. Drop-dead gorgeous. Violet fit the description perfectly.

A balding man with thick eyebrows waves, and April nods. "I'll be back," she says and saunters across the room toward him.

My phone buzzes in my purse, and I tug it out to glance at the screen. Another text from Alex:

> I'm worried now. If you don't call me,
> I'll tell your mom I think you're in
> trouble.

What? Why would he be worried? I've been texting him back. Most of the time. He has to know I'm with my friends and it's hard to talk on the phone all the time.

I text back, glancing at the girls, who gaze around the room, looking kind of stunned.

> We're at a memorial party. I'll call
> you when we get back to Zoe's.

His reply comes so fast I'm surprised he can type that quickly.

> Are there hot guys there?

He's got to be kidding me. Not, *How are you doing? That must be tough.* He's going straight there. I'm suddenly aware of the heart pendant he gave me, hanging around my neck like a shiny noose. I write back:

> No. Only a few old men. Don't
> worry.

Denise grabs my arm, and for a second, I think she's going to drag me back outside. "This place gives me a bad feeling," she says. I glance at her with a smirk, and she quickly shifts her eyes to the hardwood floor. "Whose idea was this again?"

Calista frowns and puts her hands on her hips. "It was mine. And I don't regret it by the way. We're going to find out crucial information here. Wait and see."

A brunette woman in a low-cut green velvet dress walks toward us. She grabs Denise's and Calista's hands and drags them to the dance floor. "Dance with me," she slurs. How did she manage to pick the most uptight ones? That's talent. Calista's jaw ticks, but surprisingly, she sways along with the music. Denise moves from side to side awkwardly, and the woman closes her eyes. "This is my song," she coos.

Zoe laughs, grabs my hand, and spins me around.

"Yes! That's what I'm talking about," the woman in green

says, and she pulls Denise and Calista forward until we're all in a circle, our arms on each other's shoulders. "Isn't this great?"

She's got a point. This music is kind of fun to dance to. There's no right or wrong way to move to it. I glance at the others, and I suddenly feel as giddy as I did back at camp at age thirteen, when we were all together on one of our theme nights. For the first time, all of us are smiling. Even Calista. Finally. This is the fun I was looking for.

"Got to get a drink," the woman says, and she dances away, leaving us swaying from side to side.

Zoe grins at me. "I thought you were more into pop music."

"I am," I say with a laugh. "But this isn't so bad."

*Crash.*

"What did you say?" a loud voice booms over the jazz music.

A barstool careens across the room, hitting the floor and sliding into my foot. I flinch in pain. Denise shrieks. My arms open, and I dive forward, pushing the girls toward the back wall, then I whip around, heart pounding, trying to figure out where the shouting is coming from. Zoe grips my hand. "Oh my God," she whispers.

A group of men stands next to the booth closest to the dance floor. A tall man with a baseball hat and a shorter man with a full sleeve of tattoos stand chest to chest. "Come at me," the tall man yells. He backs up and rams his body into the other man.

"I warned you," the tattooed man bellows and throws his drink on the taller man's face. He drops his glass, then charges his fist into the tall man's stomach. The tall man staggers backward, then shoots forward, lunging on top of the other guy. They're on the floor, rolling around, punching and kicking.

The music stops, and four muscular men in white T-shirts

rush out of a room behind the bar. Two of them hold each man back, and they roughly push them toward the exit.

My foot's throbbing and my head's reeling. What kind of place is this?

"What the heck was that?" Calista cries.

Denise pales. "We need to get out of here."

A stocky guy with a lip piercing comes toward us, and at first I think he's going to ask us if we're okay, but his brown eyes are cold and leering. "Watch out tonight," he says. "You girls don't belong here."

# 12
# Denise

The guy with the lip ring stands there, unblinking, glaring at us. I grab Calista's arm. Alarm travels through my body, and I break into a cold sweat. "You heard what he said. Let's get out of here."

Calista plucks my hand off her arm and shakes her head. "We can't leave yet." My heart's thumping so fast I'm surprised I'm still standing. *How could she not want to leave after all of that? I love Violet and I'd like to know what happened to her too, but I don't want to get hurt in the process.*

Holly puts her hands on her hips and sneers at the man. "Is this your bar?"

Zoe flushes and drops her eyes.

"Do you think I'm joking?" the man says in a low, threatening tone. "I warned you. Remember that."

April appears at the man's side and narrows her eyes. "Can I help you with something?" she asks, her hands on her hips.

He glares at us one final time and walks toward the exit.

"Don't mind him," April says breezily. "He's a regular. Thinks he's a tough guy."

"We should leave," I say. "That fight. We could have got hurt."

"I *did* get hurt," Holly says, rubbing one of her feet.

"Every bar has fights," April says and waves her hand like this is a typical night at Bennington's. "Just a couple of people trying to air out their differences. It happens."

"Are the police here a lot?" I ask. "They must be."

April leans in close, like she's telling us a secret, and her perfume smells expensive. "See those guys over there?" she asks, pointing across the room at a table of men who are wearing leather coats. They're talking in loud voices, chugging back their drinks, and nudging each other forcefully. One of them is smoking a cigarette. Sure, I haven't been to a bar before, but I'm pretty sure that's illegal. "Those guys *are* the police," April whispers. "They're involved in a lot of bad stuff. They're friends with most of the people who come here. Basically, beware. I wouldn't call them even if someone was robbing my house."

I shudder. "What? What kind of town is this?"

April laughs. "Stay away from trouble and you won't need to deal with them. Why don't you guys sit down for a bit? Have a drink. I'll take you to V's friends. They'll look out for you."

The slow, almost hypnotic music starts back up again, and a bouncer with wavy blond hair picks up the barstool from the dance floor and puts it back where it belongs like nothing happened. I want to go back to where I belong. Home. Alive.

We follow April through the slowly rising haze of smoke the fog machine left behind. I spot Hector at a table by the bar with some other people I saw at Mrs. Williams's house and assume we're going there, but instead, April stops at a long table where the sketchy guys from the funeral sit. The conversation halts, and they stare at us suspiciously as we approach the table.

"These are V's friends," April says, putting her arms around Holly and Zoe. "Make them feel welcome."

"I'm not sitting with them," I hiss and give Calista a light jab in the ribs.

"Don't make a scene," she whispers. "Sit down. If anything's off about them, I'll get us out of here fast."

Zoe sits at an empty chair in the middle beside the muscular guy with the eyebrow ring who she seemed to find attractive at the funeral, and Calista sits next to her. Holly makes a face and settles down across from them, beside the creepy tall guy with the thick beard. The only available seat is right next to her. Great. I glance down the other end of the table at the men I don't recognize. They nudge each other and laugh at jokes I'm too far away to hear, eyeing me and my friends with interest.

The creepy guy turns to stare at Holly intensely. "I know you."

Holly traces her finger along the wood grain on the table, and her jaw twitches. Suspicious as always. She won't even look at him.

I study the guy carefully. I knew as soon as I saw him that he looked a little familiar, but I can't place him. "Where do you know each other from?" I ask, reveling in the fact that Holly seems uncomfortable, but he ignores me.

Zoe's beaming at the guy with the eyebrow ring, and he's smiling back like he enjoys the attention. She plays with a strand of her hair. "What's your name and how do you know Violet?" she blurts out.

"I'm Levi and my friend Bradley introduced us," he says with an amused expression on his face. "I feel like I'm getting interrogated." He gestures to Bradley, who's drumming his fingers on the table, still staring at Holly. "Bradley told me he remembers you all from the camp his mom ran."

My heart rate accelerates. *Bradley? Can this nightmare get any worse?* My shallow breaths grow faster and faster. *Denise, get a grip. You have to.* The last time I saw Bradley Felmont was right after the police confirmed that it was his sister Farrah's body at the bottom of the cliff across the fence from Camp Bellwood Lake. He was hysterical. He threw himself onto the ground and wailed. No one could console him. They ended up taking him away in an ambulance. I struggle to take a deep breath; the others must notice. I glance at Bradley. He snarls at me and shakes his head slowly. *He knows something. He must know something.*

"How's your mom doing?" Calista asks.

Bradley glares at her. "Fine," he snaps and storms away from the table to sit on a stool by the bar.

Calista opens her mouth like she wants to ask more questions, but then she closes it.

Levi waves a hand. "Don't mind him, he's having a hard time right now. He'll be okay." He focuses on Zoe, and his mouth twists into a half smile. "How's your night going so far?"

"Awesome," she answers. "How's yours?" She's practically glowing.

"My night was difficult. But it'll probably be better now that you're here."

Hector and a guy with a ponytail get up and head for the exit. I have the biggest urge to get up and leave too, but how would I explain that to the others? I scoot my chair around to the head of the table, closer to Calista, who swivels around to examine each person with a suspicious look painted all over her face.

"I can't believe Bradley's here," I whisper the next time she glances my way.

"No kidding," she says. Her dark eyes flash, and she leans across the table to whisper back without anyone hearing. "I'm telling you, Denise, we're going to find out big information tonight. I can just feel it. Whoever wrote that threatening note to Violet could be here. They always say murderers end up being people the victim knows, and a lot of them are here right now. We could be sitting with the person who killed her." She looks pointedly at Bradley and cups her hand around her mouth to block the others from hearing her words. "Like, why was Bradley still friends with Violet? She was never nice to him at camp. Always using him to get things from his mom. Maybe he finally got back at her."

She has no idea how much Bradley could get back at Violet and me for. Hopefully no one does. I take a deep, shuddery breath and try to look calm, even though my jaw is tight and my muscles are tense.

Calista stops staring Bradley down, her gaze zipping around the room, resting on the DJ, the waitress, a loud guy who's staggering around on the dance floor. Everyone's a suspect. She narrows her eyes and leans across the table to face Levi. "I heard this place has a bad reputation. Why do you hang out here?"

Levi smiles and fiddles with his eyebrow ring. "Some bad people come here, but we don't mix with them. Violet would hang out with us sometimes before her shift started. Man, I miss her." His eyes become glossy, and he blinks quickly to compose himself.

A redheaded waitress approaches the table. "What are you ladies drinking tonight?"

"We'll all take Cokes please," Calista says, shooting Zoe a look before she can say vodka.

"Oh my God," Levi says, and I turn to follow his line of vision to the doorway, where I spot Damien marching into the room with a clenched jaw and hands that are balled into fists at his sides.

The other guys at the table stop talking and glare in Damien's direction, and Levi jumps out of his seat and books it over to Bradley. I have no idea what's going on, but it doesn't seem good at all.

"They think it was Damien too," Calista says, shooting daggers at him as he takes a seat by himself in the front corner by the bathrooms. She's found her number one suspect. She bites her lip to stop herself from saying more as the waitress places Cokes down on coasters in front of us.

"Why would Damien write Violet that note about fucking with the wrong crew?" Holly says when the waitress is out of earshot. She points at him. "Besides his deceased girlfriend's mom, he doesn't seem like he has a *crew*."

"There's something off about him," Calista says. "It's undeniable." She turns to Holly. "Men seem to like you. Go and talk to him and find out some info for us."

Holly makes a face. "Me? No way. You think he's a murderer and you want to send me right into his clutches? No, thank you."

"I'll do it," Zoe says. She waggles her eyebrows at us. "Might be exciting."

Calista gives Zoe a long glance. "I don't know. You seem kind of buzzed. Sending you might be dangerous for all of us."

Zoe grins and blinks for a few counts too long, making me realize Calista's right. She keeps sipping out of that flask like she's on a mission to get wasted. "I can play it cool. No one else wants to do it. Why not me?"

"What are you going to say?" I ask. I can picture her sitting across from him, silent, not knowing what to ask and then blurting out something like, *So, about Violet, did you do it?*

"I'll say sorry for his loss and ask how he's doing," Zoe answers. "Then I'll see what he says back."

"What about Levi?" Holly asks. "It seems like he likes you, and judging by what we just witnessed, he definitely doesn't like Damien."

Zoe stands and adjusts her red crop top. "A little jealousy might work out in my favor. Wish me luck." She rushes toward Damien's table and plops down clumsily across from him. He tilts his head back like he's startled.

Calista sighs. "She'll need all the luck she can get."

Levi and Bradley return to the table and glare in Damien's direction. "What's she doing over there?" Levi asks Holly.

"Just offering her condolences," she answers, gracing him with her Barbie-princess smile. "Why? Is everything okay?"

Levi grimaces. "I don't like that guy." His eyes are glued to them, and he rubs the back of his neck.

Calista's eyes widen, and she leans forward eagerly. "Why? What's wrong with him?"

"He's not a good person. Zoe needs to be careful. I should go over there." He pushes back his chair and stands.

"No, no, don't worry. Stay here." Holly stretches out her

hand and pats his arm. "She's only offering her condolences. If she doesn't come back to the table in a few minutes, I'll go and get her." She glances at Zoe uncertainly.

Levi slowly lowers himself until he's perching at the edge of his seat, frowning.

"I'm going to the bathroom," I blurt out. I've needed to get away from this bad situation since I got here. I stand and carefully wind through the tables, being sure to walk as closely as I can to Zoe and Damien. I need to check on her right away. Unlike Holly, I'm not comfortable waiting for a disaster to happen.

"I can't sleep," I hear him say, and for the first time, a contorted look of grief plays across his face. "I can't eat. The whole thing's a mess."

Zoe clasps her hands together like she's praying. "I'm so sorry."

She seems safe enough. No sinister talk. I push open the door to the ladies' restroom. A girl with short purple hair is in front of the sink splashing water on her face. She lets out a stifled sob.

I move closer, stopping a yard away from her. "Are you okay?"

"Not really. I don't even know why I'm here." She spins around to face me, and her pretty green eyes make my breath catch in my throat.

"Yeah, I know what you mean," I say softly, fighting the urge to reach out and touch her arm comfortingly. "This place is a lot."

She looks down, shuffling her combat boot along a shiny black tile. "I kind of thought being here would make me feel closer to her but it's making me feel like I didn't know her at all."

My heart races and my body tenses up. "Are you talking about Violet?"

"Yeah." She squints at me. "You knew her too?"

I nod. "Yes. We were close a while ago."

She cranks the paper-towel dispenser and takes a wad to dab her face. "At school she was all about her work. Telling me about the people she wanted to help when she was done with law school. I liked that about her."

I smile, remembering how Violet used to tell me about her plans to help people who were wrongly accused. She could be really nice. Before Grayson disappeared, at least. "Yeah. She could be great sometimes."

The girl closes her eyes as if the memory pains her. "Then, I started hanging out with her outside of school and it seemed like she was on a dark path, hanging out with strange people, always being really secretive about phone calls and texts she was getting. I'm sure some people here are really nice but a few of them seem like they're into drugs and stuff like that. I told her I'd help her find another part-time job if she quit, and she kept saying she was going to, but never did."

"I'm sorry," I say. Her expression crumples and she covers her mouth with her hand, and it's like the pain I've been carrying around with me for the last few days is displayed on this beautiful, sad girl's face. I take a few steps forward, and as if my hand has a mind of its own, it reaches out and lands lightly on the girl's arm.

She looks down at my hand but doesn't move it. Instead, she leans in closer to me, rests her head on my shoulder, and lets out a shuddery sob. "I miss her so much. What happened to her is just so horrible and it . . . it doesn't make sense."

She's quiet for another long minute. We're still strangers to each other, but her head's a comfortable weight on my shoulder and I don't mind her hot tears seeping through my shirt because for the first time since I heard about Violet, I feel like I'm griev-ing her with someone whose shade of sadness matches mine.

She sighs, lifts her head, and wipes her palms along her cheeks to clear away the tears. "I should go home. It's too hard to be at this place."

I take a scrap of paper and pen out of my bag, scrawl my number on it, and hold it out for her. "I'm Denise. Call me if you'd like to talk about it. I'm a good listener."

"Janie," the girl says. "Thanks." She gives me one last look, then leaves the restroom, the door swinging closed behind her.

I take a long deep breath and try to gather my composure. That moment was something I didn't expect at a place like this. I open the door to a faster-paced song than the ones playing earlier. The dance floor's full of people writhing around with their eyes shut. Probably high. The table where Damien and Zoe were sitting is now empty. At the other table, the girls are clus-tered together, shooting concerned looks at a closed door near the bar. *What's happening?* My heart thuds against my chest.

I slide into my seat across from Calista. "Where's Zoe?"

"She went into the manager's office with Damien," she an-swers, pointing at the door.

"What? Why?"

Calista raises one of her perfectly shaped eyebrows at me. "Your guess is as good as mine."

# 13
# Zoe

I flopped down on the chair across from Damien before he had a chance to stop me from sitting there. One hundred percent confident and not a bit nervous. He was cold at first, but I worked the Zoe magic, and he even offered to buy me a drink when the waitress came by. And without Calista hovering over me, I ordered what I *really* wanted.

"I can't sleep," Damien says with a pained expression. He runs a hand across his face. "I can't eat. The whole thing's a mess."

It's the first time I've seen him actually seem sad. I clasp my hands together and lean forward. "I'm so sorry."

Denise eyes me with a worried look on her face as she heads to the bathroom, and I give her a reassuring smile.

"Rob. It's here. Regular spot," the DJ calls over the speakers in a raspy voice that makes him sound like he smokes at least two packs of cigarettes a day. One of the guys who April pointed out as a corrupt cop stands and strides toward the entrance. I guess that's Officer Rob, heading to the spot to get whatever it is that just showed up here. I doubt it's an ice-cream cake or a floral arrangement. This has drugs written all over it.

"How did you meet Violet?" I ask, tugging on a strand of my short black hair. Okay, maybe I am a little nervous. I'm practically interrogating someone Calista's convinced is a murderer. It's only natural.

"I met her at a bar. We were friends first. I became her accountant," Damien answers. There's a faraway look in his eyes, and he presses his full lips together. I didn't think it was possible, but he's even more good-looking up close. "I definitely didn't meet her at this bar. I had no idea she worked here when we met. Probably wouldn't have continued talking to her if I did. There are some bad people here." He lets out a long breath, then turns to eye the table where the other girls and Levi and his friends are not being subtle about staring at us with varying levels of blatant distrust.

The others glance away at times, but Levi's eyes don't shift. A warm feeling travels through me, and I don't think it's just the vodka. I give him a little wave so he knows I haven't forgotten him. It's nice that he's jealous but I don't want him to think I'm not interested.

Damien clears his throat. "Tina mentioned that you and your friends went to the camp Violet worked at. Where do you live?"

"I live here in Birchbrook and two of my friends are from Shawdale," I answer without thinking twice about it. I'm about to tell him where Holly's from when my hand flies to my mouth.

I shouldn't be sharing information like this. The drinks have got me saying way too much.

Damien flicks his eyes toward me, then back at their table. "When are they headed back?"

I give him a strained smile. "Probably tomorrow." I have to turn this around and find out more about him or the girls will regret agreeing to send me over here. I remember the note about the crew. Maybe I should find out if he has one. "Have you got people to support you through this?"

"Sort of," he answers, running a hand across the light stubble on his chin. "My friends keep asking to come by to comfort me, but I just want to be alone. It's devastating. I can't believe this happened." His eyes glisten in the lamplit room. He does seem sad. Maybe our suspicions about him earlier were off. Everyone deals with things differently. "Tina's there for me too," Damien continues. "But she's dealing with her own heartbreak."

I remember the funny look on his face when we saw him coming out of Mrs. Williams's room, and I want to ask exactly how she's been there for him, but I decide to take a different approach. I gulp down the vodka cranberry he bought me and then the words bubble out before I have a chance to change my mind. "Violet was the best swimmer we knew. It was shocking to hear."

Damien's forehead creases, and he narrows his eyes at me. "Accidents happen," he says gruffly. His phone vibrates against the table, and he picks it up, glancing at the screen with a look on his face that I don't know how to interpret. "I need to go to the manager's office for a second. He wants to talk to me."

I remember my mission to find out as much information

as possible. I'm going to impress the girls if it's the last thing I do. "Can I come with you?"

Damien stares at me for a long minute. "I don't think it's a good idea. I'll be back in a bit if you want to keep talking." He stands and pushes in his chair.

I'm not going to give up on this chance that easily. Calista wanted to send Holly to talk to him. I need to find out way more than Holly ever could. I spring to my feet and almost fall back down. I rest my hand on the table to steady myself. "Wait, I'm thinking about applying to be a waitress here. It would help if I met the manager, and he knew I was a friend of Violet's."

Damien's eyes glower, and he grips my wrist, his fingers digging into my skin. "Never work here."

So much for him being a nice guy we all misunderstood. I twist my wrist out of his grip and frown at him. "Why?"

Damien blinks quickly and pats my arm awkwardly as if he suddenly realized how hard he grabbed me. "I'm sorry. I shouldn't have reacted like that. I just saw how this place and the people in it changed Violet. I wouldn't want that to happen to anyone else, you know?"

I nod. "I guess I can understand that." Pretending to forgive him is the only way to find out more, but I am most definitely going to tell the others that he's got a temper.

"You can come with me," Damien says. "I'm only stopping in for a second. He probably wants to have a drink." I follow him toward a door beside the bar, and he raps on it twice.

A gray-headed man wearing an expensive-looking suit opens the door. Violet's uncle. I remember him from the funeral. He manages this place? Well, I guess that's part of the reason why Violet chose to work here. "Come in," he says, gesturing for us to step inside. Damien sits on a black leather sofa, and I settle down beside him, surveying the burgundy walls adorned with framed black-and-white portraits of women posing seductively.

"You brought company." Violet's uncle raises his eyebrows at me. "I saw you the other day. What's your name?"

I sit up straight and shoot him what I hope is a confident smile that helps me look twenty-one. And sober. "I'm Zoe, a friend of Violet's."

"What's this about, Tom?" Damien says impatiently.

"I wanted to make sure we're good," Tom says. "Your people and my people."

"Fine," Damien says. His jaw clenches and his eyes are filled with something that looks like fear.

Tom takes shot glasses out of a bar cabinet behind his desk, fills them with tequila, and hands us each one. "To Violet," he says, raising his shot glass.

I down the tequila and tap my fist against my lips as I gag. How embarrassing would it be if I puked in here? I can just imagine being thrown out of the place. That would ruin my chances of being a badass investigator.

Tom folds his hands and leans across his desk. "So, listen, Damien, I'm going to keep this short and sweet, especially since you brought a *friend* with you. What are you doing here?"

Damien's forehead creases, and he slowly shakes his head. "I'm here for the party. For my girlfriend."

A muscle in Tom's jaw twitches. "I don't believe that. You never liked it here."

"I still don't."

"Well, now that we've established that and have had a drink to honor V, I think it's best you leave," Tom says, looking pointedly toward the door.

Damien stands, his arms tense against his sides. "Fine by me," he says gruffly and storms out of the office. I trail behind him, glancing back at Tom, who studies me carefully.

Damien's heading for the exit, and he's moving quickly.

"Wait." I rush after him and almost trip on the leg of a customer's chair.

He stops at the door, his hands balled up in fists at his sides. "What do you want?" he growls, whirling around with a scorching glare. "You heard him. I have to go."

"I'm really sorry," I say. I step closer to him with outstretched hands. My pulse beats in my ears. "I wanted to talk to you more. About Violet."

Damien's face reddens, and his gaze bounces around the room. He digs into his pocket, pulls out his wallet, and flips through it. "Here, you can have this." He takes out a card and shoves it in my hands.

I glance at the bolded words: "Damien Terrance, Accountant." Below is an address and phone number. Jackpot. I can picture the girls' admiring smiles when I show them. None of them will ever doubt me again. Could Holly manage to get his business card? *Pfft.* "Thank you," I breathe, like he's just awarded me with an Oscar. "This is . . ."

Damien rolls his eyes and barges out the door without looking back.

I head in the direction of the girls' table where they've spotted me and are gesturing for me to join them. Denise looks panicked as I slide into a seat across from her. "Why did you go into the office with him?" she hisses. "The door was closed. Anything could have happened."

"It was fine," I say, waving a hand dismissively. "Did you know the manager's Violet's uncle? Weird, huh?"

"It's not him we're worried about, it's Damien," Calista snaps.

I laugh. "Don't worry about me. I can handle him." I'm about to add that danger is my middle name, but Levi rests his hand lightly on my forearm, and the electricity that zings through me has got me suddenly tongue-tied.

"Damien's bad news," Levi says, his forehead creasing. He gazes intently into my eyes, takes my hand, and squeezes it gently. "You should stay away from him."

Holly's face lights up, and she points at me and then at Levi and makes a kissy face that he thankfully doesn't notice.

I giggle.

Calista smiles eagerly like she can't wait to find out all the new info I know.

Violet used to look at me the same way when I got back from the missions she sent me on. I used to drag out showing her the video clips for as long as possible. It was such a rush.

# 14
# Calista

It's 9:43 p.m., and the only thing we know so far is Bennington's has a bad reputation for a reason.

Everyone here seems like they're up to something. Something strange.

First of all, I can tell by the way the people at the table by the bar are leaning their heads together, listening to a guy in a leather jacket who looks like the kingpin, they're coming up with some kind of crime plot.

Second, I'm fairly sure I witnessed some kind of drug deal happening at the table across from the bathroom.

Also, ever since Levi and Bradley saw Damien, the mood at the table's changed. It's a good thing Damien left, or I could see fight number two of the night breaking out.

And finally, the waitresses, who are dressed like they've come out of a fifties burlesque club, are hiding something. I've caught them whispering by the bar, looks of concern on their faces, like they have a secret they're afraid someone's onto. April's making that face right now as she climbs the stairs to the DJ booth holding two glasses of champagne.

"And now for a sad but very special announcement," the DJ says, running his hand across his shaved head. He holds the microphone below April's mouth and nods encouragingly at her.

"I want everyone to raise their glasses in honor of a woman many of you knew and loved," April says, turning to survey each customer in the bar with a serious expression instead of her usual sultry one. "My dear friend, Violet Williams, who was Tom's niece and a waitress here, has passed away. So, at your tables now, share a good word or memory of her, and we'll have a few minutes without music."

Violet's uncle steps out of the doorway of his office and holds his scotch glass up. He bows his head in what seems like a showy display of mock grief.

The DJ takes the microphone back. "To Violet," he calls, raising his glass of champagne.

"To Violet," the crowd calls out, and I look around to see most customers and everyone at our table—with the exception of Bradley—with their glasses raised. I frown in his direction, and he draws his lower lip between his teeth and stares at me defiantly.

I take a sip of my soda and turn to Levi. "Didn't Bradley like Violet?" I ask, nodding in his direction. "He was one of the only ones here who didn't join in the toast to her."

"Bradley liked her all right," Levi says, a flicker of amusement playing in his eyes. He clears his throat. The bar's suddenly got this heavy weight in the air, now the music has stopped, and Violet's name resounds around the room. "We should share memories like April said."

The guys at the table nod in agreement. "I can go first," Levi offers and turns his right hand palm side up on the table, revealing a wolf tattoo on his forearm, similar to the one I saw peeking out from under the sleeve of Violet's shirt. "I'll never forget the day I got this," he says. "V told me she was sick of being weak, she wanted to be the leader of the pack so no one could push her around or try to control her." He pauses and glances around the table, making me wonder if Violet was talking about any of the guys here. "She said 'I'm so serious, I'm tattoo serious.' I brought her to the shop I go to, and we got matching tats. V went back a few weeks later for a dolphin. For Grayson. A permanent reminder of her goal to buy a house on the ocean for them."

I'm surprised by the wolf. The way I recall things, it doesn't seem like she'd need a reminder. She was a natural, without any effort, and I spent most of my preteen years wanting to be just like her.

Levi dabs at his eyes with the back of his hand, which is more emotion than Damien ever showed, and looks around the table. "Who's up next?"

"She always put me in my place when she didn't think I was being nice to the girls here," a man with spiky hair and green eyes says. He blinks quickly and scratches his cheek. "I liked that about her. She didn't take any shit."

One by one each of the guys at the table murmurs a few nice words about Violet until it's only us girls and Bradley left.

"Your turn," Levi says, pointing his index finger at Bradley.

"You didn't raise your glass for her either. We all know how you felt."

Bradley stares down at the table and runs a hand through his beard. "I don't feel like talking about her."

Levi smiles at me. "Don't let him fool you. Bradley used to be in love with Violet, since they were kids. Every summer he came home from camp heartbroken to be away from her, and I heard all about it. When Farrah passed, Violet was there for him in a big way."

My body stiffens. That's highly unexpected. Violet hated Farrah and always accused her of flirting with Grayson.

Bradley's eyes become glossy, and he tugs at his beard. "Don't talk about her," he croaks.

Levi nods. "Sorry, man."

Beside me, Denise fidgets in her seat and takes a shaky breath. She's dealt with a lot of tragedy in the past few years.

Farrah's accident was the closest brush with death I had as a child. One day she was there, making smart remarks and turning her nose up at me and my friends; the next she was at the bottom of a cliff and the whole camp became a crime scene. Yellow tape and police officers swarmed the place, tarnishing my view that camp was a safe haven. It suddenly became a place where someone died. Someone young. No one knows why she left her cabin in the middle of the night. There were rumors that she had been sleepwalking or completing a dare, but no one knows for sure.

"Violet was the best," Zoe says. She's slurring her words now. We probably don't have a lot of time left before we need to make a quick exit. Zoe barely even has a filter when she's sober. She'll say the wrong thing if we stick around much longer. It's 9:50 p.m., and we've found out virtually nothing, but staying isn't worth the risk. I catch her eye and make a gesture with my fingers as though I'm zipping my lips. She splutters out a burst of laughter. That's it. I'm going to announce we're leaving as soon as the music comes back on.

Levi beams at her like she's endearing instead of drunk and annoying. Wow, maybe he really does like her. "Tell us one of your camp stories."

"Okay, I've got stories for you," Zoe says, rubbing her hands together like she can't wait to get started. Everyone at the table has their eyes on her, waiting. She's grinning like she's enjoying this a little too much. "Violet used to get us to do the most hilarious things at camp," she says. "She made it fun, like every day was some kind of mysterious adventure. We were always pranking people to keep them on their toes. Sometimes we'd take things, and they'd all blame each other, but Violet said those girls deserved it. They picked on her because she was prettier than them."

Levi chuckles and his eyes twinkle. "Yep. Sounds like V."

I reach across the table to squeeze Zoe's hand and give her a meaningful look that I hope she's able to interpret to mean she needs to stop talking before she says something that will put us all in a bad situation, especially with Bradley here. Maybe she knows about The Mistake from Violet. This is the absolute worst time to talk about it. "You've had a lot to drink tonight," I say firmly. "I think we should go."

"Don't act like you haven't got drunk before," Zoe says with a laugh. "Remember that night when I brought a bottle from my dad's cabinet and we snuck into the forest to drink it? You had plenty that night. You were actually kind of fun for a change."

I flush. Drunk Zoe's rude.

Levi smiles. "That sounds like a blast. Did you guys get caught by Bradley's mom?" He turns to Bradley and laughs.

Bradley tenses and glares at Zoe. "Weren't you guys like thirteen at the time? That's not a blast, it's irresponsible."

Finally, someone at this table is sounding like they have some sense. I know it was stupid to do, but I'm not the one yapping about it proudly.

"It was super creepy," Zoe continues. "We spotted these guys there." She hiccups loudly and covers her mouth with a giggle. I tug on her hand, but she twists it out of my grip. "They were digging the ground like they were trying to find something. We got scared and started running back to the cabin." She hiccups again and looks like she's lost her train of thought.

Levi rests his hand on her arm. "What happened after you got back to the cabin?"

Zoe nods, and her glazed-over expression brightens. "Violet was waiting outside and she was mad. She knew we were all drunk and said she wouldn't tell but we owed her. Big time. Oh, I've got another story . . ."

"I want to hear the rest of *this* story," Bradley interrupts, squinting across the table at her. He looks so hateful it makes me shiver. "This is my mom's camp you're talking about and the place my sister . . . died. Have some respect. You're talking about people digging on our land. What were they doing?"

Zoe squints like she's trying to gather her thoughts. "Violet told us they were burying evidence from a heist. She said they were dangerous dudes. She asked us if we were going to tell Mrs. Felmont and we said no since we didn't want any dangerous dudes pissed at us. She said good because it would be terrible for us if Mrs. Felmont found out we were in the woods drinking."

Levi shifts in his seat and twists his eyebrow ring. This is not your everyday conversation topic. Zoe's apparently clueless. "Did you ever end up telling anyone? Like the police?"

Zoe shakes her head. "Nah. Maybe one day we can go dig up the buried treasure together."

"Like hell you will," Bradley booms. His lips stretch into a thin line. "Do you think Violet knew who the guys were?"

"Maybe," Zoe says. "She knew about their robbery, so probably."

"That's enough," Denise says, a pink tint washing across her cheeks. She stands and grabs Zoe's hand, tugging her to her feet. "You've had a lot to drink and it's time to go now."

It was time to go ten minutes ago before the blabbing started. My jaw stiffens. Being friends with Zoe takes a special kind of patience.

"Give me your phone for a minute," Levi says to Zoe. She pulls her phone out of her purse and drops it on the table with a clunk. He laughs, picks it up, and types something on the screen. "Call me later," he tells her as he hands it back. "I want to make sure you get home okay."

Zoe puts the phone back in her purse and covers one of her eyes with her hand as if she's seeing two of him. "All right." She grins and makes a hand gesture like an imaginary cell against her face. "Talk to you soon."

Denise scoops up her coat, links arms with her, and leads her toward the exit.

"Nice meeting you guys," Holly calls over her shoulder.

I stand, grab my stuff, and turn to see Bradley, back to sneering off into space, and Levi, still smiling at Zoe. Why are those two even friends? Even if they were close since childhood.

They're so different. At least we got out of there before Zoe told Bradley more of the stuff we did at camp. When we get back to the house, I'll try to convince Zoe not to call Levi. It's too risky. If she doesn't agree, I'll erase his number from her phone myself. He's bad news.

The bouncer holds the door open for us, and the biting cold wind hits me in the face, taking my breath away for a second. I trudge across a layer of freshly fallen snow toward Holly's car. Zoe slumps against it, and Denise puts her arm around her waist like she's holding her up.

"I miss Violet," Zoe says into Denise's shoulder.

Denise pats her hair. "Me too."

"I want to hear her. I want to hear her voice again," Zoe murmurs.

"We all do," Denise says soothingly.

"I have a way we can." Zoe suddenly stands up straight. "I'll show you when we get back to my house." She pulls away from Denise, crouches on the ground, and vomits on the snow.

# 15
# Holly

And the Oscar for most entertaining performance of the night goes to . . . Zoe. Obviously. Everyone else is boring. She gets a standing ovation for keeping things interesting. The barfing was like a mic drop.

We're all sprawled out in sleeping bags on Zoe's basement floor except for Calista, who hovers over Zoe like a hawk. "Drink this," she says, handing her a steaming mug of black coffee in a probably pointless attempt to sober her up and keep her wide awake enough to tell us the stuff she talked to Damien about. "Careful. It's hot."

Any money Zoe's going to spill it. I can already picture the burn injuries and us spending the night with her at the hospital. Then, she goes ahead and SHOCKS me by blowing on it cautiously and taking a tiny sip. "I . . . I didn't mean to get this drunk, you guys," she stammers.

Holy shit, this girl's lovable and all, but she can be so dense. I shake my head at her and laugh. "Well, why'd you drink so much then? What did you think was going to happen?"

"I don't know." Zoe scrunches up her face and taps her fingers against her mug. "I thought I'd just have a little buzz, maybe meet some guys, have a little fun, not barf or anything like that."

Calista opens her mouth to say something, but before any sound comes out, she snaps it shut and closes her eyes like she's praying for patience.

Denise sits up and her brow furrows as she looks at Zoe. "Why are you so into meeting someone?"

Zoe sighs. I'm expecting an answer about wanting to get laid, but her face falls and she clears her throat.

Next up in her intoxicated adventure: crying.

"You're probably all going to college next year," she wails, fat tears pouring down her cheeks. "Well, I'm not. I'll be stuck here, in Birchbrook. You know how sketchy this town is, you guys say it all the time." She lets out a long breath. "If I'm not going to get out of here, at least I could be with someone . . . maybe get married." She lets out a little burp and covers her mouth, and believe me, it takes every bit of self-restraint I have to chew on my lip so that I don't giggle at how perfect the timing is. "I've been meeting guys online but they all suck." She stares into her coffee, and a little smile suddenly brightens her blotchy face. "Maybe Levi and I will work out though."

Denise scoots closer to Zoe and rubs her back. "Married? You're so young to be thinking about that. And Levi? I don't think he's right for you. He's friends with Bradley and Bradley's not a nice person."

Zoe raises her eyebrows and blinks as though she doesn't agree with that advice.

"Why aren't you applying for college?" I ask. There are a million things she could do, even if her grades aren't that great. "I could see you studying film or something."

"College is . . . it's an overly expensive waste of time." Zoe's shoulders slump. As if he's a furry feelings reader, Bark trots across the room and curls up between her and Denise. Zoe reaches down to pet him. "Also, my dad can't afford it."

"I can help you look into loan options." Calista takes her phone out of her purse. "I'll make a note for myself to help you once I'm back home." She types something, puts it down beside her sleeping bag, and makes a face that she probably thinks looks sympathetic but looks more like she has gas. She shifts closer and awkwardly pats Zoe on the back. "Don't limit yourself," she says softly. "You have lots of talents." She stares at the ceiling like she's trying to think of a list, then gives up.

We can't just leave the girl hanging like that.

I crawl across the floor and cup Zoe's chin in my hand. "You're pretty, smart, and awesome, and don't forget it," I say. A flicker of a smile crosses her face. I want to go on about how being single isn't bad, but I don't know if I feel that way. I almost don't trust myself with that kind of freedom. Maybe Alex keeps me grounded. If I were free all the time, maybe I'd take it too far. What if I'm like Violet, and without someone in my life to keep me on the right path, I took the wrong one? Would I end up in the same place as she did?

We all wrap our arms around each other until we're in a group hug. Apart from Bark's panting and Zoe's occasional sniff, we're silent. This feels kind of nice. Like old times.

Calista clears her throat. Here we go. "When you were talking to Damien, what did he say?"

"Ummmm." Zoe looks at the ceiling and taps her finger against her chin. "We talked about a lot of stuff actually." Maybe we'll have better luck finding that out tomorrow. She probably doesn't remember what she talked about five minutes ago, never mind an hour ago.

Calista rolls her eyes. "Maybe I should have given you a notepad." She rifles through her purse. Is she actually trying to find her a notepad? Talk about an eager beaver. She pulls out a phone. "I just remembered we have Violet's phone. There's probably some clues on it. Does anyone have an iPhone charger?"

"Mine's there," I say, pointing at my charger, plugged into the outlet by the couch. I have to admit, thinking to bring Violet's phone with us was a smart idea. Calista strides over and plugs it in.

"When you said we'd hear Violet's voice again, what did you mean?" Denise asks. Her eyes are wide and eager as if she's desperately hoping that Zoe can bring Violet back from the dead. I did notice a Ouija board in Zoe's game closet, but I'm hoping that wasn't what she had in mind. We played that game with Violet herself once when she wanted advice about her beloved Grayson. Talk about freaky shit. Never again.

To make it clear: not even if someone paid me five million dollars.

Zoe stands and stumbles toward the table. Coffee sloshes out of her mug onto the beige carpet as she puts it down. It was only a matter of time. She grabs a cord from the wicker basket that rests in the center, scrolls through her phone, and plugs it into her TV. "Here you go," she calls in a singsong voice that probably means she's also forgotten about being sad. Our cabin from camp comes into focus on the large screen, which is odd because we never filmed anything there. Not to my knowledge anyway.

I crawl across the carpet for a closer look then swing around to face Zoe. "What the fuck is this?"

"Memories." Zoe bats her eyelashes and tries to flash us a smile, and I bet she's thinking she looks cute, but with all her smeared mascara, she looks more like the Joker.

"Well, play it already," Calista says, lowering herself onto her sleeping bag, her eyes glued to the screen.

"Okaayyy." Zoe presses Play, and her image comes onto the screen. I can make out the four twin beds with familiar red-and-white plaid comforters and clothes piled up on two of the bedside tables. Zoe's still got her long hair in the video, and I'd forgotten what her face looks like without makeup until now. It brings me back to the time when she'd hug us all at least twice before she'd get into bed because she missed her dad so much. The camera's right in her face, and it seems like she's finding a spot for it. I remember there was a shelf with a bunch of old books, and I bet that's where she's putting it. She backs away and sits down on her bed with her hands folded in her lap, looking innocent. Then there's the creak of the door opening. Calista and Denise step into the frame, holding tennis rackets. We started playing tennis all the time at thirteen. So, this must be from the last year we were together at camp.

"Come sit with me," thirteen-year-old Zoe says to them, her voice more high-pitched than it is now. She taps a place beside her and gathers her long dark hair in a messy bun. The girls dive onto the bed to sit cross-legged beside her.

"How was it?" Zoe asks. It's as if she's reading lines, and I'm surprised to see Calista's and Denise's neutral facial expressions. How could they not tell that something suspicious was happening?

I hear heavy breathing, and I whirl around to see Denise suddenly next to me. "I remember this day," she whispers. "It was right after the woods thing that we're not allowed to talk about." She crawls even closer to the television as if she'd like to climb inside it and return to that time.

I turn back to the screen. "It was fine," Past Calista answers. She looks almost the same as she currently does, except her springy, curly hair barely skimmed her shoulders then and it's longer now. "You should have come."

"Are you feeling better?" Denise asks with a friendly smile. She's so cute with her short spiky pigtails and braces. She's got a light about her that the years since have snuffed out.

"Yeah, the nap helped." Past Zoe smirks and shifts on the bed.

What a LIAR. Are they seriously buying this shit? If I were in this video, I wouldn't be falling for it.

I remember this day now too. Denise is right. It was a few days after the woods thing. Zoe said she was sick even though she didn't seem the least bit sick before or after, for that matter. This was a few days after I asked Bradley to be my boyfriend. I don't want to even try to imagine what Violet used to do while I distracted him. At the time I thought it was silly things, but now that I know her better, I think it was a lot more sinister.

I watch my younger self step into the room and toss my racket on the bed. "Hey, guys," I say in a cheerful tone. My hair's in braided pigtails, and I'm wearing an oversized red Camp Bellwood Lake T-shirt. I look cupcake-sweet, like I could do no wrong, which might be why Violet gave me the tasks she did. "Heads up," I hear myself whisper. "Violet's on her way here."

I watch Past Zoe's face closely on the screen and notice the flush in her cheeks and the way she fiddles with her friendship bracelet. What was she up to? Obviously something to do with Violet. "Come sit with us," she says to me, patting a place on the other side of her, so I can be in the video I have no knowledge of. "Violet's been kind of strange lately, don't you think?"

"Yeah," I say, pulling on a thread that's hanging from my cutoff shorts. "She asks us to do some weird stuff sometimes and I don't really get it."

"Like what?" Zoe asks, and the corners of her mouth stretch into a sneaky smile.

What the actual hell? Why am I falling for this? I thought I was smarter than that. "Like all the spying we do," my past self answers. "Yeah, it's fun and all, and she gives us some cool stuff, but don't you ever worry that we're going to get in trouble?"

"Not really," Zoe answers, glancing right into the camera.

"Violet's great." Younger Denise beams eagerly. "She makes camp more exciting. She'd never do anything bad, just harmless stuff like pranks. No big deal."

Past Zoe grabs Denise's hand and looks into her eyes. "So, you aren't going to tell on her?"

"No." Denise shakes her head quickly. "Why would I?"

Past Zoe lets go of her hand and grabs Calista's hand. "What about you, Callie?"

Younger Callie's eyes widen, and she sits up straight. "I can't."

My younger self tilts my head back, and my eyes narrow. Finally, I seem a little bit skeptical of this whole phony scene. "What do you mean, 'can't'?"

"I wouldn't," Calista corrects herself in a firm voice.

"Violet told us to drop it and we need to listen." Zoe nibbles on one of her fingernails. "We won't get in trouble unless we tell and then we all get in trouble, and we might not get to come back again next summer. I don't want that. You have to swear right now that you won't talk about anything she's asked us to do."

"I swear," Younger Calista and Denise say in unison.

"I guess I swear too," I say with a shrug.

Then there's a rustling at the door, and I watch us all jump. Me and Denise clutch each other.

"It's me, silly," I hear Violet's voice say. It punches me in the gut to hear it. I exhale slowly. Her voice amplified in Zoe's basement. It's almost like she's actually here again.

I sit upright, my heart in my throat and my hand over my mouth as I wait to see her on screen. She steps into the frame. She's blond, just like she used to be. "What were you girls talking about?" she asks in a playful voice that has just the slightest hint of an edge to it.

"Nothing," Younger Calista says quickly.

"Good." Violet tosses her beautiful hair over her shoulder. "You're doing great with the pranks. Making summer a lot more fun. You know what I think we should call this cabin?"

"Prank Club?" Denise props her face up on her hand and grins at her.

"Hush Cabin," Violet says with a sly smile. "I think it sounds exciting, don't you? We know stuff the others don't, but we'll never say anything. It's like a secrets club, and secrets are exciting."

We all nod like obedient pets. This is pathetic. Talk about having us wrapped around her finger.

"Okay." Violet places a hand on Zoe's shoulder, and Zoe looks up at her like she's checking to make sure Violet's proud. "So next subject, campfire. Tonight, there's a talent contest and I've got a perfect idea for our cabin's act. Let's go practice out front."

Our younger selves spring to our feet like marionettes whose strings have been jerked at the same time. All of us head outside. Past Zoe lingers back, and I watch her finger move toward the screen. Before she stops the recording, there's a smile on her face I've never seen in real life. It's a sly smile, and there's something in her eyes that looks almost evil. Goose bumps run up and down my arms. Is there another side of Zoe I don't know about?

The clip stops, and the room's full of a tense silence. Calista moves so she's face-to-face with Zoe. "Why did you record us?" she demands. "Like, what was the point?"

"This is honestly pretty screwed up," I agree. It's so unexpected that I'm sick to my stomach.

"Don't tell me that she didn't get you to do stuff for her too." Zoe rolls her eyes way more boldly than she does when she's sober. "Come on. She was always giving us tasks that made no sense whatsoever."

"No," Calista says, but the guilty expression on her face says otherwise.

"How did you earn your candy then?" Zoe asks. I totally forgot about the candy. We did so much stupid shit and were rewarded with sour gummy bears. "You got just as many bags as I did," Zoe continues accusingly. "What did you have to do for it?"

"Nothing," Calista snaps. She crosses her arms tightly over her chest and glares at her.

Zoe lets out a short laugh. "I know that's not true. But you can keep pretending if that's what you want to do."

"What's that supposed to mean?" Calista asks, but she's losing her fire. "Do you have other clips?"

"No," Zoe says. But I can tell by the way she quickly looks away that she's lying.

# 16
# Denise

*I'm thirteen years old, the others are riding the paddleboats, and I stayed back—told them I had a stomachache.*

*I'm alone in the cabin with Violet like I wanted. But it isn't going the way I want it to.*

*Violet faces the mirror, combing her hair, and I watch her reflection, the shadows under her eyes darker than ever. "You're going to do it, right, Denise?" she says softly.*

*"I . . . I don't know," I stammer, hugging my legs to my chest. "One a.m.? You want it to happen at one a.m.?"*

*Violet spins around and tosses her hairbrush in my direction— it grazes my thigh and lands beside me. "You said you'd do it and now you're changing your mind?"*

*"I . . . I'm sorry. It's mean . . ."*

*"Mean?" Violet bellows, grabbing handfuls of her hair and*

*yanking like she's going to rip them out.* "Mean? She's the mean one. She had no respect for what Grayson and I had. I deserve a little fun at her expense." *She pauses, blinks, lets go of her hair, and takes a breath, one corner of her mouth turning up in the hint of a smile.* "I'm sorry, Denise. I get so . . . mad when I think about it."

"It's okay," *I whisper, hugging my legs tighter against my body. Violet settles on the bed next to me and runs her hand across my knee. Her face is so close to mine that her hair skims my cheek.* "So, are you going to help me, or not?"

———

THURSDAY, DECEMBER 30

Light's streaming into the room through the spaces between the basement windows' blinds. The others are still snoring in their sleeping bags on the dingy beige carpet, and I'm curled up on the couch under a quilt with Bark on my lap and my phone in my hand. I've already texted Mom to let her know I'm staying until the afternoon and that Calista will drive me home. **It's going better than I expected it to,** I texted, which isn't exactly true. The truth is, being away from home is putting my grief in another setting and I'm processing things differently. I'm still mourning, but I'm not being crushed by the weight of a house of memories. And last night, instead of sadness, I felt something I never thought I'd feel again.

Mom responded, **As long as you're back before Saturday to get ready for school,** and then added a thumbs-up and a smiley-face emoji, which was nice and all, but another text came through that made my stomach flutter. I can't stop rereading it.

I press the Messages icon to look at it again.

It's Janie. I met you last night.

I type the reply that I've written and erased at least ten times so far.

Do you want to meet up today?

This time I hit Send. I exhale slowly. *Holy moly, I did it.*

Calista sits up and stretches. Maybe my deep breath woke her up. She yawns and rubs her eyes, then springs to her feet and yanks on the pull cord to turn on the light. She looks at me curiously. "Who are you writing to?"

"My mom," I lie. "I told her you offered to drive me home later."

"Your mom," Calista repeats with her eyebrows raised. "Okay then."

I touch my face. It's a little warm. *Am I blushing or something? She doesn't seem to believe me.*

Calista leans down to nudge Holly. "It's time to get up now."

Holly rolls over onto her back and stretches, exposing her flat stomach and gold navel ring. "What time is it?" she murmurs.

I glance at my phone. "Ten." No text back from Janie yet. Maybe asking her to hang out right away was too forward. Hopefully I didn't creep her out.

Calista rifles through her suitcase and pulls out jeans and a blouse. "I'm hungry. God knows there's nothing here to eat. How about I drive us somewhere we can grab breakfast?"

"I'll drive," Holly says firmly. She grabs her bag and bounds across the creaky floor to the bathroom. "Give me a second to get ready."

Calista nudges Zoe, who moans like she'd rather sleep for at least another two hours. "We're going out to eat, wake up."

Last night, finding out she recorded us at camp was a shock, but the others reacted like she was a killer or something. They can never, *never*, find out what I did.

Zoe sits up halfway, then flops back down. "Ugh, I feel like crap."

Calista makes a face. Holy moly, has she ever got a big repertoire of annoyed-looking expressions. "Obviously."

My phone buzzes in my hand, and my stomach flutters again as I look at the screen. A reply from Janie:

> Name the place. I'll be there.

I bite my lip to stop the giant smile I feel is threatening to take over my face. In the two minutes I spent talking to Janie, I knew I liked her. Maybe hanging out with us today would help her. She seemed really upset last night.

Calista raises her eyebrows. "Another text from your *mom?*" She's definitely on to me. She leans against the wood paneling with her arms folded and studies me carefully. Not sure why she's so set on being a lawyer; she'd make an excellent detective.

"Yeah," I answer. "Where do you want to go for breakfast?"

"Rise and Shine," Zoe says. She springs to a sitting position like her hangover suddenly disappeared, her eyes widening eagerly. "Because—"

"Let me guess," Holly interrupts. She steps out of the bathroom dressed in tight jeans and a yellow top, grinning. "Because the guys that work there are hot?"

"No." Zoe giggles. She tosses a pillow across the room, and

it hits Holly in the stomach. "Because they've got the best french toast. Do you guys think I'm that shallow?"

Holly tosses the pillow back at her and sticks out her tongue. "Maybe."

I wonder how much Zoe remembers from last night and if she recalls telling us how she feels she'll be stuck in Birchbrook and thinks her best shot is finding someone to marry. It's pretty upsetting that she feels that way. Now when she talks about guys nonstop, I'll find it more sad than silly.

"You passed out before you told us what you and Damien talked about," Calista says. "Did he say anything incriminating?"

Zoe tugs on one of her earrings. "He seemed sad. But I can also tell he's got a temper." She fills us in on how he blew up on her for lying that she wanted to work there and how Violet's uncle told Damien to never come back. She rolls up her sleeve, examines her wrist, and points at a red mark. "See the little bruise right here. That's from him."

I grab her arm and peer at the blotch. "He gave you a bruise? No wonder people say he's a bad guy."

"Yeah, he really freaked out when I said that," Zoe agrees.

"Maybe he had a similar temper with Violet," Calista says and runs a finger along Zoe's bruise. "What happened next?"

Zoe shrugs. "Then he left. He didn't argue. He just walked out." She trudges up the stairs. "I'm going to change and get some Advil. I'm not feeling so good."

"Shocker," Calista says with a sniff. She picks up Violet's phone that's plugged in by the couch. "That's unfortunate. It has a four-digit passcode." She taps her fingers against the screen, her eyes narrowed in concentration. "Any guesses on what it would be?"

"Her birthday? Grayson's birthday?" Holly suggests. "April

fourteenth and May twenty-sixth, so, what, zero-four-one-four or zero-five-two-six? Or maybe day, then month, or year even?"

Calista jabs at the screen and sighs loudly. "Nope. We've got to figure this out."

Holy moly, she could probably spend a whole day trying to figure this out. "Bring it to breakfast and we'll keep trying," I suggest.

I type a text to Janie:

> We're going to Rise and Shine right
> now if you'd like to meet us there.

Her reply comes quickly:

> That's right by my house. See you
> soon.

Calista steps into the bathroom to change while I pet Bark to calm my nerves. What if I meet up with Janie and it's awkward? What if the others are quiet and cold around her? Maybe I should meet her on my own first. Bark sighs as though he can hear my racing thoughts and puts his paw on my forearm comfortingly. Being around animals always helps me feel calmer.

When everyone's dressed, we bound up the stairs, get our coats and boots on, and head outside. The sky's bright blue and cloudless, and the sun's so bright I squint.

I'm just about to open the car door when Holly stops in her tracks. "What's that on my windshield?" she says.

I look at where she's pointing. On the windshield there's a little scrap of paper.

"It's probably an ad for something. The salespeople around here are ruthless. I wouldn't put it past them to come onto people's driveways to promote stuff," Zoe says with a laugh. She rushes toward the car and peers at it.

Holly snatches the small square of paper off and turns it over. "It's not an ad," she says softly. There's a low tone in her voice, and I know something's wrong. Everything inside me stills, and I hold my breath. Suddenly I'm acutely aware of every sound. A bird squawking in the distance, brakes squealing, something rustling in the trees.

Calista grabs the paper out of her hand to read it herself.

"What does it say?" Zoe asks cautiously.

Calista flips it around so Zoe and I can see. In thick black block letters, it reads, "I KNOW ABOUT THE DEADLY NOTE YOU WROTE. HERE'S ONE FOR YOU: GO BACK TO SHAWDALE. OR ELSE."

"Did one of you write this?" Calista demands, her eyes blazing. "Who did this? What the hell does it mean that someone here wrote deadly notes? Who?"

I take the paper from Calista's hand, reading it again and again. I'm breathing hard and fast, hyperventilating.

"Hey. Take a deep breath," Zoe says softly, her hand on my back.

"I . . . I can't," I gasp.

Zoe leads me by the arm toward her front steps. "Sit down."

I slump down on the cold step and put my head between my knees. My heart's pounding. *Deadly notes" doesn't mean what I think it does. Someone else is hiding something. This isn't about me.*

When my breathing slows, I glance up at Zoe, who's got a trembling hand over her mouth. Calista's eyes are darting around everywhere like she's hoping to spot whoever left this letter. Holly, on the other hand, looks unbothered. She passes her car keys from one hand to the other and taps her foot. I frown at her.

"Are you okay now?" Zoe asks.

I nod weakly.

"It's the same writing," Calista says, gesturing at the note frantically. "It's the same writing as the note we found in Violet's purse. And the paper's the same size too."

Zoe shakes her head. "How the hell do they know where I live, whoever it is?"

"And how do they know where *I* live?" I add. My stomach's suddenly rock-hard, and I can feel my legs shaking.

"I'm not from Shawdale," Holly says, a hint of a smug smile on her face. "They don't know where I live."

"Good for you," Calista snaps. "But that doesn't mean you're safe."

"Oh shit." Zoe grows pale. She moves her sunglasses to the top of her head and runs a hand across her face.

"What?" Calista demands. She reaches out and grabs Zoe by both shoulders, giving her a little shake. "What do you know?"

"I told Damien," Zoe says softly. "He asked where you guys were from, and I told him Shawdale. I didn't mention Holly's from Devonville."

"So, this was definitely Damien then." Calista pumps her fist in the air triumphantly. "I knew it. I was right. Did you tell him your address too while you were at it?"

"No!" Zoe cries. Then her face lights up like something helpful has occurred to her, and the corners of her mouth twist upward into a hint of a smile. "But I know his."

"What do you mean?" Calista demands, stepping closer to her.

Zoe reaches into her purse and pulls out a card. "He gave me this. It's got his name, title, address, and phone number. Can you guys believe he's an accountant?"

"Accountant slash murderer," Calista says and opens Holly's passenger-side car door. "We should check out his office before I leave this afternoon."

"We should get breakfast before that," I say firmly. "We should eat first." I open the door and climb into the back seat.

Calista grunts. I'm sure she'd rather skip breakfast and get straight to investigating, but there's no way that I want to stand Janie up the first time meeting up with her.

My heart thumps against my chest as we pass a laundromat, a convenience store, a school, the cemetery, and I'm trying to think about something, anything, to distract my thoughts from returning to those two words, *deadly note*. I turn to glance out the back window to make sure no cars are tailing us.

Holly pulls into the restaurant parking lot, and I spot Janie standing by the door in a long coat that's almost the same shade of purple as her hair. My heart pounds even faster, and I squeeze my locket with Dad's picture in it to center myself. Maybe inviting her was a mistake. I can't focus on her now that someone's threatening us.

"Hi, Denise," Janie calls as I step out of the car, a warm smile stretching across her pretty face.

I wave, then shove my hands into my pockets. Despite the cold they're clammy. "You're here," I shout back. *That was probably a dumb thing to say.*

"Who's that?" Calista whispers.

"Janie," I answer. "She's a friend of Violet's. I met her yesterday."

Holly scowls at me and clicks her tongue. "You didn't ask us if it was okay to invite anyone."

I glare at her. "I didn't think I needed permission."

We reach the doorway and stop in front of Janie. I nod toward each of the girls. "Janie, this is Calista, that's Zoe, and this is Holly."

"Hi," Janie says, smiling shyly at us. "Nice to meet you. I've already met Holly before."

I frown at Holly, who's staring at the ground, then turn back to Janie. "You mean yesterday at the club?"

"No," Janie says. "Before that."

Holly looks up, blinking quickly. "I've never met you before. You must be getting me mixed up with someone else." She smiles widely at us. "I get that a lot. People confusing me with other people. Let's go inside. I'm starving."

I glance at Janie, and she just shrugs and shakes her head.

# 17
# Zoe

My head throbs as we follow the waitress across the sticky check-ered floor toward our table. The Advil hasn't kicked in yet, and I feel like literal crap. Holly and Calista climb into the booth first, I slide in after them, and Janie and Denise settle down across from us. The waitress places plastic-covered menus on the table and pours each of us a glass of water.

I guzzle mine back in one long dehydrated gulp.

"I don't see any hot waiters in bow ties." Holly swivels around to check out the staff, who are mainly women in their forties. "I'm surprised you still like this place, Zoe," she says with a laugh.

I shrug. "Sometimes it really is just about good food." What the hell? I'm tired of these girls thinking they've got me all fig-ured out. I vaguely remember them asking me last night about why I want a boyfriend so badly. None of them get what it's like to feel stuck somewhere. They're all going back to their lives any day now with college just around the corner; things are about to get exciting for them. All I've got to look forward to is another pointless semester of high school and maybe a job at a fast-food joint or somewhere like this. If this is my future, hopefully the tips are good.

Janie nibbles on her lip and fidgets nervously. I can't figure out how old she is. She looks a little older than us, but her anxiousness makes her seem younger. Denise has got her beat in that department though. That note left her absolutely rattled.

"Can you believe that I've lived in Birchbrook since I was a baby and I've never been here?" Janie asks.

I pick up a greasy menu, turn it toward Janie, and tap one of the food pics. "You've got to try their french toast. It's to die for."

She looks at the photo and nods. "Good idea. Thanks. Maybe I'll get it with some scrambled eggs. And bacon. Bacon for sure."

I'm about to ask Calista what she's going to get, but she's facing Janie with crossed arms and narrowed eyes. "So, how did you know Violet?" she asks. Calista doesn't mess around, I'll give her that. She's not about to make small talk when there's stuff she could be finding out. I wonder how she feels about Denise inviting Janie without asking us what we thought first. I know Holly's not pumped about it, but if we're going to find out what happened to Violet, we need to talk to people she hung out with recently.

Janie's face clouds over, and she traces her fingertip along the S + T initials someone's carved into the table. "We went to university together," she says softly. "Violet was the best. It kills me that she's gone."

Denise puts her hand on Janie's shoulder, her eyes filling with concern. "It's so sad," she agrees.

Calista moves the bouquet of dusty fake flowers from the center of the table to a spot by the window so she can stare at Janie unobstructed. "Did you ever meet her boyfriend?"

Janie nods, running a jerky hand through her purple hair.

Calista leans forward. "And? What's he like?"

"He seemed controlling," Janie answers, looking back down at the table. "He was constantly calling to check up on her. I always thought that Violet could do better."

I peek at Holly, and just as I thought, that statement seems to have affected her. Her lips are set in a thin line, and she looks down at her lap. It seems as though she's in a similar situation. Her boyfriend calls her nonstop, and she ignores him and keeps making comments about liking to feel free.

"Did you tell her that she was better off without him?" Denise asks.

"All the time," Janie says miserably. She wipes a tear from the corner of her eye. "Apparently he didn't even want her hanging out with her own family members."

Calista clucks her tongue. "Hmm. That must have felt suffocating." She stares at Holly pointedly, but Holly doesn't look up. "Nobody should put up with that."

My mind drifts to last night when Damien grabbed my wrist. He seemed nice up until that moment. Like the kind of person who is happy and pleasant until someone does the wrong thing. Then he just snaps. But can I picture him purposely drowning his girlfriend? Can I picture him writing threatening notes and giving them to Violet or leaving them on Holly's car? I don't know.

A waitress approaches our table, and we give her our orders. We make awkward small talk until she returns with our food. Then we eat in silence. I'd be able to hear the other girls chewing if it wasn't for the sounds of garbled conversations and clanging cutlery coming from the surrounding tables. Janie being here has quieted us down, but despite seeming panicked, Denise has more of a glow about her, like Janie's a long-lost friend that she's just been reunited with. They must have met when I was in the manager's office with Damien, which wasn't for very long at all.

"You were right about the french toast," Janie says after a while. "It's excellent."

"The coffee tastes burnt though," Calista says, looking as though she's bitten into a lemon. "It's gross." She reaches into her purse and pulls out Violet's phone. "Do you have any idea what Violet's passcode is, Janie? Four digits."

Janie plays with a strand of her purple hair. "I don't know. Her birthday maybe? Why do you have her phone, if you don't mind me asking?"

"Long story," Calista snips. "And I tried the birthday code. Other guesses?"

"Try thirteen-thirteen," Janie says with a shrug. "She liked that number."

Calista taps the screen. "Nope."

"After we eat, I'm going to hang out with Janie for a bit. I don't think I'm up to going . . . where we were discussing," Denise blurts out, running a hand along her pale face. She looks at Janie shyly. "If it's okay with you."

Janie nods, and a smile slowly spreads across her face. "I could use some company."

Calista looks up from Violet's phone. She seems relieved. I

doubt she would have wanted Janie to accompany us to check out the scene at Damien's office. That would have taken a lot of explaining, and we can't trust someone new right away.

After we pay, we head back out to Holly's car, and my stomach clenches as I think about how Damien will react to me just showing up at his office. Without the liquid courage, I don't know if I'll know what to ask him. It could be dangerous.

Janie points at a silver Honda Civic. "I'm parked over there."

"I'll text you guys in a bit," Denise says and follows Janie to her car.

I get into the passenger side and take Damien's business card out of my wallet. His office is on Glass Street, which is just outside of Birchbrook. It will probably take us twenty minutes to get there.

"She likes her," Holly announces as she turns on the ignition.

"Who likes who?" I ask.

"Denise likes Janie," Holly says matter-of-factly. "It's obvious."

I squint at her. "Likes her as in likes her, likes her?"

Holly nods and gives me a look as though she thinks I'm the opposite of observant. "Yeah. Can't you tell?"

"I guess," I answer. Denise seemed edgy at breakfast, but I did see her glancing at Janie a few times like she might be interested in her.

"She's been a nervous wreck since she arrived," Calista remarks from the back seat. "Maybe she needs a distraction."

Meeting someone has been the least of Denise's priorities since she got here, and now *she's* found a love match? It's hard to see that as fair. Yes, Levi seems as though he could be into me, but if I was even half of the drunken mess last night that Calista makes me sound like, I doubt he'll want anything to do with me again. "Speaking of love matches, do you think I should call Levi?" I ask. "He gave me his number and I didn't let him know I got home okay like I was supposed to."

"No," Calista says firmly. "I don't like him. You said you're into online dating. Show me your app and I'll find you a match."

I haven't checked my VenusLove app messages since the girls arrived, which might be a record for me. I wasn't planning on it, but I'm also curious about the guys Calista would pick for me. I'm picturing a guy with a shirt buttoned all the way to the top with a tie, maybe holding a book or briefcase for added smart points. Basically, a male version of her. My inbox has twelve unopened messages that I'll check later. I pass Calista my phone, and she swipes through, stopping on a guy with a plaid shirt and a crew cut. I was close.

"This guy's from Birchbrook," Calista says eagerly. "His screen name is Salinger and it says here that he's a skilled pianist."

"Zoe might be more interested if he's skilled with his penis," Holly says, and if she wasn't driving the car, I might have punched her.

"That's bullshit," I say. "And he's not my type. Can I have my phone back now?"

"Let me pick someone else," Calista says. She swipes again and lands on someone with shoulder-length brown hair and a Nirvana T-shirt. "This guy plays in a band and he looks like he has a similar style to you." She presses the heart button before my mouth even opens to reply.

"You can't do that," I cry, reaching my hand out to grab my phone out of her hands. "Now he's going to think I like him."

Calista frowns. "Well, don't you?"

"He—he's okay," I stammer.

"Well, what's the problem then?" she snips.

Calista only shows an interest in helping people when it benefits her. Why are she and Denise trying to get me to forget about Levi? What do they have to gain from doing that?

"So, next stop, Damien's?" Holly asks as she turns down Main.

"Yes," Calista replies. "Make it snappy. We'll find some incriminating evidence before I head home."

Holly tilts her head up to look at her in the rearview mirror. "Are you sure it's safe for us to go there?"

"We'll stay parked far away," Calista answers. "We need to find out if he sent those notes. What else are we going to do? Just sit back and let him threaten us?"

I read the business card. "It's on Glass Street, which is a little west of my house. Turn right at the lights."

Holly follows my directions, and we coast along Richmond Road toward the cemetery. My chest tightens, just like it has every day since the funeral. I should have taken her the longer way. I look at the line of headstones, wondering which one belongs to Violet.

Calista clears her throat. "We should probably visit her on our way back to the house."

I murmur in agreement.

We continue along the road until we reach Glass Street. I eye the street numbers on either side of the intersection. "It looks like the even numbers are on the left," I tell Holly. "We're looking for number fifty." We drive toward the flashing lights of an ambulance and several cop cars that are parked in front of one of the apartment buildings. Hopefully that's not the building we're heading to.

"I bet that's it. The one with all the police cars," Calista cries. "Maybe they figured out he hurt Violet."

Holly drives a little faster. "You're right. I see the sign. That's number fifty." Just as she's about to turn into the parking lot, the ambulance speeds off, lights flashing and siren blaring.

Holly pulls into the visitor parking lot, turns off the car, and swivels around to look at us. "Who do you think that was for?"

"Maybe Damien murdered someone else," Calista says, leaning as far forward as she can between the two front seats without taking off her seat belt. "Maybe someone else knew what he did to Violet. What if it was Mrs. Williams?"

I eye the tall building with its stained balconies and crumbling bricks. "I expected this address to be his office. A classy-looking one. This looks like a sketchy building. The police could be here for loads of reasons. Maybe someone was dealing drugs."

"Let's find out what's going on by getting closer," Calista says. "I bet you ten dollars it's something to do with Damien."

I tap my fingers against the dashboard and shift in my seat. "What if the police aren't here for Damien and he sees us?"

"He gave you his card. It's not like he was trying to keep where he lives a secret," Calista points out. "I bet they caught him for something he was doing, and we don't have anything to worry about anymore."

A black BMW backs out of its spot just as we pull in next to it. The driver's got straight brown hair and wears large sunglasses. "Is that April?" I ask, pointing out the window.

"I don't think so," Calista answers. "She looks older than

April. Besides, why would she be here? She doesn't like Damien and I doubt she'd live *here*."

We get out of the car and walk up the sidewalk toward the front of the building. There's a large area that's been sectioned off with caution tape and four police officers are scattered around, speaking to people. All of a sudden, visions of my last day at camp hit me in a swift swoop. With all the cops and the tension in the air, it's like déjà vu. The day they found Farrah all over again. I chew on my lip and push away the urge to run back toward the car.

Calista gestures for us to join her at the edge of the yellow tape, close to a male officer with a deeply lined face who's talking to a middle-aged woman in jogging pants. There are red splotches in the snow. I gulp. They look like blood.

"Did you know the deceased?" the officer asks.

"Deceased?" Holly whispers, her eyes widening in alarm.

"Not well," the woman says. "I've seen him in the building from time to time and we exchanged hellos here and there. He looked a little worried sometimes and always seemed like he was in a rush, but I didn't get the vibe that he was depressed."

A man with white hair walking a dalmatian approaches the police officer. "Excuse me, officer. I live here. Is everything okay?"

"There's been an incident," the officer says. "A man jumped from his balcony, I'm afraid."

The older man makes a *tsk* noise. "What a shame," he says, shaking his head.

"We're trying to gather information at this point, find out the names of the family members we'll need to contact. Perhaps you knew him?"

"What's his name?" the man asks, leading his dog closer to the line of caution tape and looking over it as if he expects to see the body still lying there.

The police officer peers down at his notepad, then looks up again with a grim expression. "His name was Damien Terrance."

# 18

# Calista

THURSDAY, DECEMBER 30

My blood runs cold.

"Is Damien dead?" I blurt out. Beside me, Zoe makes a noise that sounds like a stifled gasp.

The police officer eyes us curiously. "Yes, he is. Did you know him?"

"Not really. We had a mutual friend." I cross my arms and press my lips together. I'm not interested in answering a bunch of questions. I could tell him about the note we received and how we came here because we thought it was Damien.

But what if it wasn't him?

We'd really piss off whoever sent it if we got the police involved. And I doubt we'd want to. April warned us about the police here.

"What floor did he live on?" a man who's walking a dog

asks. "I always got off before him when we were in the elevator together."

"The fourteenth," the police officer answers, glancing up at the top of the building solemnly.

I follow his gaze. The fourteenth floor must be one of the balconies at the very top. I picture Damien gripping the railing, staring down at the ground below, then hoisting himself over the ledge. He was young, presumably well educated, an accountant. Sure, he had some issues, like A) he may or may not have killed his girlfriend, B) he might have been dating her mother, and C) his apartment building's a little on the rough side, but he had a whole future ahead of him. Opportunities galore. What was going through his head to cause him to do that, and did he regret his decision as he plummeted to his death? I turn and step away from the crime scene. I need to process what this means. I head toward a bench several yards away, brush the snow off it with my gloved hand, and sit, facing where the officers still stand, speaking to people. Holly and Zoe sit beside me. "You guys owe me ten dollars," I say. "I told you this was about him."

Zoe shakes her head sadly, making me aware of my poor timing with that comment. She's the one out of all of us who seems to have some sympathy for him. "He must have been more devastated about Violet than we thought," she says softly. "I knew from talking to him yesterday that he seemed on edge and sad, but I didn't think he was commit-suicide upset."

Holly draws a zigzag in the snow with her shoe and purses her lips. "Maybe something else went down after he left the club last night."

"Do you still think it was him that left the note at my house?" Zoe asks in a shaky voice, her eyebrows drawing together.

"No one else knows where we're from. You said yourself that you forgot to say where Holly's from." I'm about to add, *Thanks again for having a big mouth*, but Zoe's already looking rattled, and this isn't the time to start pointing fingers at each other. Who knows what kind of danger we're already in? I clear my throat. "My take on this whole thing is that he got in an argument with Violet, drowned her, felt like we were asking too many questions, threatened us, then felt so guilty that he took his life." Sirens wail, and another police car pulls up. An officer gets out of the car and steps over the caution tape, kneeling on the ground, looking at God knows what.

Holly whistles softly. "This keeps getting more fucked up."

Right on cue, a white Range Rover speeds into the parking lot, and a woman jumps out. I immediately recognize her slim figure, although her blond hair isn't as carefully combed as it was yesterday at her daughter's farewell party. It's wild and spiky around her shoulders like it's dry from overbleaching. She runs across the parking lot toward the officers. "Where is he?" she yelps in a frantic tone, pacing in front of them and wringing her hands. "Where did you take him?"

"I'm thinking she's the deceased's next of kin," an older-looking male police officer says to a younger officer as he slowly approaches her. The younger officer goes to his trunk to retrieve a folding chair and a blanket. He looks familiar, but I can't put my finger on where I know him from.

"That was one of the cops who were at Bennington's yesterday," Holly says as if she can hear my thoughts.

My pulse quickens. If he's into crime and really is friends with people at Bennington's and one of them did this, he's finding every reason to make this look like a classic suicide. He says something to Violet's mother, who sits uneasily at the edge of the seat he brought her. The older officer drapes the blanket around her shoulders and crouches in front of her.

My insides clench up as a dark memory hits me: the officers trying to calm Bradley down after they found Farrah had stumbled off the cliff.

From where we sit, we hear the murmur of a calm tone from the officer, and a few words are audible, such as "unfortunate" and "tragedy."

"He wouldn't do this!" Mrs. Williams shrieks, covering her face with her hands. "You need to investigate. Damien would never do something like this. He's the last person. You have to believe me."

I stand, tempted to move closer so I can hear how the officer responds. "Did you hear that? She thinks he was pushed," I murmur, in case Zoe and Holly aren't following.

Holly tugs on my arm. "Sit down," she orders. "We can hear fine from here. If we go any closer, the cops will think we're being suspicious and will definitely be asking us questions about why we're hanging around."

She has a point.

I lower myself back down, leaning forward as much as I can, my face propped up on my hands. Thoughts race around my mind a mile a minute, and I'd type them in my notes app if I wasn't scared they'd get in the wrong hands somehow. If Damien was pushed, maybe he wasn't the one who wrote us the note after all. Maybe someone else has been watching us and wonders why we're still here. I don't know what deadly note they were referring to though. Maybe one Violet wrote and blamed us for.

We need to figure this out, and fast. I managed to finish

my cover letter for Mr. Molina, but I know it could be better if I wasn't so distracted. Dad keeps texting that Mr. Molina can't wait to meet me and that I better get home so I can prepare what I'm going to say. I promised my parents that I'd be home today. If I go back on my word, they'll lose it, and I'll be the dead one.

"We should tell Denise what's going on." Zoe takes her phone out of her purse and types a text message. "If someone else did write the messages and then pushed Damien, she needs to know she's got to be very careful."

The older officer steps away from Mrs. Williams and approaches another officer standing in front of the police car parked closest to us. "She's coming to the station. We'll give her a ride there. She's in shock." They continue talking in hushed tones.

Mrs. Williams's eyes zip around the parking lot, her face red and puffy. Her gaze rests on us. Our eyes lock, and she beckons for me to come closer.

"I'm going over there," I announce, and Holly doesn't try to stop me this time. She's probably just as curious as I am.

"I need to talk to you," Mrs. Williams whispers as I approach. Her eyes are wild and her hands tremble as she takes her phone out of her coat pocket and thrusts it toward me. "Give me your number," she says. "Please."

I quickly type in my number and hand the phone back to her.

Her fingers move across the screen and my phone dings with a text from her, just her initials, TW.

"I knew when we talked that you suspected something wasn't right," Mrs. Williams continues. "Now, I'm sure. Whoever killed Damien killed my Violet too."

The older police officer steps away from the other officer and heads back in our direction. He eyes me suspiciously and opens his mouth to say something. "I'm cold," Mrs. Williams wails. "Dizzy and chilled to the bone."

The officer takes Mrs. Williams's arm and helps her to her feet. She sways slightly, trembling violently beneath the blanket that's still draped around her.

She shuffles toward the police car. The officer opens the door of the back seat for her, and she climbs in, shoots me a desperate look, and mouths, *Please, help me.*

The officer shuts the door and drives out of the parking lot.

# 19

# Holly

My day so far in a one-word understatement: eventful.

Zoe unlocks the door to her house, and we follow her into the living room. She tiptoes in cautiously as if she expects the murderer to be sitting on the couch, waiting for us, gun in hand. Now that we know Mrs. Williams thinks someone killed Violet and Damien, Calista spent the drive home listing every person we've met since we got here and what their motive might be, and Zoe's been so high-strung I'm surprised she hasn't passed out. I, on the other hand, am getting kind of over this whole situation.

Here's the thing: I did what I needed to do, and it's time to leave. I didn't want to spend half of my Christmas break sleuthing it up like a wannabe detective. School starts in four days, and I need to have some actual fun first.

"Has Denise written back to you yet?" Calista asks Zoe, cringing as Bark dives onto her lap. She pets him awkwardly.

Zoe glances at her phone. "Yeah. She says she'll be on her way back here soon." She opens the curtain a crack and peeks out at the front yard.

"She's not bringing that girl with her, is she?" I grab a seat on the armchair and rest my clammy palms on my jeans.

Zoe shrugs. "I don't know. I didn't ask."

Janie recognized me, and I'd rather spend as little time with her as possible, instead of needing to explain that I actually HAVE met her before. Recently.

"Okay, so let's get this whole story straight," Calista says, waving her hands around dramatically. "First of all, Violet drowns, which is weird because she was a strong swimmer. Then, we meet Damien, who acts like he doesn't care about her death. Then, he supposedly commits suicide by jumping off his balcony. Then, Mrs. Williams pulls up in complete meltdown mode and says she thinks both Damien and Violet were murdered. We got a threatening note. If Damien didn't send it, we're still in danger."

I glance across the room to meet Calista's serious expression and try to look more interested in her detective work than I feel. "As Denise would say, Birchbrook is definitely a sketchy place."

Zoe nods. "Welcome to my world."

I came to Birchbrook expecting some time to breathe, to feel free, but I'm starting to feel trapped in a situation I didn't sign up for. Hanging out with Alex doesn't seem as suffocating anymore. It's less work.

Calista clears her throat. "So, now we wait to hear what Mrs. Williams has to say." Bark licks Calista's face as if he wants her to stop talking and pet him. She grimaces, lifts him off her lap, and begins pacing back and forth across the carpet. "Maybe she can give us more information. Do you think I should call her yet?"

I stifle a sigh. I thought we'd already been through this. Five times at least. "No. She's definitely still at the police station. Give it a few hours. If you call now, the officers will ask her questions about us." I rest my head back against the cushion. "Hey, I just thought of something. Violet's phone. What if the passcode is the day she *met* Grayson. November fifteen. One-one-one-five or one-five-one-one, or the year even?"

Zoe tilts her head back in surprise. "How do you remember the day they met?"

I shrug. "Sharp memory. I dunno."

Calista fumbles through her purse and pulls out the phone. "Bingo," she says, shooting me a look of admiration. "It was one-one-one-five." She scrolls through the phone, and Zoe and I settle on either side of her to flip through selfies of dark-haired Violet when she was alive. In every picture she's in a different place: a mall, a park, Bennington's. In every picture she's with a different person: April, her cousin, her mom, Levi, Bradley, Damien. But in every picture her expression is the same. Sad. She may be alive, but her eyes are dead. A version of herself died the day Grayson left during the last summer of camp. Someone threatened him is what she told me. Someone told him if he stuck around, he'd be in danger, so maybe he ran away somewhere, and maybe once it was safe he'd have come back. She kept waiting. Until the day she died.

There's a short knock at the door, and Zoe jumps so high she almost hits the dusty ceiling fan.

Calista tilts her head and looks at her with concern. "Are you doing okay?"

Zoe blushes. "Yeah. Just kind of on edge. Some creep knows where I live and it's scary as hell." She peeks outside again and rushes toward the front door. "It's Denise," she calls over her shoulder.

I stare down the hallway and watch Denise enter and stomp her boots on the welcome mat. Relief courses through me. Thank God it's just her. Then, Janie steps in and my heart drops. Shit. She catches me looking at her and narrows her eyes like she's studying me carefully, like one of her practice cases. Denise grabs her hand shyly, and they sit on the shabby corduroy couch by the window. Denise looks across the room at me and shakes her head slowly with a snarl on her face like she's disgusted by the sight of me.

"What?" I ask, glaring at her. "Why are you looking at me that way?"

"You know why," Denise mutters.

Zoe's eyes widen, and she props her chin on her hand like she's ready to settle in for the show. If her dad had left groceries, she'd be making popcorn right now. Calista looks from me to Denise with interest. Janie stares at her lap which makes me so furious that I clench my fists. The bitch. Couldn't she just have kept her mouth closed?

"No," I say. "I don't know why. What the hell is your problem with me? You've been giving me a hard time since the day you arrived."

"Why don't you tell everyone why you lied to Janie." Denise's eyes are blazing, and her voice rises to a thundering volume that I didn't think she had in her. "Earlier at the restaurant you said you'd never seen her before but that's bullshit, isn't it?"

"No, it's not," I say sharply. It's not like they can prove it.

"I thought you'd deny it, but you can't anymore. Take a look at this," Denise says, and Janie holds out her cell phone. Denise grabs it and walks around the room to show us the picture on the screen. It must be recent because Violet's dark-haired and thin. I move my eyes to the left of her where I see myself in the background. This is from the pub night Violet invited me to.

"When was this?" Calista demands. "There are Christmas decorations in the background, and you look exactly the same as you do now, so it must be recent."

"It was a week and a half ago," Janie says, staring down at her lap. "At a bar near my school."

"You mean to say that after pretending it's been, what did you say again, two years since you saw Violet, you saw her the week before she died?" Calista says incredulously, wagging her finger at me like I'm a kid and she's my teacher. "Why the heck would you lie about something like that?"

I chip away at my nail polish and frown.

Here's the thing: I don't have to tell them anything.

"I didn't want to get into it," I say crisply. "I wasn't in the mood."

"You weren't in the mood?" Calista repeats, approaching my armchair and standing in front of me in a poor attempt to seem intimidating. "Obviously there's a bigger reason than that. And how did you know her hiding place? The passcode to her phone? What else are you hiding?"

"I saw them fighting," Janie says softly. She glances at Denise who nods at her encouragingly. "She probably didn't want to share what it was that they were arguing about."

"Spill it." Calista's eyes are cold as she leans her face close to mine. She pokes my forearm roughly. "No more secrets."

"You all have your secrets, and you know it," I say, my voice sounding even more bitter than I expected it to.

Just then my phone rings, blaring Beyoncé's "Crazy in Love," which is way too cheerful of a song for a moment like this. I knew I should have changed my ringtone to something like "The Sound of Silence." Much more fitting.

Calista glowers at me. "Don't even think about answering that."

My finger hovers over the Answer button. As much as I don't want to talk to him, this call is going to buy me some time.

Calista snatches the phone out of my hands and holds it behind her back, staring at me with narrowed eyes. "As I was saying, why did you lie to us?"

"Give that back," I growl.

Calista shakes her head. "No way."

I lunge forward, wrap my arms around her body before she has a chance to react, and pry the phone out of her hands.

Calista gasps. "What the hell are you doing? You dug your talons into my hand. What's wrong with you?"

The ringtone's stopped, and there's a shocked silence in the room. They're all staring at me with beady eyes like I stabbed Calista or something. The Beyoncé ringtone starts playing again, and this time I answer. Screw all of them.

"What's up with you?" Alex says gruffly before I say a word. "Why are you ghosting me?"

"Oh, hi, baby," I say brightly. "It's so good to hear your voice. You have no idea." I shoot the girls a triumphant look and flick my ponytail over one shoulder. "I'm going outside to take this call privately," I tell the others, whose tense expressions are probably even colder than the icy temperatures I'll face in the front yard.

Calista's hands are clenched fists at her sides, and she's practically breathing fire. "You pissed off the wrong person. Enjoy your phone call. It'll be the last pleasant conversation you'll have, believe me."

# 20
# Denise

I watch Holly stride outside—tossing her hair over her shoulder, clutching her phone against her ear smugly, like she dodged a bullet—and I have to sit on my hands to stop myself from jumping up and physically wiping the big phony smile off her face. I knew she was acting suspiciously the first day I saw her again. I got a bad vibe, a strong one I couldn't ignore, but Zoe and Calista made me feel like I was an overreacting weirdo. Violet must have told her about me, about the note I sent, and now she's playing with my head.

"Why do you think she'd lie to us about the last time she saw Violet?" Zoe asks. Her lower lip's jutted out and she looks deflated. Probably because Holly replaced Violet as her role model, and now she's finally realizing her new idol isn't as great as she thought she was.

"There's obviously something she doesn't want us to know," Calista says, pacing back and forth across the threadbare paisley-print carpet with her arms crossed. "That boyfriend of hers has been calling multiple times a day and all of a sudden she's all about answering his calls? Very convenient." She shakes her head, then marches toward the living room window, flings the long curtains aside, and peers outside.

Janie squeezes my hand, and despite everything that's going on, I turn to smile at her. She's on the couch beside me, our thighs resting together, hers quivering just slightly. Meeting Janie was the one silver lining on this trip so far. It's been a long time since I felt like this. The last time was with Violet.

"Oh, come on," Calista grumbles. She slaps her palms against the window and makes a clicking noise with her tongue. "She caught me watching her and she's heading through the gate to the backyard." She dashes toward the hallway, grabbing Zoe's hand and dragging her along. "Let's open the sliding door before she notices so we can hear what she's talking about. She's acting shady."

Zoe glances back and motions for us to join them, but I shake my head at her. I'd rather get a few more minutes alone with Janie. When she brought me to her apartment earlier, she spent the whole time showing me photos of her and Violet; then we both got choked up. We held each other for what felt like minutes but was actually over an hour. The next thing I knew, Zoe was texting me the Damien bombshell, and we left to meet her back here.

Janie strokes her thumb up the center of my palm and turns to look at me with her stunning green eyes. "Despite the shitty circumstances, I'm glad I met you."

My pulse is suddenly in my throat, making it hard for me to get my response out. "Same." I had no idea that my house was full of a stifling sadness until I left and came to Zoe's, a house with no memories. Things started looking up. Then I met Janie. She's the icing on the cake for me. With sprinkles and cherries.

Janie draws her lower lip between her teeth and blinks quickly. "I do have to tell you though; I'm still dealing with some heartbreak so it might take me some time."

Of course, there has to be a catch. This had too-good-to-be-true written all over it. "Heartbreak?" I repeat, my voice coming out like a squeak.

Janie looks down at her lap. "Violet," she says softly. "I think I was in love with her."

Who wasn't? That girl had an intense magnetic force everyone was drawn to. "I used to be too," I admit. "I get it. Last time I saw her was four years ago, but we talked often. She used to promise that she'd come see me. I'd keep asking when, but something always seemed to come up."

Janie fidgets with the hem of her sweater. "It's going to sound kind of stupid, but she used to call me her sunshine. She'd sing that song, 'You Are My Sunshine' to me all the time. Do you know it?"

"Too well," I answer, my chest tightening. That was her nickname for me too. *How many people had she used that name on?*

"She used to say that I made dark days brighter and I was the only one who made her happy." Janie's voice breaks, and I scooch closer and put my arm around her.

"It's okay," I whisper, speaking to both her and myself.

Janie sighs and runs her hand across her chin. "She said she wanted to be with me and that she just needed time to sort her feelings out. Stuff was complicated between her and Damien and she was still heartbroken about that guy Grayson who disappeared."

I take a gasp of air and blink back the tears that prickle in my eyes. *How could she?* Except for the Damien part, those were the things she'd say to me. Almost word for word.

Janie studies my face. "Denise, what's wrong? You look sad all of a sudden. I'm sorry, maybe I shouldn't have told you that."

Silence hangs heavily in the air until I finally speak. "She used to say the exact same things to me," I whisper. "But she never ended up sorting her feelings out." After Grayson disappeared, Violet changed. She became completely preoccupied with finding him and with making money to buy their dream house as if that would somehow bring him back. I was always there for her, through everything. She said she was falling for me and just needed time. Even four years wasn't enough.

Every time I called her, she found an excuse to let me go.

Janie wipes her eyes with the back of her hand, removing the blotches of smudged mascara. "That sucks to hear. I didn't think she was the type to lead people on."

I slump against the back of the couch, my eyes roving across the stucco ceiling. My heart feels like it's ripping out of my chest. My childhood crush, the breathless excitement of it all, was nothing more than a lie told by someone who wanted to manipulate me. It was comforting to convince myself that it was just bad timing, but now even that has been taken from me. "I'm learning more about her now that she's gone than I knew about her during all the time she was alive," I say softly. "It feels wrong to say but not much of it is good."

"Was she wrapped up in the wrong crowd, even then?" Janie

swings around on the couch to face me, pulling her legs up to her chest and resting her chin on her knees.

"Kind of. When we were kids, we saw some people digging something in the woods on one of the nights the manager wasn't around. They couldn't have been up to anything good. I think Violet knew them, the way she wanted to make sure we weren't going to say anything."

Janie slowly shakes her head. "I wonder what the hell they were doing. That sounds creepy. I know so many dark, dark things about all the twisted people in her life. Sometimes she'd get me to follow them like I was her private investigator or something. I can't believe I actually went along with it."

Me and her both. I can't believe my friends and I did half the things Violet put us up to. Especially the last thing. That haunts me every day of my life. Violet had the power to get anyone to do anything. I squeeze Janie's hand. "She had that effect on most people. Not just you."

The front door swings open, and Holly barges into the room. She perches on the edge of the armchair and gives us a look like she's daring us to challenge her.

Little does she know, I'm not in a timid mood today. I glare back at her. "As we were saying before your *important* phone call, why did you lie?"

"I didn't," Holly snaps.

Calista and Zoe rush back into the room and lower themselves onto the sofa across from us, looking from Holly to Janie and me.

"Why didn't you tell us you saw Violet last week? What was the point of lying about that?" My booming voice echoes in the room, and I realize that all my feelings about the note and about Violet leading me on are fueling my anger. I'm fuming to the point that my hands are twitching, and I'm scared that they have a mind of their own and I'll slap the pretty right off Holly's face.

"We're not exactly close anymore," Holly says, picking at her cuticles. "I didn't think I needed to tell you guys everything."

"You didn't tell us you saw Violet just before she died? That's important," I bark.

Calista moves so she's standing directly in front of Holly. Her arms are crossed, and she squints angrily. "Zoe and I heard you talking to your boyfriend, telling him you were coming home tonight. You're not leaving until you tell us everything. We're all in this now."

Holly snorts. "Really, Calista? I can leave whenever I want to. Believe me."

Calista inches closer. "At the funeral when you and I went up to the casket and I was shocked Violet looked so different, you didn't say anything. You didn't say anything because you already knew what she looked like nowadays. Did you know where she worked too?"

Holly avoids our gaze and stares straight ahead at the gap between the curtains. I bet she's wishing she left while she was out there.

Calista moves forward until Holly won't be able to get up without colliding with her. "Well?"

Holly's jaw tightens. "Yes."

Calista lets out a low whistle and clenches her hands. "Are you kidding me? You had so many chances to tell us the truth, and at the funeral would have been a perfect opportunity. How many lies have you told us?"

Holly tilts her head to stare past her, refusing to look into her eyes. "I didn't exactly lie. I just didn't tell the whole truth."

Janie stands. "I . . . I should get back home."

I gently tug on her hand. "You don't have to go." Hopefully this tense situation doesn't get in the way of what we have. I can't imagine a worse introduce-your-crush-to-your-friends experience than what's unfolding right now like a nightmare.

"I really should go." Janie gives me a fragile smile. "You all need to talk. Without me. I'll text you later." She leans over and kisses me lightly on the cheek, and I'm flooded with warmth. She slowly retreats, and my fingers tingle as I resist gently pulling her back toward me.

I follow her to the foyer. "I'll walk you out."

Janie steps into her boots. I hold out her coat, and she slips into it. The front door creaks as it opens, and the cold wind whips against our faces. The snow's hard and deep, and we leave a trail of footprints as we huddle together, clutching hands, to make our way to Janie's car.

"I can't believe Holly willingly came out in this just to talk to Alex in private," Janie says.

I squeeze her hand and tilt my head to glance at her. "Really? I can. She's sneaky as hell. If your car wasn't blocking hers, I bet she would have taken off."

Janie nods. "Yeah, maybe." She leans against the car door and wraps her arm around my neck. "Now I can say good night the way I wanted to." She leans into me, her breath warm against my cheek. My heart thumps faster and faster, and she presses her lips gently against mine, and I kiss her back. The only thing I can focus on is how soft her lips are, how much I want to stay in this moment. "See you soon," she says, her nose nudging my cheek. She opens her car door, puts the key in the ignition, and pulls out of the driveway onto the road.

I stand right where she left me until my heart starts beating at a regular pace again. That was beautiful. When I turn back toward the house, the curtains move, and I see Zoe darting away, probably hoping I didn't catch her spying on us.

As I climb the front steps, I notice something that I didn't see when I was walking Janie out in a giddy daze. A coldness hits me in the pit of my stomach. To the left of the door is a scrap of paper pinned down beneath a large rock, and I freeze, goose bumps rising on my arms.

# 21
# Zoe

Denise walks into the house and stands motionless in the foyer. I guess that kiss really knocked her off her feet. The early evening darkness creeps inside the open door, along with a gust of bitter wind. The bare tree branches are black silhouettes against the navy-blue sky.

"Denise? Why are you just standing there? Are you okay?" I call, stepping closer to her. Unfortunately, she doesn't look lustful.

Denise's face is as pale as it was when she dressed up as a corpse bride for costume day at camp. Only back then, she was giggly and wired because of too much candy. Right now, with her moon-wide eyes and trembling lower lip, she looks scared out of her mind. Bark must sense her fear because instead of jumping up and down, bugging her to pet him, he stands still, peering at her silently as if he's waiting to see what she'll do next.

Calista steps away from Holly and zips to Denise's side like a bolt of lightning. "Why are you just standing there like that? You didn't even close the door behind you." She pulls the door closed, locks it, and nudges Denise. "Well? What's going on?"

Denise still doesn't move or respond. Her eyes close and she hangs her head. She holds up a small slip of paper, and I rush toward her.

"What is that?" I ask, but she doesn't answer. My stomach twists in knots because judging by the familiar paper size and Denise's reaction, it's another note.

Denise's outstretched hand shakes as Calista takes the paper from her.

"'Don't talk to the police. Ten reasons why . . .'" Calista reads, then stops, leans against the wall, and slowly lowers herself until she's sitting on the floor. Her breath is coming out in bursts, and her hand flies up to cover her mouth.

"What does it say?" I cry and crouch beside her.

"It lists every one of our family members by name. And the last name is Farrah. It's a threat," she says softly, whipping her head around to face Denise. "Is it possible that we missed this when we came in earlier?"

"No," Denise whispers. "It was right in the doorway. I know I would have seen it. It has my mom's name on it and my brother's. I . . . I can't lose them."

I swipe my suddenly sweaty palms against my leggings and take the paper from Calista so I can see it for myself. Who the hell knows my dad's name? And how do they know Jill? How do they know any of our family members' names? It's not like we've been talking about them in any of the places we've been.

"Why do you think Farrah's name is on there? Does anyone know another person with that name?"

The other girls shake their heads. Denise's face is paper white, and her lips are bloodless. She lets out a whimper.

Calista rubs her temples. "Maybe whoever is writing it is trying to say that our family members will end up dead like Farrah if we tell. Maybe the same person who killed Violet and Damien pushed Farrah off the cliff. Now we know for sure that person wasn't Damien."

I sneak a glance at Holly, who's sitting on the couch spinning her thumb ring. She never seems to react in the same way the rest of us do. She used to before, when we were at camp. Not now. She looks way too calm for someone whose snooping has put her own mother in danger.

Holly catches me looking at her and narrows her eyes at me. "What?"

"Aren't you scared?" I ask, my voice rising. "You don't seem like you are."

Holly rolls her eyes, crosses her legs, and leans back against the worn cushions. "Oh my God, Zoe. Now you're going to start with me too?"

Denise finally unfreezes and steps forward, her face still a ghostly white. "Don't you get it, Zoe? She's not scared because she was the one who wrote the note. Doesn't it seem strange to anyone else that she was just out front and it suddenly turns up? She wants us to stop hunting for information so we don't find out what she did."

I lower myself onto the sofa across from Holly and study her nearly expressionless face. Denise can't be serious. Holly can be rude sometimes, but she hasn't set off my creepy radar, and it's usually pretty sensitive. "Did you see anyone when you were on the phone?"

"Of course I didn't," Holly says in an overly sweet tone. "I was only in the front yard for a few seconds before I realized you and Calista were spying on me."

"What's your boyfriend's name?" Denise asks, slowly walking across the foyer until she stands at the edge of the carpet.

Holly sighs. "Why do you want to know?"

"Answer the question," Denise snaps. "What's your boyfriend's name?"

Holly throws her hands up in the air, and her cheeks redden. "It's Alex. What does that have to do with anything?"

"Look at the list." Denise snatches the slip of paper out of my hand and points at the names, written in the same thick block letters as the last notes. "Calista's boyfriend's name is there. Where's your boyfriend's? If someone else wrote this, why wouldn't they put Alex's name on here too?"

"No idea," Holly snaps. "But whoever wrote that note is pathetic. Someone with no life. I would never do that. Even if I am getting bored. I don't know why you're so preoccupied with me, Denise. Get a fucking life."

"Oh, I have a life. And it entails more than brushing my hair, looking pretty, and murdering people." Denise steps across the carpet with her hands on her hips and stops a foot away from Holly. "Why don't you let us all know what you've been up to. Last night after Zoe passed out, where did you really go?"

My mouth drops open. I didn't know she went anywhere. I wish I didn't pass out. I would have followed her.

"She left?" Calista splutters. "Why is this the first time I'm hearing about this?"

Denise shrugs. "She told me she needed some air and I believed she was telling the truth. Not anymore though."

Holly shifts in her seat and looks down at her nails. "I went for a drive. I didn't know I was a prisoner here. Like Ms. Drama Queen said, I needed some air."

Denise narrows her eyes. "You must have gotten plenty of air on Damien's balcony."

"You've got to be kidding me." Holly stands and Denise steps closer until they're inches away from each other, neither of them blinking. "Leave me the fuck alone," Holly growls. "Or else."

Denise makes a clicking noise with her tongue. "Oh really? Another threat? Didn't you get enough of that in your little letter? I knew there was something dangerous about you the minute I saw you again." The timid voice she had a few days ago is long gone. Her lips stretch into a frightening snarl. "Admit it. Either you know what happened to Violet and Damien or you did it yourself."

"The only thing I know about Violet's and Damien's deaths is that I had nothing to do with either of them." Holly tilts her face even closer to Denise's. "Now move."

Denise doesn't budge. The silence in the room is so heavy that I just want to say something, anything, to break the frightening intensity of this moment. If one of them throws a punch, who am I going to hold back? I glance at Calista who's got her hand over her mouth. I wonder if she's thinking the same things as I am.

"I didn't write that note but you should listen to whoever did. Give up playing detective and go home." Holly shoves Denise and she stumbles backward and falls on the floor at the foot of the sofa.

Denise's eyes blaze with fury as she jumps to her feet. "What the hell's wrong with you, Holly? That hurt."

"Good!" Holly yells and storms downstairs.

Calista rushes to the basement door and secures the sliding lock at the top of it. She spins around and leans against it with her hand pressed against her forehead. "This is so screwed up. She's going to stay down there until we figure out what we're going to do about her. Denise might be right. What if the person we've been terrified of has been staying in the same house as us the entire time?"

# 22
# Calista

"Thanks for covering for me," I say.

I'm thirteen, and Violet and me are talking privately in the woods near the cabin. The sun's setting and the crickets are humming, and even though this is the calmest, most beautiful time of day, my heart's racing and adrenaline still charges through my veins.

"Don't sweat it," Violet says, rolling her eyes slightly. She runs her hand along the trunk of an oak tree. "Don't do anything like that again. Once you're eighteen and you do something like that, you go to jail. Did you think of that?"

My stomach clenches. "Jail," I repeat. No one would want to hire a lawyer that's done jail time. That would ruin my life.

"You put it back, right?" I ask.

"I couldn't." Violet tilts her chin and squints at me. "I saw her coming back to the house and didn't want to get caught."

*I nod. "But you are going to put it back, right?"*

*Violet shakes her head. "No. I'm not."*

*I don't get why she's acting so annoyed with me if she gets a bunch of money out of it. "What are you going to use it for?"*

*"I'm saving for that house I showed you a picture of. On the ocean. When I get it, Grayson will come back and we'll live there. I'm saving every cent," Violet says firmly, her eyes gleaming. "He'd never leave me. He told me he wouldn't. I believed him. I still do."*

———

THURSDAY, DECEMBER 30

Great.

Here I was thinking my time away from my real life couldn't get any more terrible, but now I'm sitting on the floor next to Zoe's locked basement door with Holly, who may or may not be a murderer, on the other side, slamming her fists into it. If she manages to break it down, I have a plan. 1) I'll tackle her to the floor, and 2) I'll put her somewhere else until we can figure out what to do.

"Let me out of here," she shouts. "I swear to God, whoever locked me in here is going to regret it." I feel the vibration of a thud against the door like she's bodychecking it with all the force she can muster.

Zoe crouches down next to me and chews on her lower lip. "She's been down there for a while," she says nervously. "She's yelling so loudly my neighbors are going to call the police."

I sigh and pull my knees to my chest. "Let's hope they don't." Locking Holly in the basement was an impulsive decision. I was half-hoping Holly would just admit she killed them, or we'd find proof she didn't. Sitting here on the hallway floor isn't getting us anywhere, and I needed to be home hours ago.

"Should we tell the police we have reason to believe it was her?" Denise asks, a note of bitterness creeping into her voice. She's never been a Holly fan, and she'd probably love to see her taken away in handcuffs.

I shake my head. "Not yet. I think we just wait until she's ready to talk to us calmly and we can figure things out."

Zoe tugs at the hem of her crop top and bounces her legs anxiously. She's a bundle of nerves. We all are.

My eyes dart from Zoe to Denise, and I flash them a reassuring smile. "Holly won't be able to get out. We're okay. We're safe. We should all just take a breather for a few minutes and figure out what we're doing next." Zoe and Denise nod halfheartedly, and I take a deep, shuddery breath. I try to tune out Holly punching the basement door and channel a sense of serenity. There's a pang in my chest as I realize the things that usually calm me down—homework, writing, Javier, my family—are miles away. I said I'd be home today. But how can I go home when people are threatening my family? I need to protect the people I love.

My phone buzzes. A text from my dad:

> Email me your cover letter. I haven't
> read it yet. Why aren't you home?

I open my cover letter. *My name is Calista Diaz, and I believe I'm the perfect candidate for this internship . . .* My dad's going to hate this. He knows I can write better, but there's no way I can focus enough to do that now. I grudgingly attach it to an email and press Send.

"Are you on VenusLove?" Zoe asks, peering over my shoulder with the first smile I've seen on her face in hours.

"No," I say indignantly. "I'm on my email. I don't go on dating sites, I have Javier. Have you gotten any new messages lately? From the guy I chose for you maybe?"

"He wrote to me but I'm not sure I'm interested," Zoe says and twists a strand of hair around her finger. She flashes me a wide grin and perks up. "I'm more into Levi. I messaged him and he wants to meet up with me. Even though I acted like an idiot in front of him."

Denise stares at her lap. "That's a terrible idea. I never want to see Levi or Bradley ever again."

I close my email and turn to face her. "I agree. Look, Zoe, I told you, I don't get a good feeling about that guy. No offense, but you were extremely wasted that night. That's the only time he's met you. If he liked you then, he's probably looking for a wild party girl. He said it himself that he hangs out at Bennington's on a regular basis. He's not right for you."

Zoe's face falls, and she nudges the wall with her foot. "That sucks. Maybe you're right, but I want to see him one more time while I'm sober so I can make up my mind."

I frown and cross my arms. "I still don't think it's a good idea." I need to figure out a way to convince her not to see him. I don't want her hanging out with Levi and Bradley and telling them something about The Mistake. I don't want Mrs. Felmont to ever know about that.

"Let. Me. Out," Holly screeches, and it sounds like she's kicking the door now.

"I can't be calm when she's freaking out like that. We need to let her out," Zoe says, her eyes widening pleadingly.

"There's no way we can do that," I answer. "She needs to calm down and be rational. Who knows what she'd do if we let her out now." I can fully picture Holly attacking all of us. She sounds furious. I take Violet's phone out again and scroll through it. The pictures haven't given me any clues yet. The last photo was a selfie with April at Bennington's on December fourteenth. Nothing seems weird yet. She has a banking app, a music app, some games, nothing out of the ordinary. I tap on her voice memo app. There are three files. I tap on one marked December fifteenth. A familiar voice sings a Katy Perry song. I'd know that voice anywhere.

"Is that Holly singing on Violet's phone?" Zoe asks.

"They got together to sing?" Denise says, her face crumpled. "Why?"

I shake my head. "No idea."

"That was great, Hol," Violet's voice says. "You sounded beautiful."

I open the second file. "He said he'd be back and I believed him," Violet's voice says in an eerily calm voice. "And I think I know what happened."

I tap on the third file marked December twenty-first. The day before Violet died. "Holly's in too deep now," Violet whispers. "I probably shouldn't have involved her. They won't let this go. She asked about him and they'll kill her for knowing too much. That's what they do. Even if she never asks another question. Never comes back here again. They'll kill her, just because she hung around snooping. It's dangerous if we keep doing it and dangerous if we stop. The only thing we can do now is take them down. It's the only way to stay alive."

"What?" Zoe yelps. "Are we going to ask Holly who Violet's talking about? Who did Holly question?"

I take a long breath. "No. There's no way she'll tell us now. She's completely losing it down there."

All the color drains out of Denise's face. "But what was that about?" She presses her fingers against her mouth and swallows hard. "So, it's too late for us too? They've noticed us hanging around. Violet said whoever these people are will be after us whether we stop investigating or keep on doing it. What choice do we have? We can't go to the police. Now they're naming our family members. Holly's behind those notes. She's working with someone now. I know she is."

"This is getting bad," Zoe says. "This disaster keeps getting bigger and bigger. I'd lose my mind if something happened to my dad. Even to Jill. She's annoying but she and my dad are all the family I've got."

Suddenly, I want nothing more than to go home. Get bothered by my parents about my chores and homework, have David harass me about hanging out with him. I miss Javier. He has the best hugs, the way he wraps his arms around me when he can tell I'm stressed about something, how he kneads the tension out of my shoulders. I slip my phone out of my purse and type him another I miss you text. God knows I'm in danger, I might as well be sure he knows how I feel before it's too late.

His reply comes quickly.

You too, mi amor. When u back?

Later today

It's getting late. I'm surprised Mom hasn't called me yet. I usually help her make the soup for the party around this time.

"This is getting too dangerous," I say. "This needs to be over."

"It's not dangerous when the person who wrote the note is trapped in the basement," Denise says. "She's the only one who would know all of the names of our loved ones. She didn't put her own boyfriend's name because she obviously doesn't like him and probably forgot about him when she was writing the note. She uses people. Just like Violet used to."

"I can hear you, you know," Holly yells, and it sounds like she's punching the door again. "How many times do I have to tell you, I didn't write the fucking note. Stop obsessing over me and maybe spend your time worrying about the actual person who wrote that. Who knows everything about us. Let. Me. Out."

"If that's true, why would Holly include Farrah's name?" I ask. "Why did she bring her up?"

"To scare us? Probably to scare us." Denise runs a hand across her face and takes a ragged breath. "How would *I* know?"

Behind us, Holly's phone buzzes against the coffee table, blaring Beyoncé's "Crazy in Love" and sending us all jumping.

"Give me my phone," Holly yells.

"No way," Denise whispers. "Does she think we're dumb?"

I scoot closer to the table and see Alex's name flash across the cell phone's screen. The call ends, and then he calls back again. I pick it up. "Hello?" I whisper.

Zoe shoots me a shocked look. *What are you doing?* she mouths.

"Who is this?" Alex asks. His voice is deep and low. I can see how someone would think he sounds intimidating.

I step out of the room, so Holly won't be able to hear me. "You're Alex, right? Holly's boyfriend? This is Calista," I say, trying to sound positive and upbeat as though we just spent the day painting our nails and watching movies. "Holly's taking a nap right now. Long day. I saw that you called twice so I answered in case something bad happened. Is everything okay?"

"I want to talk to her." There's a note of desperation in his voice, and I can't figure out if it's irritating or sad.

"She's really tired today," I lie, stepping into a dimly lit room. I sit cross-legged on a dingy-looking quilt that's been haphazardly thrown across the bed. "I don't want to wake her. Is there a message you want me to pass to her?"

There's a long pause on the line, and the only sound is his heavy breathing. "What's that noise?" he finally says. "It sounds like someone's yelling."

"We're watching a movie," I say coolly and open the curtains to survey the bare tree branches and single streetlight. It's dark and the sidewalks are empty, basically. Hopefully if any neighbors do decide to go for a walk, they're not the neighborhood-watch type because Holly's probably loud enough to be heard outside.

Alex clears his throat. "Tell her that I'm mad she did this to me again."

"What is it she's doing to you?" I ask, wondering if he'll open up or tell me to go to hell.

"She's lying. She said she'd be gone for a day, and it's been days now. She did the same thing the other week. Makes me wonder what she's up to."

"How long was she gone then?"

"She said she'd be gone for an afternoon to visit a friend and she was gone for three days. She asked me to tell her mom she was staying at my house if she called. I have no idea who she was really with." He sighs. "It was probably a guy."

"That's really crappy," I answer. "Who did she claim she was with?"

"She said her name's V."

She spent more than just one day with Violet and got Alex to cover for her? Be her alibi? Goose bumps rise on my arms. Maybe Denise is right after all. "V?" I repeat. "That's interesting."

There's a beeping sound in the background, and a man's voice muttering something I can't quite make out.

"Okay," Alex says. "Well, I have to go back to work. Tell Holly I'll see her very soon."

"I will," I say, wondering how Alex would react if he knew what we suspect and where Holly is at this moment. It sounds as though she's still throwing her body against the door in an effort to break it down.

I end the call and stand, flinging the curtains aside to take another look out the window. The bushes sway, and I freeze, ready to yell for the others. Then a cat steps out and wanders slowly across the snow. An eerie feeling hits me, like someone's watching me out there. I dash out of the room and back to the living room.

"What did he say?" Zoe whispers when I sit back down on the floor beside her.

"He confirmed that Holly spent days with Violet the week before she died," I whisper back. "And she lied to him about how long she'd be gone."

All of a sudden, headlights beam through the spaces between the curtains, and I turn to Denise. "Is that Janie again?"

"No," Denise answers, her face growing pale. "She's home. I just texted her."

"Then who is that?" Zoe cries. "Who's here?"

"What's going on?" Holly shouts. "If someone's trying to break in, you can't leave me stuck down here. Please."

I run across the room to peer out the window at the unfamiliar black car parked at the end of the driveway. The headlights switch off, and a man gets out of the vehicle and strides toward the front door.

# 23
# Holly

I sit on the top step with my ear pressed up against the door. My heart pounds so hard I feel like it's going to burst out of my chest, and my hands ball into tight fists. Are these girls for real? How dare they leave me down here, especially now that someone's trying to break in.

"The guy's opening the door," I hear Denise scream.

Bark growls.

"I'm taking Bark to hide in my room," Zoe yells.

"Hide here," Calista shouts, and then there's silence.

Blood rushes to my ears. "Let me out," I snarl, but it's pointless. I'm stuck here, waiting to be attacked by whoever's breaking in. I can't believe those bitches.

Heavy footsteps are approaching the basement door, and I hold my breath. My fists are raised, trembling, but ready to pound into whoever opens the door. First step: ram my fist into his temple before he has time to react. Second step: run.

"Zoe?" a raspy male voice says. "Where are you, Zoe?" Holy shit. I've got my money on it being Levi. He seemed all right at first, but it was odd how Zoe being drunk didn't completely turn him off. If she wasn't part of the plot to lock me in the basement, I might have helped her. Sorry about your luck, Zoe.

"Dad?" Zoe says in a shaky voice. "What are you doing home?"

"Good lord," I mutter, my heartbeat starting to slow back down. *Dad?* It's her dad? All that panic for nothing. Why didn't anyone suspect it was her father, just coming home to his own house like a regular person?

"Jill and I are going to New York City after all. I came home to pack some nicer clothes," he answers.

"I thought you were an intruder," Zoe says, relief in her voice.

He laughs. "An intruder? Why would someone want to rob us? What have we got that anyone would want?"

"I guess," Zoe says, forcing a laugh. "Where's Jill?"

"I dropped her off at the mall. I'm supposed to go back and get her before eight thirty. She convinced me to buy her a new dress for New Year's. I see your friends are still here. Hello."

"I'm Calista and this is Denise," I hear Calista say.

"I remember you two from dropping Zoe off at camp. I didn't think you'd be in Birchbrook as long as this," Mr. Callahan says with a chuckle. "As my girlfriend would tell you, there's shit all to do around here."

"We didn't think we'd be here as long as this either," Calista says crisply. "But we'll be heading back tonight. I need to get back home."

"Why not stay and ring in the new year with Zoe?" Mr. Callahan says. "She could use the company." Here's some Zoe 101: she'd prefer her father's company to ours, but he's either clueless about that or he doesn't care.

"I've got a family party tomorrow that I need to get ready for," Calista begins, and I don't want to hear about Mr. Molina, the internship, her stupid cover letter, or any of that garbage.

I've got to cut this conversation short and take my chance to get out while I can. "Hello? Mr. Callahan?" I call in the sweetest voice I can pull off even though I'm so mad that smoke's practically swirling out of my ears.

"Who's that, Zoe? Where's the voice coming from?" he says.

"It's Holly and I'm stuck in the basement," I call. "I hid down here when you came in and the door must have locked behind me. Can you let me out?"

"Absolutely," he says, opens the door, and stands there grinning at me. He's wearing baggy jeans and a faded blue sweater. No wonder he came back for better clothes, but I'm not going to think anything negative about the guy who saved me. "I can't believe you locked yourself down here. Sorry I caused such a panic."

I nod. "That's okay. At least I'm out now." I plaster on a smile and turn to the girls. "Right, ladies?" There's no way any of them have the guts to tell him the real reason I was down there. Zoe's eyes are bugging out of her head, and Denise is pale and twitchy. Calista's lips stretch into a thin line, and I can tell by the expression on her face that she's coming up with a plan about what to do with me. There's no way she'll be able to lock me back down there. I'm ready to fight them if I have to. As in: they'd better watch out.

Mr. Callahan shoves his hands in his pockets and nods his head in the direction of the bedrooms. "Well, I'd better go get some of my wedding outfits out. They're the only fancy clothes I own. I'm more of a jeans-and-T-shirt kind of guy." Hmm. I never would have guessed.

"Wait, you're leaving right away?" Zoe's face clouds over with disappointment. If I didn't want to slap her so badly my fingers twitch, I might even feel sorry for her. "Couldn't you stay for a bit longer? I haven't seen you in days."

"Sorry, Zoe. We're driving out there right after I pick Jill up from the mall. You don't want to hang out with your old dad. You've got friends over." Mr. Callahan leans down to pet Bark, who rolls over onto his back like he's making the most out of the small amount of Mr. Callahan's attention he can get. Zoe might want to give it a try.

Zoe's face crumples. "But I *do* want to hang out with you."

Mr. Callahan runs a hand through his wavy gray hair and shifts his weight from one foot to the other uncomfortably. "I'll be home on Saturday, Zo, I promise. Jill's going to her mother's to celebrate New Year's Day with her. It will just be us two."

"I want you to stay with me now though," Zoe says softly.

"Saturday," Mr. Callahan repeats. He pats her on the top of her head awkwardly and heads for his bedroom.

Zoe stares at the carpet. "This really sucks."

Denise puts an arm around her. "Saturday's the day after tomorrow. It'll be here before you know it."

Mr. Callahan walks back along the hallway with blazers, collared shirts, and dress pants draped over his arm. "Okay, I'm off. You girls have fun. Help yourself to anything you'd like."

Meaning rotting vegetables and a bag of some weird chip

alternative. No, thank you. He calmly slips on his boots and scoops up a pair of dress shoes. I'm surprised he doesn't seem to sense the tense energy in the room.

"Love you, Zo Zo." Mr. Callahan gives Zoe one last smile before he closes the door behind him.

Now that he's gone, I can say what I really want to.

I spin to face the girls, my fists clenched at my sides. "What the fuck. Why the hell did you lock me down there?" I step toward them, and it takes every ounce of restraint I have not to tackle them to the ground.

Zoe backs up, her eyes wide and her hands raised in surrender. "It wasn't me, it was Calista. I told her to let you out."

My fist rises, ready to strike, and Calista glowers at me.

"I don't regret it," Calista says snidely and tilts her chin up defiantly. "We were right about you. You've got a violent streak. Are you going to attack me now?"

My hands vibrate with rage as I slowly lower them to my sides. Punching her isn't worth it. Knowing her, she'd probably charge me. "Believe me, I'd love to, but it's a waste of my energy."

"Oh, please," Calista huffs. "Anyway, I'm calling my parents. I'm going to ask them if I can stay over one more night if I promise to practice what I'll say to Mr. Molina. I'll leave first thing tomorrow. All of this drama is making me too tired to drive and also, this isn't over. The last thing I want is for this dangerous situation to follow me home, have murderers stake out my high school."

Denise glares at me from beneath her long bangs. "What about you? Why don't you leave now?"

"I'm tired too," I snap. "You girls are so annoying, it's exhausting." I'll leave as soon as I wake up, make it home in time to plan something for New Year's Eve. Part of me wants to drive off on my own tomorrow, somewhere random, stay in a hotel and celebrate the evening on my own, but knowing me, I'll drive home and watch a movie on the couch with Alex. And even though it might be boring, it'll be better than all this stupid drama.

Denise crosses her arms and shakes her head. "I'm not going to feel safe in this house with you."

"We can sleep in my room with the door locked," Zoe says. "I can push my dresser up against the door."

I point at myself, my face flaming. "What if *I* don't feel safe? Where am I going to feel protected from you three? You locked me in the basement for fuck's sake."

"You can lock yourself in my dad and Jill's room." Zoe opens a closet, takes out a bedding set with sailboats on it, and hands it to me. "But you should probably change the sheets first."

Gross. I follow her down the hall to their room.

———

I wake to someone pounding on the door.

"Holly," Zoe yells. "Come out here. We need to talk to you."

It takes me a second to remember where I am. The lights are still on, and my eyes rest on a row of nature landscapes in bronze frames that remind me of the ones my grandfather used to have at his cottage. And obviously? I wish I was at the cottage instead of locked in Zoe's dad's bedroom. The sheets Zoe gave me smell like they haven't been washed in a decade. My gaze drifts to the window. It's still dark outside. I feel around beneath the blankets for my phone. "What time is it?" I holler. "Why are you waking me up now?"

There's another loud knock on the door. "It's eleven fifty p.m. Open up," Calista shouts. "Is she in there with you?"

"What are you talking about?" I fling open the door and come face-to-face with Calista in full bitch mode, with her hands on her hips, scowling.

"I'm talking about Denise." She storms past me, opens the closet door, then proceeds to kneel down to look under the bed of all places. "Where is she?"

"How the hell should I know?" I shout.

Zoe rushes into the room in her unicorn pajamas, her arms wrapped around herself. Bark runs in after her and circles around whining. "Seriously, Holly. Just tell us."

"I went to sleep. I have no idea." Is this actually happening in the middle of the night? These girls need to get a grip.

"So did we. Then I wake up to go to the bathroom and she's gone." Zoe presses her face against the window. "I still don't see her out there. The door was unlocked. She has no car and she keeps saying this place is sketchy. I seriously doubt she'd go walking on her own in the middle of the night."

"I bet you she's with Janie. She might have wanted to say goodbye to her before we all head back." I move past them, out into the hallway. "Did you try calling her?"

Calista nods and gives me a look as she lifts her phone to her ear. Denise's melodic ring resounds from another room, and Calista leaves and comes back with it in her hand. "See. She's in trouble."

"That's definitely odd," I admit, brushing at the goose bumps that have risen on my arms. "There has to be a reasonable explanation.

"What if she's dead?" Zoe cries.

A reasonable explanation besides that.

Calista grabs both of Zoe's shoulders and leans forward so she's talking right in her face. "Calm down," she says firmly. "You freaking out is not going to help anything. We need to find her."

"Should we call the police?" Zoe asks. "I think we should."

"We don't even know if she's missing." I open my bag and take out some clothes. "I'm telling you, she probably went to meet Janie. Janie drives. Maybe she came by to get her and Denise just forgot her phone behind because she was so excited to see her."

The phone rings again in Calista's hand, and she jolts. "So much for that theory," she snaps. "It's Janie texting that she can't sleep. Denise isn't with her."

Zoe stares at me with a cold expression. "If you know, tell us, Holly. Did you do something to her?"

I throw my hands in the air. "Seriously. If you don't stop it right now, I *will* do something. To you. Stop being so annoying."

Zoe looks down and shakes her head.

These girls have been complete bitches to me, and really, I should leave now, but as much as Denise pisses me off, I don't want her to die or anything. "Listen," I say. "Let's get dressed and go look for her. Are you sure she didn't get freaked out and catch a bus back home?"

"And leave all her stuff here?" Zoe says. "Not likely."

"Let's go," Calista orders and storms out of the room.

Zoe and I follow her outside and trek through the snow to my car. We pile inside and I pull out onto the dimly lit road. "Where should we even go?" I ask, eyeing Zoe in my rearview mirror. "If she's not with Janie, where would she be?"

"Well, let's think of the only places she knows around here. Mood, Bennington's, that place we went for breakfast." Calista lists the options on her fingers.

"It's almost midnight, Mood's closed, and obviously Rise and Shine is too. Do you think she went to Bennington's?" Zoe asks.

"It's kind of hard to believe she left in the middle of the night to go to a bar that freaks her out. On foot." I turn onto Main.

"It's worth a try," Calista says. "Drive there." She slaps the dashboard with a leather-gloved hand.

I raise my eyebrows. "Okay, boss."

When we pull into the parking lot of Bennington's, April's outside, smoking a cigarette. I roll down my window.

"Look who it is," April says with a grin and saunters toward my car. "I thought you girls would be heading home by now. I didn't think you'd be back here."

"Denise," I say. "She's not here, is she?"

April shakes her head, and her long hair cascades around her shoulders. "Nope. She's definitely not here. You probably want to go home for New Year's, but if you're still around, you should come by here. It's going to be an epic party."

I bite my tongue to hold back a *hell no.* Hopefully we can hurry up and find Denise so I can get back home and make the most of my New Year's.

"We'll definitely be gone by then," Calista says.

"Thanks anyway," Zoe adds.

I wave, roll up my window, and drive out of the parking lot. "Where should I go? She doesn't know anywhere else. Do you think she went to Damien's building? To see if the investigation is still on?" I glance over at Calista.

She arches her eyebrows and frowns. "She doesn't even know where he lives. She wasn't with us."

I head in the direction of his apartment anyway because I have no clue where else to go.

Zoe points at the cemetery. "We have to remember to go see Violet before you guys leave."

"That's it!" Calista cries and slaps the dashboard again. "Turn into the parking lot. I'd bet a hundred bucks she's in there."

I snort. "In a graveyard at midnight? She strikes me as being too big of a scaredy-cat for something like that."

Calista's eyes gleam. "Maybe. Or maybe you're wrong."

I drive into the dark parking lot, and chills immediately run up and down my spine. I turn off the ignition, and it's eerily silent. "Now what?"

"Now, we look for Violet's grave," Calista says. She opens the car door and steps out, her breath making little puffs of smoke. She switches on her phone's flashlight and shines the light across the deserted cemetery.

Zoe gets out and stands beside her, looking anxious. She jiggles around to keep warm.

I link arms with her, and Calista slips her arm around mine on my other side. A few hours ago, I never dreamed I'd let them within a yard of me ever again. There's nothing like an emergency to bring people together. We step slowly forward along the stone path, peering along row after row of headstones. I think I see someone crouched behind a tree, but it's so dark I can't be sure. I blink quickly, straining to focus, and there's no one there—it's just a shadow. I inhale sharply as fear prickles along my flesh.

"This is so creepy," Zoe whispers. "I don't think she's here. Maybe there's somewhere else we can check."

I scan the names on the stones, eyeing the elaborate arrangements of fake flowers. "I don't see hers. Is there some kind of order these things are usually arranged in?"

THE GIRLS FROM HUSH CABIN

"Denise would know but she's the one we're looking for," Zoe whispers.

There's a whimpering sound, like a hurt animal, and Zoe grips my arm even more tightly. Fear grips my chest, and I swivel around to figure out where the sound's coming from. Whoever hurt that animal, or person, could be coming for us next. Time's passing in slow motion, and I get this feeling like someone's moving in on us.

One step.

Two steps.

We're going to find ourselves cornered somewhere and then it will be too late.

"What the heck is that?" Calista swivels around.

"We should go." Zoe stops in her tracks and takes a step backward, tugging us along.

"We need to find her," Calista hisses and pulls us forward. She shines her flashlight across the rows of tombstones and stops at a dark figure hunched over on the ground. "Denise?"

The whimpering sound becomes louder. The figure turns to face us, a hand blocking the glare of our flashlight.

# 24
# Denise

A glare of light beams onto Violet's headstone, and I whip around in a panic. "Who's there?" I cry, my heart thudding against my chest. Someone knows what I did. They might have followed me here.

There's no reply.

"Please don't hurt me," I yelp, then spring to my feet and back up.

I can make out the silhouettes of three people in front of me.

"Denise?" a familiar voice finally says. I squint through the bright light and see Zoe step forward with a panicked look on her face.

I release a pent-up breath—I'm relieved and disappointed at the same time. *How did they know where I was? I'm not ready to talk. Not yet.*

Zoe rushes forward and crouches on the ground beside me. "You scared the shit out of us. Why did you come here on your own?"

"She thought Holly murdered you," Calista says dryly.

Zoe shoots Calista a dirty look. "So did you."

Holly heaves an exasperated sigh. "Stop with that, already." She moves closer and runs her hand along Violet's white marble headstone just like I did when I found it—it's smooth and cold like Violet herself. Holly glances back at me with a faraway look in her eyes. "So, tell us. Why did you come here?"

I shake my head. I'm afraid that if I open my mouth, things will come somersaulting out in a tangled mess. They won't understand. Their Violet secrets are tame compared to mine. If I tell them everything, none of them will look at me the same way again. It will make it even more real, and maybe I'll end up getting the punishment I know I deserve.

"Say something," Zoe says, nudging me gently. "What happened?"

I'll tell them one thing that's hurting my heart so they'll be satisfied. I can't tell them anything more. "She led me on," I blurt out.

Zoe clicks her tongue and rests her hand on my forearm. "Who did? Janie? I'll punch her."

"No," I whisper. "Violet." I lean forward and trace her name, etched on the headstone in large gray letters, and it hits me in the gut all over again. She's gone. She's in a coffin, sealed up under the ground. I'll never be able to ask her why she lied to me. I'll never be able to see her again.

"What do you mean?" Calista steps forward and crouches in front of me. "When did this happen?"

I avoid her eyes and bite my lip. *Why does she have to inter-rogate everyone? Can't she tell this isn't a good time?* I gaze up at the moon, a half-full flash in the sky. *Maybe if I just keep star-ing at it, Calista will look at it too. Maybe she'll understand that with all the loss and lies, I feel half-full too.*

"During the last year at camp," I finally say. "I thought Violet and I would end up together, but we never did. She lied to me."

"You thought you'd end up dating her?" Calista repeats. "And she was just leading you on?"

I nod.

She sits in the snow next to me and rests a hand against my back. "I'm sorry."

Holly and Zoe sit beside her, and now we're in this tight little circle like the one we made in the woods when we played with the Ouija board. Only back then we were best friends, and we'd have rather died than snap at each other or accuse each other of anything.

"We need to stop fighting," Zoe says as if she's reminiscing about the same things. "We should come clean about all our secrets and start fresh."

"No one actually thinks I killed Violet, right?" Holly asks, and for the first time, her voice sounds shaky instead of smug. "Because that was shitty how you blamed me. I didn't tell you guys about seeing her recently because we did some strange stuff together. She had a job for me and I got some money for doing it. Mom's killing herself working long hours and I needed stuff and didn't want to bug her for it."

Calista tilts her head and surveys her curiously. "What did you have to do?"

Holly looks at her fingernails. "She asked me to go to a bar and find this guy she showed me a picture of. She told me to talk to him for a while and then somehow bring Grayson into the conversation. She wanted me to describe his reaction."

"Why would she ask you to do that?" Calista asks. "What was his reaction?"

Holly's mouth sets into a thin line. "He looked kind of pissed. He changed the conversation topic and then he left. I told Violet and she asked me to do more. She wanted me to meet him again and ask him if he knew who killed him. I said I wouldn't. I was scared. Then we got into a big fight because I stood up to her. That's the night Janie saw us. I don't know why she got me to do all this stuff, only that there were probably bad reasons. It was fucked up seeing Bradley the other day considering what I did to him back at camp."

Calista folds her legs against her chest. "What did you do?"

Holly makes a face and massages her temples like the memory pains her. "She got me to pretend I was into him. He liked Violet better but she made it clear to him that it would never happen. Anyway, she convinced me to start this whole secretive relationship with him. She said dating someone like him would be good for me. I could practice kissing on him so I'd be good at it with someone I actually liked. She convinced me to find out where Mrs. Felmont kept her money and valuables. One day when she wasn't home, I got Bradley to show me her bedroom. I started making out with him to buy myself some more time. Then I heard Mrs. Felmont's car pull up and hid in the closet. That's when I found the safe. I reported the information back to Violet and a week later Mrs. Felmont was robbed."

Calista stares at her lap and fidgets with her charm bracelet. "Wow."

"I know it's kind of twisted but I think we all did some stuff
we're not proud of." Holly looks at the ground. "So, who's spilling next? Calista?"

Calista runs her hand along the back of her neck and stares
at her lap. "I don't have a secret."

"Yes, you do," I whisper. "Let's face it. We all do."

Calista blinks. She opens her mouth and then closes it again.
"I . . ." she begins. "I was the one who stole from the safe," she
blurts out. "It was my idea."

Zoe's brow furrows. "Aren't you rich though?"

"Violet told me Mrs. Felmont was paying her staff less than
minimum wage," Calista says. "She told me how Mrs. Felmont
had a safe with lots of money in it and how unfair it was that
she had all of that money when her staff was doing all the work.
'I bet the code for the safe is Bradley's birthday,' she said to me
one day. 'Mrs. Felmont's out today and I know Bradley's occu-
pied.'" Calista pauses and runs a hand across her face. "Anyway, I
climbed in the back window and tried the code and it worked. I
took a box out and I didn't even open it myself. I took it straight
to Violet. I thought she'd be so proud, but she frowned at me
and said, 'Why did you do this, Calista? This was a mistake.'
She told me she'd put it back but she didn't end up doing that. I
felt awful about it, especially when Farrah had the accident not
long after that. Mrs. Felmont's been through so much. I wish I
could go back in time and erase my mistake."

"It wasn't just *your* mistake," Holly jerks her head back.
"Violet gaslit you. It was her idea and she made you feel like it
was yours? She should have put it back like she said she would.

Bradley told me the reason the camp closed was because his mom went bankrupt."

"It's my fault," Calista says softly.

"No," Holly cries. "Violet was older than us and she knew exactly what she was doing. She was nice at one point, but after Grayson went missing, she changed. All she cared about was making money for that house he wanted to buy. She got evil."

Calista stifles a sob. "All of these years I felt so terrible that I'm one of the reasons the camp shut down."

Zoe rests her hand on Calista's back. "Don't let it eat at you. We all did bad things."

Calista sniffs. "What about you? What's your secret?"

Zoe shrugs and pulls on her hoop earring. "You already know. I recorded stuff."

"Was that clip you showed us the only one?" Calista asks.

"No," Zoe admits. "I have at least sixty others."

Holly shakes her head slowly and lets out a low whistle. "Shit. That's more than I expected."

"What was the purpose of that?" Calista demands. "Violet just wanted to document things? Or was it like the other time where she wanted to have it on camera that we vowed not to tell?"

"Blackmail," Zoe says. "She'd get me to film the other counselors doing crap, like smoking weed, drinking, and hooking up with each other, and then show them the clips to get them to do stuff for her so she wouldn't tell on them."

Holly makes a face. "That's twisted."

"So was what you did," Zoe says with a shrug. She turns to me. "I still want to know more about what happened with you and Violet."

I close my eyes, and it's like I can see her in my mind. Her hand around the back of my neck, her clear blue eyes, her soft lips. I'm frozen for a few seconds, and it takes a minute to find the right words. "I loved her. She made me feel special. She collected things. Little knickknacks she wanted to put on the mantel of her dream house. I'm the only one she showed her treasures to. I think. She gave me my first kiss. She said she wanted to be with me, and I believed her. She said the exact same things to Janie. It was all lies. Everything I ever felt about Violet was a lie. All of it." *And to think that Violet got me to do something terrible and I did it, without really protesting, because I loved her so much.* A lump grows in my throat, and it hurts when I swallow. I bite my lip hard.

Zoe hugs me. "I'm sorry," she says.

"Yeah, that really sucks," Calista agrees.

"But what did you used to do for her?" Zoe asks. "What's your secret?"

I hesitate, trying to arrange my words, to find the right version of the truth. "She was good at lying to me and I guess I was good at lying *for* her," I admit. "She'd confide in me and tell me I was the only one she trusted. Then she'd use me as an alibi for things. Like the night the stuff from the safe went missing, I said all of us, including Violet, were in our cabin all night. She told me I had a face that anyone would trust. No one would ever accuse me of lying."

"What else?" Holly asks.

"What do you mean what else?" I ask, my hands flying up like she's pointing a gun at me. "That's it."

Holly stares at me for a long time. "Why did you get so freaked out about the notes? Both times you nearly hyperventilated. What does Farrah mean to you? I think it's something about her."

"No," I say firmly. "It's nothing to do with her. The notes are scary and that's all there is to it."

"I feel like you still have something to say," Holly protests.

*I have to tell them something. Somehow change the subject.* I clear my throat. "Well, there might be one thing, something Violet told me. That night, the digging. Violet admitted she knew the guys in the forest. They told her they buried evidence of a heist but she told me she was starting to think it was something else. Something worse."

Calista's brow furrows, and she leans forward. "What do you think it was?"

I shake my head. "I don't know. I'm scared to think."

Zoe's eyes widen, and she clasps her hands together eagerly. "Let's go and see for ourselves. We could go now."

Holly snorts. "Hell no. People are threatening us and now you want to go and dig something up at summer camp? Who knows what it is, but it's obviously something that people took great pains to keep hidden."

"Who's going to know? It's not like anyone would see us there. Aren't you curious about it?" Zoe asks. "I know I am. Maybe it will help us figure out who killed Violet. We could find some kind of clue."

Maybe bringing up the digging was a bad idea. I should have known that it would turn into them wanting to investigate, and that's the last thing I want. "No." I shake my head hard. "I don't want to go back there."

"What choice do we have?" Calista faces Holly. "When you were downstairs, you know . . ."

"Locked up in the basement?" Holly butts in, her eyebrows arched.

"Yes," Calista says, tucking a curl behind her ear. "While you were down there we got into Violet's phone. She made a recording about you. She said that you weren't safe after asking those questions. I didn't know what questions, but you just told us. She said anyone who acts like they think something suspicious is going on is in danger. I don't know about you guys, but it's after midnight, meaning my family party starts today. My mom's furious with me for staying here so long and not helping her prepare. My dad thinks he stuck his neck out to help me with Mr. Molina and all I'm going to do is disappoint him. We have to figure out who did this before they take us down. Where else are we going to look?"

My high-pitched ringtone blares, making us jump. Zoe takes my phone out of her coat pocket and gives it to me. "Why did you leave without your phone anyway?"

"I wasn't thinking. Feeling sad." *More like terrified. More like I just opened the door and ran because I didn't know what else to do with myself.* I glance at my screen, and a jolt of electricity surges through me when I see Janie's name, followed by a tightening in my chest. It's late and I hope she's okay. "Hello?" I say into the phone.

"Sorry it's so late. I didn't know who else to call," she blurts out. "I can't stay in my house anymore. I saw someone outside my window."

# 25

# Zoe

I turn to glance at Denise and Janie, curled up together in the back of Holly's car. Calista sits beside them, looking a little squished. Oh well. I called shotgun this time, fair and square. Denise takes off her black fleece coat and drapes it over Janie, who shivers in her navy-blue Henley shirt and ripped jeans. She must have been freaking out so much she forgot her jacket. I can relate. Ever since someone started leaving us notes, I've been majorly on edge.

"Did the person look familiar?" Denise asks Janie, her eyes filled with concern.

Janie shakes her head. "I . . . I don't know," she stammers. "I was trying to fall asleep, and when I glanced out my window, I saw someone wearing a black hoodie behind the bush, but they were gone by the time I got outside."

"You went outside?" Calista repeats, blinking incredulously. "Wouldn't it have been better if you stayed inside and called the police? What were you going to do if there was someone out there? Just hand yourself over to them?"

"I brought some things outside with me," Janie says softly, her green eyes gleaming. "For protection." She rifles through her bag and pulls out a Swiss Army knife, a can of pepper spray, and a lighter.

Holly looks back at her in the rearview mirror. "What were you planning to do with that? Start a campfire?"

Denise nods and brushes her bangs out of her eyes. "They're right, Janie. Next time you think someone's outside your house, call the police or hide. It's a good thing whoever it was wasn't out there anymore."

"Do you think whoever was threatening us was the one outside of Janie's house?" I ask.

"It's possible," Calista says. "Or it might just be one of those people who try to get change out of unlocked cars."

Denise pats Janie's knee. "You're safe with us now."

How safe we are is the question. I've never felt as far from safe as I have this week, that's for sure.

"Where to?" Holly asks as she turns out of the cemetery parking lot, leaving Janie's car behind. "Do we go and sleep or do we go where we were discussing?"

"Where were you discussing?" Janie asks. She tugs on a strand of her unusually tangled purple hair and looks from Denise to Calista and back at Denise. "Can you tell me? I can come with you."

Maybe it's just me, but Janie's asking a lot of questions suddenly and it's sort of suspicious. I wish my suspicion radar was always on—as the queen of online dating, it might come in handy.

"It's a terrible idea. Remember what I told you about those people digging?" Denise asks.

My eyebrows shoot up. Wait, she told her that? I guess I shouldn't judge. The girls said I started telling that same story at Bennington's.

Janie nods calmly like that event is as normal as a walk on the beach. "Yeah, that was creepy."

Denise might have told Janie everything there is to know about us, and she's only known her for a matter of days. Even *I* keep my lips sealed longer when I meet someone new. What's Janie doing with that information? I study her carefully. Could she be the one leaving the notes?

"We . . . we can't go there," Denise stammers. "We can't. It will be traumatic after what happened to . . ."

"To Farrah?" I ask.

Denise stares at her lap and nods.

"We should go," Calista says firmly. "We only have a few more hours to figure this out. How else are we going to get to the bottom of this?"

"We can't," Denise yelps. "Tell them it's a bad idea, Janie."

"It seems like a good idea to me. Like Calista said, we need to find whoever hurt Violet, because whoever it is, they're planning to hurt us next. Don't worry." Janie takes a hold of Denise's hand, and a strange smile creeps across her face. "Swing by my house first. I've got the perfect shovels in my garage."

"I don't know about this," Denise whispers.

Maybe Holly was right about Denise. She hyperventilated

over the notes, and now she's bringing up Farrah and freaking out about going back to camp. What's she hiding?

———

"There it is," I say and point at the large wooden Camp Bellwood Lake sign. Instead of looking welcoming like it did in our camp days, it appears so ominous beside the snow-covered pine trees that it might as well be smeared in blood.

"It feels surreal being here again, especially in the winter," Holly says as she turns into the narrow entranceway. Normally she's smirking like everything's no big deal, but today her jaw's tense and she blinks quickly. "This is kind of creepy," she says as we drive down the winding dirt road. The bare maple tree branches on either edge of it intertwine overhead like a sky full of tangled arms.

The last time I felt this scared here was the morning after Farrah died. Before that, this place was blissful and predictable with campers hiking, wildflowers, Mrs. Felmont's big red van. Then one morning we left the cabin and entered a crime scene. Campers were pacing around in a panic, most of them crying, and yellow tape and police were everywhere. Mrs. Felmont rode in the ambulance with her daughter's dead body, and Bradley was wailing, despite several officers trying to console him. Eventually he was taken away in an ambulance too. Nothing could calm him down. That was the last day I was here.

This time it's scary for a different reason. This place is like a wintry ghost town.

Holly taps her fingertips against the steering wheel anxiously, and I shiver. This doesn't feel like a good idea anymore. I regret saying it was.

Like she can hear my thoughts, Denise says, "It's not too late to forget all about this, you know."

Calista shakes her head. "We're here now. We should do it. We're running out of ideas."

Holly parks in front of Mrs. Felmont's deserted house. Judging by the missing shingles and broken gate, flapping open and shut in the wind like a hand shooing us away, I don't think she's been up here much since the camp shut down. Or at all.

We climb out of the car, Holly pops her trunk, and Janie takes out the shovels and flashlights she got from her garage. We stand in an uncertain huddle, and I notice Denise's upper lip twitching. "This is a bad idea," she whispers. "This is a very bad idea."

"It's okay, Denise," Janie says, grabbing her hand. "We're all here together. You guys want to figure out what happened to Violet before you leave later. This is going to help." The gleam in her eyes is a little too eager. She hands Denise one of the shovels, tucks the other one under her armpit, switches on her flashlight, and starts down the trail with Denise trudging behind. We follow them, through the pine trees, the hard snow crunching under our boots. Without the sounds of cicadas and campers, the woods are disturbingly quiet, and every creak of a branch has my heart in my throat.

Out of the corner of my eye, I see a dark silhouette flash by. An animal. Or a person. I can't be sure. "Did you see that?" I yelp, staggering backward into Holly, who grabs my arm. Tremors shake my body.

Holly leans into me. "What did you see? Where?"

I point to the right. "I saw something moving."

Janie swings around, nearly hitting us with her shovel. "No one's here but us. It was probably a deer. Let's keep going."

I stumble forward, still gripping onto Holly until the lines of log cabins peek through the branches.

"There it is," Calista calls, pointing at our log cabin. It's smaller than I remember it, like a garden shed almost. How did we not feel claustrophobic in there?

Holly tiptoes forward and pauses in front of the door. Her eyes dart around like she expects someone to step out from the bushes and grab her, ask her what she's doing here. She slowly reaches her hand out and turns the knob, and surprisingly the door creaks open. "It's not even locked," she whispers. "I figured Mrs. Felmont would want this place secured. She seemed so uptight and careful. Especially after the robbery . . ." She looks at Calista, who frowns.

I step inside, Janie shines her flashlight around the room, and it's like I've entered a time machine that's transported me back to life at thirteen. Besides being dusty, everything's exactly the same. The red-and-white checkered bedspreads, the nightstands. The only thing different is there aren't mounds of our clothes laid out everywhere. And instead of the scent of the vanilla-rose body spray we all bathed ourselves in nonstop, there's a stale, damp odor lingering in the air.

Janie lets out a low whistle. "So, this is Hush Cabin."

"The magical place where Violet manipulated us and made us keep secrets from everyone, including each other." Calista rolls her eyes. She points at the table. "I bet our initials are still there. I wonder if anyone ever went under here and saw them."

I crawl under the table to check it out. Our initials are deeply etched in the light wood. Larger than all of our letters is Violet's V.W. surrounded by a heart. I can't believe that I used to think she had one.

Outside the window there's a loud thump. We all jump. My hand flies to my chest, and my heart pounds against it. "What was that?" I cry. First the silhouette, now the noise. Someone's here. It's the perfect place to kill all of us.

Calista inches toward the window. "Maybe it was an animal? Or snow falling off a cabin roof?"

"Someone's here," I whisper. "They followed us."

Calista cautiously peers outside. "I don't see anyone out there."

"There are animals in the woods," Janie says in a patronizing tone, like she wasn't scared shitless by some guy outside her house less than an hour ago. "Of course we're going to hear them. I say we go and see what those men were doing. The animals are probably more scared of us than we are of them." She taps her foot against the wooden floor impatiently and fiddles with her flashlight.

I study her curiously. "Why are you so into this?"

She smiles. "It seems exciting, don't you guys think?"

Calista raises her eyebrows. "I don't know if exciting is quite the right word."

"I'm ready as I'll ever be," Holly says with a shrug. "Let's just do it. We always wondered about it. Let's find out." Holly and Janie step out of the cabin and lead the way down the path into the forest, and Calista follows behind.

Denise plunks down on the edge of the bed with her head in her hands.

I hesitate in the doorway. "Come on, Denise."

Denise looks up, her eyes wild with terror. "No one's listening to me. Go without me. I'm going back to wait in the car."

"We need to stick together." I offer her a hand, and she

reluctantly takes it. I pull her to her feet, and we step out and start along the trail. Denise has her arms wrapped tightly around herself, and she's muttering something under her breath.

We walk for what feels like ten minutes until we get to the fence that separates the camp from the escarpment. Denise stops in her tracks and presses her face against the chain-link fence.

"Come on, Denise," I say in a voice that comes out more sharply than I expected it to. We're all scared. Why is she acting like such a drama queen?

Denise doesn't turn or acknowledge I've said anything. She grips her shovel with a shaky hand.

"Denise!" I yell. "Please, snap out of it." I don't want to be left in the middle of the woods with her. She's acting unpredictably lately, and it's freaking me out.

"That's the place they found her." Denise points her finger through a chain-link diamond at the steep cliff on the other side. The side every camper knew was dangerous and off-limits because of the thirty-five-foot drop and the sharp rocks below. "That's where they found Farrah's body."

"I know," I grumble. "Denise, I know that. Everybody knows that. It's weird being here, I get it, but can we just hurry up and catch up with the other girls?"

Denise finally comes out of her daze and turns toward me, but her eyes are blank and her face looks more ghostly white than ever in the glow of my flashlight.

"Let's go," I say again and start along the path before I can be sure she'll follow me. I can't see the others anymore. They're too far ahead. How rude of them not to wait when they realized we weren't with them anymore.

Denise staggers behind me, and every time I shine my

flashlight on her, she reminds me of a zombie, frenzied, her mind someplace else. And it's hard to forget that she's got a large metal shovel in her hand. I start running. I can hear her grunting behind me as she tries to keep up. I think I'm lost, or the other girls are lost—they can't be this far ahead.

I sprint through the branches, adrenaline crashing through me. "Calista?" I shout. "Holly?" My heart clenches at the sound of raw panic in my voice. "Janie?" I shriek.

"Zoe?" a voice calls. "Zoe, is that you?"

I clamber through the branches. Calista, Holly, and Janie are gathered in a clearing up ahead. "Where the hell did you go?" Holly asks. "We were going to go back for you."

"Denise . . ." I begin, but then there's rustling in the bushes and Denise lurches toward us, her face red, panting. She glares at me, and I swallow my words. "Denise and I needed to rest for a second."

Janie puts her arm around Denise. "Are you okay? You're so out of breath."

Denise rests her head on Janie's shoulder and crumples against her. "I think so," she croaks.

"This is the place we went to drink that night," Calista says, pointing at the row of tree stumps we sat on. "Remember?"

"Of course Zoe remembers," Holly says with a laugh. "It was the highlight of her time at camp."

"Shut up," I snap, and Holly's mouth drops open. Tough. She wasn't the one lost in the woods with a shovel-wielding, zombified Denise.

We walk for a few more minutes until Holly stops in her tracks and kicks her boot against the snow. "This is it. Right where that rock is. This is where they were digging."

"I thought it was over more. Are you sure?" Calista asks.

"I'm positive," Holly answers and nudges the rock with the boots I lent her as if she expects it to easily roll away and expose what's buried beneath. Then she grabs Denise's shovel out of her hand and smashes it against the ground, and I heave a small sigh of relief. I'm glad someone besides Denise has got a hold of it now.

"It's frozen," Holly says. "This is going to be impossible."

"Not if we light a fire first to soften the area." Janie gives Holly a sly grin. "I guess the answer to your question earlier is yes, I'm going to light a campfire."

Holly squints at her. "Are you sure you know what you're doing?"

"Let's grab some of the dry branches from the ground under the trees," Janie says in a strange tone that sends a shiver zipping up my spine. Like an expert pyromaniac, Janie ducks under the low-hanging branches of the pine trees, grabs an armful of wood, and piles it on top of the spot Holly pointed out. Janie flicks her lighter, holds a branch against it, and waits. "Yes," she whispers as the thin stick she's holding goes up in orange flames.

# 26
# Calista

It's 1:10 a.m.

We've set a fire.

I may regret this.

Red-and-orange flames flicker and crackle, and we stand in a circle around them, a thick layer of uneasiness in the air.

So thick that I could take Violet's pocketknife out of my purse and slice through it.

Zoe and Holly are huddled together, leaning into it and jiggling in place to stay warm. I stomp my feet to keep my circulation going and cross my arms tightly across my chest. "How long should we let this burn?" I ask.

Janie stares into the fire as if she's hypnotized by it. She blinks and tilts her head in my direction. "The ground's probably soft enough to dig by now."

I gesture toward the tall flames. "How are you going to put it out? Are we going to wait until it goes out on its own?"

Janie doesn't answer. Instead, she smiles and lifts a shovel full of snow, tossing it on top of the fire. It sizzles and hisses and the flames shrink. Janie piles another shovelful on, and it extinguishes. She pushes the firewood away with her shovel, then cracks it down against the ground, heaving out a mound of dirt. "It worked," she says triumphantly.

It's almost like she's done this before.

I glower at her. "How do you know so much about this stuff?"

Janie shrugs, and her eyes glint in the silvery moonlight. "I've always been kind of interested in those wilderness survival shows."

I frown. My suspicion of Janie kicked into overdrive as soon as it became clear that she was too invested in this excursion. Maybe she plans to toss us all into the hole after we help her dig it.

But she's not the only one with a knife.

Denise gives me a look as though she can tell what I'm thinking. "Give the interrogation a rest for a while, Calista." She paces back and forth, her face contorted in worry. She's been acting guilty too. Maybe she's covering for Janie.

Janie tosses another pile of dirt over her shoulder and leans on the handle to take a break. "This is hard work."

"I can take a turn whenever you're tired," Zoe offers brightly. "Are you absolutely sure this is the spot, Holly?"

"I'm positive," Holly says and stops digging to catch her breath.

Minutes pass, the hole slowly grows deeper, and my hands

itch to be involved. Waiting is harder when I have no control over how long it takes.

"I'll take a turn," I say and gesture to Holly. She hands me the shovel. I crash it against the ground and lift out a mound of soil. I do it again and again until my hands ache.

Janie crouches down. "Stop for a second. I think I see something." Her hand trembles as she points her flashlight's beam to the ground, illuminating a scrap of blue fabric.

"Maybe it's a bag they hid evidence in," Zoe says.

Janie starts digging faster. I'm surprised by the amount of strength she suddenly has. The hole's a good three feet deep now and about two feet wide. I match her pace, and the pile of discarded dirt climbs higher and higher.

My shovel slams against something hard. "I need a light," I call, and Holly shines it on something blue. "It's that fabric again." I crouch down and run my hand along it. My heart pounds as I process the meaning of what I've found. "I think it's clothing."

Zoe's mouth twists. "Part of the evidence. The outfit they wore when they committed the robbery. They should have just burned this stuff, don't you think?"

"I doubt that's what it is," I whisper, my voice trembling, and I swallow a mouthful of bile.

It's something worse. It's something much, much worse. I wobble on my knees and close my eyes for a long second, hoping they were playing tricks on me. I open them again to see it, beneath the blue cloth, blistered and gray, sharp bone protruding. I spring to my feet and take a step backward. "This looks like decomposing flesh."

Janie moves the light along the stretch of blue and dusts the soil off with her gloved hand. "It's a body part," she whispers.

"How . . . how do you know?" Denise stammers.

Janie fiddles with the fabric and rolls it up, revealing a flash of gold.

"That's a watch," I cry, backing away. "Attached to an arm." Vomit rises in my throat again and I spit out a mouthful on the dirt.

"We weren't supposed to find that," Denise says, her voice sounding almost hysterical. She starts running through the dark forest toward the car. She stumbles and comes crashing down in front of a fallen tree. "Help," she shrieks and begins sobbing.

I rush to give her a hand to haul her to her feet.

Zoe zips ahead of us, her flashlight piercing through the darkness.

The tree branches whip against our faces, arms, and chests as we clamber through the trees, gasping to catch our breath.

Zoe reaches the car and leans over, panting, her hands on her knees.

"Where are Janie and Holly?" Denise shrieks. "What's taking them so long?"

"No idea." I look back at the trail. Hopefully Holly's okay and Janie didn't throw her in the grave.

Zoe takes a shaky breath and holds her head in her hands. "Who the hell's body do you think that was? Who did those people kill?"

I wrap my arms around myself. I need to keep my composure even though my insides are contracting and every morsel of my being is clenching in fear and disgust. "Why would Violet want to cover something like that up? That's sicker than anything else she did."

"Maybe she really didn't know what they were hiding," Zoe says. She points at the path. "They need to hurry."

Holly and Janie come running toward the car. Holly hits the unlock button, and I thrust open the door and dive into the front seat. Holly looks rattled as she gets into the driver's seat.

"Why were you so far behind us?" I grab Holly's thigh and give it a shake. "What happened?" Suspicion of Janie creeps into the forefront of my mind. Is she the one leaving notes? Or is she working with the person who is?

"We threw the dirt back in the hole and shoveled some snow on top of it," Holly says. "You just left us to do it ourselves."

"I'm sorry, Holly," Denise cries, covering her face with her hands. "Janie, I'm sorry. I felt out of it the whole time I was here and I got so scared, I just ran. I shouldn't have just left you there."

"It's okay, Denise," Janie says. "Thanks for the apology." She clears her throat. "Maybe you should apologize too, Calista." I turn around to catch her glaring at me. "I sure as hell don't want the murderer knowing we uncovered the body. Do you?"

"We—we should call the police," Zoe stammers.

"Do you remember what April said about the police?" Holly asks. "They might even be involved in this." She zips down the long, winding dirt road and onto Main Street. "Do you think whoever buried that person was the one who killed Violet? Maybe she threatened to tell someone."

She's driving so erratically. I summon my sense of calm. "Drive slower," I say firmly and lean forward to rest my hand on her forearm. "No one saw us there."

"I really think I saw someone," Zoe says. "Someone was watching us."

"It was probably an animal like Janie said," I reassure her. "No one knows. We're not in trouble."

"Wrong," Holly says. "Remember at Bennington's when

Zoe blabbed to everyone there about Violet getting mad about us drinking in the woods? We have a whole table of people who know about us seeing people digging."

"Well, I know Levi didn't do it. He cared about Violet. He was her friend," Zoe protests.

"You trust people too easily," I snap. "You were pro-Damien and it seems like he was wrapped up in some pretty sinister shit or he'd still be around now. We need to get out of this place. I've never wanted to go home as much as I do right now."

I slip my phone out of my pocket. All I want right now is to reread my texts from Javier or my brother—complaining about being put on soup duty. Someone who feels like home to me. Instead, I see Mrs. Williams's name and a message from her that freezes my blood.

> You girls are in trouble. I need to talk to you. Now.

# 27

# Holly

"This is just a silly game. It's fake. Right, Violet?" Denise whispers.

This is us: thirteen years old, at camp, sitting in a circle on the ground in the woods. Violet's beside me, and Denise? She's bent into a frightened ball on my other side. Callie and Zoe are across from us, their faces spooky-looking in the candlelight.

Violet doesn't answer, only swipes her eyes with the back of her hand. She regains her composure, scoops her tousled blond hair back in a low ponytail, and leans forward, resting a finger from each hand on the small flat stone Callie found her.

Zoe's the one who wrote the alphabet on the inside of the cereal box she swiped from the kitchen, just like Violet asked her to do. She wrote the letters in red marker and laughed about how much the ink looked like blood. Here's the thing: she's not laughing now. Her upper lip twitches, and she steals glances at Callie, maybe hoping she'll talk some sense into all of us. But Callie's quiet, solemn, and seems ready to do this. Seems ready to do anything Violet asks her to.

"It's fake. Right, Violet?" Denise repeats, her voice trembling. She grips my hand, and I gently shake it loose. I'm going to need it in a minute.

Violet's face floods with color, and her lips stretch into a determined line. "I hope not." She looks around frantically. "Now put your fingers on it with me, don't be such babies," she says hoarsely.

As if the stone's magnetic, like Violet herself, our fingers are drawn toward it. We're kneeling, our faces fearful. The only sound apart from our breathing is the cicadas buzzing around our heads.

Violet nudges me, and her eyes are glassy. I know this look. She's about to cry and will if she keeps talking. "Ask for me," she whispers.

"Okay," I whisper back. "Are you there?" I ask the board, and the stone moves from Y to E to S. Denise yelps and pulls her fingers off.

Violet shoots me an eager glance.

"Where is Grayson?" I ask.

The stone zips across the cardboard, and I know my fingers aren't even quite touching it. Who's moving it? It can't really be moving itself. It starts on D then E then A then D.

Violet swings around to look at each of us, her face wild with fury. "Why did you write that?" she yells. "Why did you do that to me?"

"I was barely touching it," Callie shouts. "And I'd never spell something like that."

"Same," Zoe adds. "Maybe it was a bad spirit. We can ask again."

Denise holds her fingers like they've been scorched and shakes her head.

"*I wasn't moving it either,*" I whisper. "*Don't worry, Violet, we can try it again.*"

*Violet jumps up. She's going to cry again. I see her glassy tears in the candlelight. Then the flame's blown out. I don't think it was the wind. It's so dark I can only faintly make out the others.*

"*We should go back now, Violet,*" Callie says, but Violet runs away from us, through the woods, leaving us feeling around in the darkness for each other's hands.

---

## FRIDAY, DECEMBER 31

Talk about fucked up. This is a whole new level. We arrive at Mrs. Williams's house and I turn off the ignition and clench my eyes shut to process what we've just seen.

I'm far from naive, but a dead body? It wasn't even on my radar. Now even Mrs. Williams is telling us we're in trouble. The obvious thing to do would be to call the police, but April told us about the police around here. I've seen it myself. The good guys? They're just as bad as the bad guys.

Basically: this is a twisted nightmare that never ends. I take my phone out of my purse. It's almost 2:00 a.m., but Alex wouldn't care if I called him. Even if I woke him up. But what would I say? It's not like I could tell him anything. He hasn't called or texted since the call Calista picked up. For him, that's unusual. His name wasn't on the list of people who were threatened, but if whoever is doing this knows about all of them, they know about Alex too.

I step out of the car and follow the others up the front

walkway to find Mrs. Williams sitting on a bench on her porch wearing a fluffy pale-pink coat. Her hair's in a ponytail at the top of her head, and the loose tendrils fall around her face. Her Christmas lights are still up and blinking, making her glow white then dark like a wax figure under a strobe light. She's so still I wonder if she's asleep or dead.

"Hello? Are you okay?" I call cautiously from the bottom of the stairs.

"No, no, no," she murmurs and rests her chin on her clasped hands.

I don't see any wineglasses, but if she's sitting outside in the cold for the hell of it, she must be drunk again. "Why are you out here?" I ask, scuffing the snow with one of the old suede boots I borrowed from Zoe. "You could have waited for us inside."

"It's hard being in there without him . . . and her." She seems to realize what she's said and covers her mouth with her hand. "Damien looked after me. Comforted me when Violet was awful to me."

"What do you mean Violet was awful to you?" Calista asks.

Mrs. Williams lets out a short sob, then dabs under her eyes with the back of her hand. "After Grayson went missing, she changed. She became completely preoccupied with finding him. With making money to buy this ridiculously expensive house. She used Damien because he knew about money. She never loved him. She used me too, but I still loved her. She was my baby. When she died, I was devastated, and now that he's gone, I'm lost."

"Yikes," Zoe whispers and nudges Calista. "Is she okay?"

Calista steps forward, one hand on her hip. "What happened at the police station? Are they investigating now?"

A cloud of anger passes across Mrs. Williams's face, and

she holds up a trembling fist. "Can you believe that the police didn't believe me? I could tell by the way they were talking. Like I was old and confused. They said Violet's death was definitely an accident and Damien's was a classic suicide. They didn't even take notes. They looked at each other and nodded at me like I was making things up." She lets out another sob. "I wonder how many supposed suicides are actually murder. The police just want to be done with it. Case closed."

Calista climbs to the top stair, leans against the railing, and crosses her arms. "Why did you say we're in trouble? What do you know?"

Mrs. Williams squints at her. "Have you seen this article?" She pulls a newspaper clipping out of her coat pocket.

Calista grabs it from her and reads it aloud.

*Police say foul play is suspected in the disappearance of Birchbrook, NY, man Grayson Dante. Over four years have passed since Grayson went missing on August 9, and now investigators believe he may have been killed.*

*"Mr. Dante was said to have mentioned to several friends that individuals were making threats to his life," Officer Delvin Foster said. "However, the reasons surrounding his disappearance and presumed murder are still unclear and anyone with information is asked to come forward."*

We exchange petrified glances. Denise's eyes look as though they're going to burst out of their sockets. We're all thinking the same thing. The body in the forest. That must be him.

"Don't you see?" Mrs. Williams cries. "Everyone who gets

close to Violet ends up dying. Tell me this: why were you at Damien's apartment?"

We all stay silent. Calista makes a pattern on the snowy porch with her leather boot. "We were trying to figure out what happened to Violet."

"I knew it." Mrs. Williams pounds her fist down on the bench with a loud thwack. "And whoever killed Grayson, Violet, and now Damien—they know it too. You're all next. Me too." She lets out a wail, steps toward Denise, and crumples against her shoulder.

"We'll figure out who did this," Denise whispers into her hair.

"Will we?" I ask. At this point, our best bet might be going to the cops, corrupt or not.

"We will," Calista says firmly. "We're an army now, versus what, one person?"

Janie's watching all of us silently. Bottom line: I don't trust her. At all. She just showed up out of nowhere and has been hanging around like a bad odor. How does no one else seem to be concerned about the suspicious timing?

Calista rests a gloved hand on Mrs. Williams's back. "Do you have someone you could stay with right now? We could drive you there." She clearly wants to get down to making a plan, and it doesn't include Violet's mom doing any detective work.

Mrs. Williams presses her fingers to her lips and exhales deeply. "No. There's no one left that I can trust. Believe me. My husband's dead and his entire family are money-hungry, selfish assholes."

"How about your parents?" Zoe says softly. "They seemed supportive."

"They're having a hard time with the loss of Violet. I don't want to add to their worries." Mrs. Williams sighs. "It probably is too cold to stay out here. Not to mention dangerous. I guess we should go inside." She stands, her body trembling, and Denise and Janie help her to the door.

We follow Mrs. Williams to the living room, and she lies down on the white sofa. "I haven't slept in days," she says. "But I feel unsettled here. This is where she . . . died. Do you think I could stay at your house until it's light out? We could protect each other." Ha. She's got to be kidding. She's not capable of protecting anyone. Mrs. Williams turns on her side. "I'm not used to sleeping alone."

I look at the others. Zoe's eyes light up because she knows it's the perfect time to ask. If they're not going to say something, I am. "Some people wonder if you and Damien were together." I swallow hard. "Like, romantically."

Janie and Denise give me matching glares, and Calista's lips twitch like she's holding back a smile. Zoe's wide-eyed expression is pure admiration.

Mrs. Williams suddenly sits upright, then stares at her lap for a long moment, and finally takes a shaky breath. "It's true," she whispers. "It kills me to admit but it's true. I did that. To my daughter. I think she died not knowing and it's best that she didn't." Mrs. Williams spins around to gauge our reactions. "Don't look at me like that. I didn't mean for it to happen. Violet didn't love him anyway. The only person she ever loved was Grayson. She used everybody else." There's silence in the room, and she narrows her eyes at us. "What are you thinking? Say something."

Calista crosses her arms. "I think we're all still processing this. It's not every day a mom announces that she was having an affair with her daughter's boyfriend." I picture my mom and Alex making out and have to bite my lip to stop a smile.

"You make it sound so sordid." Mrs. Williams sniffs and looks down at her hands. "It was beautiful. We were so much more compatible than he and Violet were. But now he's gone."

Calista leans forward until she's on the very edge of the couch. "Do you think you know who would have wanted him dead?"

"Pretty much anyone in Violet's life," she answers. "They thought he was trying to control her. But he was just trying to help her."

Calista nods. "Okay, but who do you suspect the most?"

"Her friends from her work." Mrs. Williams rubs her temples. "Very typical that my husband's brother has a bar for the scum of society. Why would Violet work at a place like that? She could have worked as a law intern."

"We were invited to a party there tomorrow—oh, I guess that would be today now," Zoe says, glancing at the clock on the mantel. "For New Year's Eve, but the girls need to get home."

Calista nods. "My parents are already pissed."

Mrs. Williams sits straight up and brushes the strands of hair out of her eyes. Thank goodness she did because they were bugging me to the point that I was about to move them out of her face myself. "Can't you stay for at least the beginning of the night? We should go there. If I see Violet and Damien's killer, I'll know. I know I'll know. There has to be some justice."

Calista fiddles with a book charm on her bracelet and takes a deep breath. "My parents will disown me but it's better than . . ." She pauses and sighs. "Them being killed or something. I didn't want to mention it before . . . but we're getting threats."

Mrs. Williams crosses her arms and frowns. "Being careful

is impossible. This is dangerous territory," she says in an uncharacteristically deep tone. "Whoever is doing this isn't going to stop until every one of us is shut up. For good."

Denise takes short, panicked breaths, and Janie puts her arm around her and whispers something in her ear. They're both super shady lately. Janie seems to be having too much fun with this, and Denise is acting twitchy and guilty. She's hiding something. Something major.

---

Our extended sleepover at Zoe's continues with Janie and Mrs. Williams added to the guest count. We finally got a few hours of very much needed sleep, and against our better judgment, we're definitely spending New Year's at Bennington's.

Calista bursts into the room with a tearstained face. "They're furious. They said I'm grounded for two weeks. My dad says he doesn't know who I am anymore. He said Mr. Molina's going to think I'm unreliable if I'm late and I'll have no shot at the internship. I've never done anything like this before. Ever. And the first time I don't keep my word, they act like I'm a monster."

I shrug. "Like you said, what's the alternative? What does it matter if you're on time for the party if you're all dead the next day?"

"What the heck, Holly!" Calista snaps, rolling her eyes toward the ceiling. "Why do you need to put it that way?"

I shrug again. "Uhhhhh, because it's true. We're not here because we want to be anymore, we're here because we saw with our own eyes what these sick people are capable of."

"Girls, girls, enough with all that. Let's forget our worries, it's

New Year's Eve," Mrs. Williams says. She huddles in her pale-pink coat and regards Bark with a look of distrust. She reaches out her hand, gives him a stiff pat on his back that makes Calista look like the dog whisperer in comparison, then leans forward and props her head up on her hands. "So, has the pre-party started yet?"

Zoe laughs. "Is that your way of asking for a glass of wine? Coming right up."

"Let's hope she doesn't want snacks with that. We've yet to buy any groceries," Calista quips, swiping at the mascara smudges under her puffy eyes. Even when her world's falling apart over her parents learning she's not their perfect little girl, she still can't resist a smart-ass comment.

Zoe comes back with a glass of red wine, and Mrs. Williams takes a long sip and turns my way. "Can I borrow some clothes for tonight?" she whispers. She gestures at Calista and Denise, who sit on the couch together in their fitted dress pants and blouses. "The others dress too frumpy"—she points at Zoe, who's got on a Rolling Stones crop top and jeans—"and too punk rock for my taste." She smiles at me with admiration and takes another sip of her drink. "You're the right balance of trendy and provocative."

Ouch. Note to self: maybe my New Year's resolution can be to rethink my look. If I'm able to stay alive, that is.

"I don't want to look like an old woman tonight," Mrs. Williams continues. "Where's your suitcase?"

I doubt she's going to stop bugging me, so I point to the spot beside my sleeping bag, and she bounces off her seat eagerly and rummages through my stuff until she finds the short, low-cut dress I wore to Violet's funeral. "I think I'll borrow this one," she says with a smile. "It's perfect."

I take out my makeup case and start applying a coat of mascara when Bark rushes to the door and barks so much that it's clear why he has his name.

Janie looks out the window. "There's a guy out there."

"Driving a black car?" Zoe asks eagerly, bolting toward the window to join her. "Maybe it's my dad again."

"What if it's the killer?" Mrs. Williams shrieks and runs into the bathroom with my dress in her hand. She pulls the door closed, and I hear it click as she locks it. Geez, this lady. I shake my head. So much for strength in numbers. She's no help to us.

"He looks too young to be your dad." Janie gestures for Denise to join her. "Gray car, not black."

I know someone with a gray car, but there's no way he'd be here. At least I don't think so.

"Oh shit," Denise says, backing away from the window. "He looks mad."

"What?" I cry and rush toward the window to look for myself. When I get there, I see someone's face pressed up against the glass, and my heart jumps into my throat. The guy steps back, moves toward the front door, and bangs a fist on it. It's Alex.

"What the actual fuck," I say. "That's my boyfriend."

Calista closes the curtains and whips around. "Why did he scare us like that? What's wrong with him?"

I march to the front door. "A lot of things apparently." I put Bark on the leash that's hanging from a coat hook so he doesn't rush out and attack Alex, even though after scaring us like that, he probably deserves it.

Calista knocks on the bathroom door. "Don't worry, Mrs. Williams, it's just Holly's weird boyfriend."

Mrs. Williams comes tottering out of the bathroom in my
dress and stilettos, looking like she's trying way too hard to be
sexy. She's got her hand pressed up against her chest dramatically. "I nearly had a heart attack, you know."

"Sorry," I say. "I wasn't expecting him either, believe me." I
wind the leash around my wrist so Bark's safely at my feet and
open the door. Alex's face transforms from enraged creep to
loving boyfriend like someone performed a magic trick on him.

"Holly," he says softly. "Why have you been avoiding me?"
He steps inside, and Bark growls and tugs on his leash as he
tries to get closer to him.

"Outside time, boy," Zoe says, amusement flickering in her
eyes. "Sorry about that." She takes the leash from me and leads
a growling Bark to the backyard.

If Bark doesn't like Alex, I'm sure that's a bad sign. He likes
everybody. Alex wraps me up in a hug that's too tight, and I twist
around to break free from his grasp, but he just grips me harder.

I catch Denise's eye and give her a look that she thankfully
understands. "Hi, I'm Denise. You must be Alex," she says.

Alex steps back. "Hi," he mumbles. He turns back to me.
"Can we talk somewhere? Privately?"

Denise raises an eyebrow, and I nod at her. She grabs Janie's
hand, and they disappear down the hallway, leaving Calista silently
regarding us, her arms crossed. Mrs. Williams stands beside her,
and maybe it's just my imagination, but I'm pretty sure she's batting
her eyelashes and giving Alex a smile that's on the flirtatious side.

I point to the couch. "We can talk right there." During my
break from Alex, my feelings have been all over the place. I didn't
know what I used to feel more: comfortable or stifled. Right
now, there's something about his tense energy that's got me on

edge. Even though I've been alone with him for days upon days over the last months, I don't want to be alone with him now. And this week I could have taken off at any time, but I hung around. I had freedom, but I didn't make terrible choices. I didn't need anyone to help keep me in check. Maybe I never did.

Alex sits with his thighs pressed against mine. "Are there guys staying here too? Is that why you've been ignoring my calls?" he whispers.

"No," I snap, inching toward the arm of the couch so there's more of a comfortable space between us. "Believe it or not, I'm reconnecting with friends I haven't seen in years and it's been nice. We all lost someone who was important to us. It's been a lot. You should be sympathetic about what we've been going through, not aggressive like this. It's not a good look."

Alex studies my face, his brow furrowed. "Why are you talking to me like that? You've been gone for days and I was worried about you. You should be thanking me for coming here. For caring enough to want to make sure you're okay."

"Thank you," I say simply. "But my friends and I are having bonding time. I planned on coming home later tonight."

"How late are you talking? It's New Year's Eve," Alex says, his voice rising. "If you don't want to be with your boyfriend on New Year's Eve that's basically breakup worthy. New Year's is for spending time with people you love, not some girls you faded apart from years ago." He glances at Calista, who frowns at him from across the room. "No offense."

"How did you know where to find me?" I whisper.

Alex shifts uncomfortably. "I tracked your phone." Is this guy serious? He glances at my surprised face and grabs my hand. "Come on, don't judge me for that. I thought you were in trouble."

"I'm not in trouble. I'm spending time with my friends, and you should respect that," I say, pulling my hand away.

Alex stares at me with pleading eyes. "Come home with me. Let's spend tonight together."

Calista steps forward. "We have to start getting ready and go pick up Janie's car," she says firmly. "You'll see your boyfriend again when you get home."

I walk toward the foyer with Alex on my heels. "If you want me to go, we need to talk privately first," he whispers. "Come out to my car with me." I nod my head reluctantly. Calista glares at us as we put on our coats and shoes.

We step out into an orange sunset and a blast of cold air.

I trudge toward his car and stand in front of the driver's-side door. "Like Calista said, I'll be back later."

"What's gotten into you? You're acting like a different person. Didn't you miss me?" Alex runs a hand through his hair and gives me a smoldering look like he's staring into my soul. And honestly? I used to find this sexy, but now I'm finding it irritating.

I clear my throat and look down at the driveway. "Since I've been with you, I've barely hung out with anyone else. I don't have friends anymore. I have people I call from time to time but it stays on a surface level. We talk about makeup and clothes. Now that I'm here, I'm remembering what it's like to have real friends who care about each other. And it's nice. I miss that."

Alex steps closer to me and wraps an arm around my waist. "What are you trying to say?"

I arch backward, angling my body away from him. "I'm trying to say that I need a bit more time with them, just them."

"That's it? So you're forcing me to leave right now?" Alex's nostrils flare. "If you are, just say it."

I sigh. "I am. I'll be home in a few hours and we can spend the weekend together, but I want you to go home now."

"How dare you?" Alex huffs. "With all I do for you, how dare you just kick me out like this?"

"It's not like I invited you here in the first place."

"You're fucking unbelievable, you know that?" Alex gets into his gray Toyota Prius and books it out of the driveway and onto the street.

I try to slow my breathing down, but my throat is tight. The necklace Alex gave me feels like it's closing in around my neck. I unclasp it, put it in my coat pocket, and exhale deeply. The girls are at the window when I get back inside.

"He's got some temper," Mrs. Williams says, her hands on her hips. "He reminds me of my dead husband."

"No wonder you're such a bitch sometimes, with a boyfriend like that," Calista adds.

I ignore both of them, sit on the armchair, and stare at the closed curtains.

Zoe crouches beside me and twirls a strand of my hair around her finger. "You can do better," she whispers. "Don't forget that."

I remember Violet, her singsong voice when she used to tell me, "Boys are like tools. You use them to get what you want. You're lucky you're pretty like me. There are so many more tools to choose from that way."

Calista leaves the room and heads to the foyer. "We should go now." She bends down to zip up her boots.

Zoe and Mrs. Williams start toward the door.

Janie stands. "Let's go," she says softly to Denise, but Denise just sits there, staring across the room with haunted eyes.

I squint at her. "Are you okay, Denise?"

She jumps and sits upright. "Yes," she says hoarsely. "Yes, I'm fine. Just thinking."

"About what?"

Denise takes a shaky breath. "The person who's threatening us. They have a grudge. What are they going to do to me?"

# 28
# Denise

It's seven o'clock on New Year's Eve, the snow's coming down hard, and the dim sky's glowing. We have one night to figure out who killed Violet and turn them in before we all head home, and who knows what hell will break loose. Janie and I are in her car in front of Bennington's. "I guess we should head inside now," she says, gesturing at the door. It's amazing how deceptive the outside of this place is. If I passed it on the street, I would barely notice it, would maybe think it's an office, and inside, with the trippy music, low lighting, and shady characters, it's like stepping into a different reality.

I sigh and make a face. "I really hate it here." The truth is I'm terrified.

I glance out the window at Holly, who's staring at me from inside her car. *Ready?* she mouths, and without waiting for my reply, she opens her car door. Fear shoots through me, and my stomach drops.

Once we're all outside, we stand in an uncertain huddle, and I'm hoping they're having second thoughts.

Calista straightens her long white coat. "Remember what we talked about—we need to make this fast. In and out. I've got to get going. Mrs. Williams says she'll know who did this when she sees him. Do you think it will be the same bouncer as last time?"

Mrs. Williams clutches her stomach in an exaggerated show of laughter. "I forgot you're underage. You girls are so mature I feel as though I'm hanging out with my peers. Or maybe that's just because I feel so young. Perhaps I look it too." She glances at us hopefully.

"You do," Zoe quickly assures her. She glances at me. "Denise, do you want to text April to meet us at the door?"

"No need." Mrs. Williams takes off her puffy pink jacket, drapes it over her shoulder, then wiggles her hips seductively. She's got on one of Holly's dresses, and it's so low-cut I can almost see her belly button. With my dark jeans and feather-print top, I look like a librarian compared to her.

Mrs. Williams winks and struts toward the door, staggering backward in her four-inch stilettos as she pulls on the brass handle. "You're definitely getting in now you've got me with you."

Zoe holds the door open for us. Unfortunately for me, it's the same bouncer, and he cracks a smile as we step inside. "The law students again. You like this place, don't you? Happy New Year." He opens the second door to reveal the packed bar, decorated with red-and-gold helium balloons. Instead of the trippy music that was playing last time, pop music blares through the speakers. The dance floor's full of people writhing around like they're either drunk or high, or both.

"Isn't it bad luck to say 'Happy New Year' before midnight strikes?" I whisper to Janie. "What if we don't make it to midnight?"

"Whatever happens, just know I'll do whatever I can to protect you. We'll be okay," she whispers back, her breath warm on my neck.

We trail behind the others. Calista leads us toward the table we sat at the last time we came. I want to sprint ahead, grab her by the arm, and tell her that it's the last place we should sit, but I'm so terrified I'm frozen.

"It's okay," Janie says, tugging on my hand. "You can sit by me."

Bradley and I lock eyes. He glares at me, and his body stiffens.

Levi stands when he sees Zoe, and he wraps his arms around her in a hug, his eyes twinkling and his face breaking into a wide smile. He's wearing black dress pants and a tight gray dress shirt with the sleeves rolled up to show off his muscular arms and tattoos. "Well, well, well, look who's back." His friends at the table chuckle, all except Bradley, who tugs on the collar of his white turtleneck, takes a sip of beer, and gives me a cold stare. My legs wobble and I stumble, steadying myself by grabbing onto Janie's arm. "Calm down," Janie whispers and helps me onto a chair.

The others didn't seem to notice me losing my footing; they all take seats and bob their heads along with "Love on the Brain."

"Hi, Tina," Levi says, reaching across the table to pat Mrs. Williams's forearm. "I'm sorry for all you're going through." His eyes gloss over.

Mrs. Williams tosses her hair back and blinks at him. "Are you really?"

"Of course I am," Levi blurts out. "Violet was one of my best friends."

Mrs. Williams nods distractedly and waves her hand to a redheaded waitress in a sparkly black dress who approaches our table. "Shots of tequila for the table, please." She spins her finger in a circle. "And a glass of red wine. Your best." She flashes the waitress a smile, then turns back to the table. "Violet was your best friend but how did you feel about Damien?" Someone's giving Calista a run for her money on being the interrogator. If Levi and his friends really did do something to Violet and Damien, Mrs. Williams's pit bull approach is probably not the safest idea.

Levi crosses his arms and leans forward. "Damien was bad news and you know it. He tried to control Violet."

Mrs. Williams scowls. "Has it occurred to you that maybe she needed that? Look at this place, she worked here. She could have had a part-time job that would have benefited her career, but instead she worked in my brother-in-law's mobster joint." She gestures to the other tables, where shifty-eyed people sit, their heads close together in probably sinister conversations they want to be very sure no one will overhear. "Violet was going to be a lawyer, for God's sake. What law firm would like waitress-at-the-notorious-Bennington's on a résumé?"

"It's not like that. There are good people here too." Levi clasps his hands together emphatically "And the waitresses? They're empowered people who use their gifts to make money quickly. Violet was smart."

"Well, not smart enough to dodge whoever it was who killed her." Mrs. Williams pats under her eyes with her fingers and chokes back a sob. "God rest my baby's soul."

"She drowned, Tina," Levi says quietly. He looks at Zoe beside him and takes her hand. She smiles sadly, and Levi turns back to Mrs. Williams. "I know it must be tough to accept that."

"Well, who killed Damien then?"

A smile twitches at the corner of Bradley's mouth. He glances at me, and I shudder. I want to tell the others everything now. I don't think I have a choice anymore.

"Damien killed himself," Levi says. "He was probably upset that the woman he loved was gone. Your daughter was the most beautiful woman I've ever met. You need to honor her memory and let her go. Not try to blame people."

Maybe Levi's in on it too. Making all of Bradley's murders look like accidents.

Mrs. Williams stares at the table for a long time. The waitress puts a glass of wine and the tray of shots down in front of her, and she brightens. "Grab a drink, everyone," she finally says, and the guys and Zoe pick up the tequila shots and hold them in the air. "Cheers to my daughter," Mrs. Williams says and downs hers in a thirsty gulp. She points at the remaining shots and gives Janie, Calista, Holly, and me confused looks. "You're not drinking?" We shake our heads. "More for me," she says and plucks each of our shot glasses off the tray and shoots them back.

The DJ's voice booms through the intercom system. "It's New Year's Eve in the place to be. Here's some Beyoncé for a special somebody. And Fred, it's here."

I spin around to look for Fred, but no one leaves their table.

April struts toward us in a gold sequined dress. She leans in toward me, resting her sharp chin on my shoulder. "You decided to stay," she says, arching her eyebrows.

I nod. "Yes. But I'm so ready to go home, believe me. What do you think the DJ was talking about a minute ago? Who's Fred?"

April bites her lower lip. "Are you sure you want to know?"

"Yes. Why?"

April gestures toward a table where a group of rowdy men in leather jackets sits. She pointed them out as police officers the last time we were here. She cups her palm around her mouth. "One of them is Fred and someone dropped something off for him."

"Drugs?"

April shrugs. "Could be? Whatever it is, it's something bad. Anyway, don't worry about that. You should enjoy your last night." She runs a hand through my hair, then saunters away.

*Last night? Does she mean last night here? Or last night, period?*

I glance at Bradley. He's scowling at me, a vein in his neck bulging. He reaches over and smacks the table in front of me, spilling some of Mrs. Williams's wine.

She glares at him. "Watch it."

Levi grabs Bradley's arm. "What did you do that for?"

He ignores them and faces me with a cold stare. "You keep looking at me like you're scared or something. What's wrong with you?"

Like my legs have a mind of their own, I'm standing, I'm backing up, I'm running, pushing people out of the way, barging past the waitresses and the bouncer, crashing through the exit, into the blowing snow.

# 29
# Zoe

I watch Denise bolt out of the door. Calista springs to her feet to follow her.

"Calista, wait," Janie calls and stands. "Don't worry, I'll go."

Calista surprisingly returns to her seat and silently watches Janie leave the bar with a look of suspicion on her face.

"Why did you scare her like that?" Levi says to Bradley, who ignores him and takes another sip of beer.

Mrs. Williams leans across the table and pats my hand. "Your friend's on edge," she says. "She should have accepted the tequila shot."

"Should I go out there and try to overhear what they're talking about?" Holly whispers.

I grin and that's all the encouragement Holly needs. She rushes outside almost as fast as Denise did.

I turn back to the table. Levi's smiling at me and everything—the Denise drama, the sultry waitresses gliding around the room, the scent of alcohol in the air, the pumping bass reverberating in my chest—it all fades away into a dull blur. It's just me and him, in a beautiful bubble. God, he looks so sexy in his fitted gray shirt, and it takes everything in me not to grab one of his muscular arms and squeeze it. He folds his hands and leans forward, his eyes twinkling. "I didn't think you ladies would be back again."

My hands are instantly clammy, and I discreetly rub them on my jeans. "April invited us last night. I was hoping we'd run into you." I take a long sip of the rum and Coke I ordered and fiddle with my straw.

"Can I ask you a question?" Levi asks. He's wearing a small diamond stud in his nose instead of his usual gold ring, and it catches the light as he tilts his head closer to mine. I catch a whiff of his spicy cologne, and if my hands weren't so sweaty, I might grab his face and plant a kiss on him.

I nod and take a deep breath, hoping it will help my voice to sound calmer than I feel. "Shoot."

He points at my glass grimly. "Why are you drinking that?"

I giggle. "I take it you're not a rum fan?"

He shakes his head. "It's not that. It's that I can tell you don't like it. Every time you take a sip you make this face and shudder."

My body tenses up. I thought this was a romantic moment, not an intervention. All my lustful jitters fade away, and I stare at the table. This is the definition of a buzzkill. On New Year's Eve of all nights.

"I'm not trying to put you on the spot," Levi says, gently

resting his warm hand on top of mine. "I wanted you to know that you're fun and interesting without that. You're bright and funny. You don't need to amp that up, you've got it naturally."

My eyes stay glued to the table, and I shrug. "I don't know about that."

Levi cups my chin and gently lifts my face so I'll meet his gaze. "Trust me, you do."

His expression looks so sincere that I have to tell the others there's no way we can doubt him. He isn't a murderer; he's a motivational speaker. How could anyone suspect someone so lovely? Calista gives me a pointed look. She's told me a million times already that she needs to go home. She wants me to find out as much information as I can, but all I want to do is ask Levi his zodiac sign, where he'd travel if he could go anywhere, if he'd bring me with him. Not *Where were you on the night of December twenty-second?*

"So . . ." I clear my throat. "I can't believe about Damien." Zero segue, but I'm feeling too lustful to be a suave detective. "Do you think it's possible someone pushed him?"

Levi's expression transforms from sweet to serious. "I guess it's possible," he answers with a shrug.

"Do you know anyone who would do that?" I ask, almost afraid to hear his answer, especially if it's someone in this room, or at this table even.

He hesitates. "If it really wasn't a suicide, it was probably someone from Violet's family. Tina and Damien were making their romance pretty obvious. Violet's dad's brothers have constantly accused Tina of having affairs. Some people think Violet's dad wasn't her real father. Her uncles brought that up a lot. Except her uncle Tom. He didn't want to say anything to piss off Violet because he wanted her to keep working here. She was the best waitress he had. Customers would come in just to see her." Levi takes my hand. "Enough about that, I want to find out more about you."

I grin and bat my eyelashes at him playfully. This is new. All the guys I meet on VenusLove seem to prefer talking about themselves. "What do you want to know?"

Levi laughs and taps my nose with his finger. "Everything."

Out of the corner of my eye, I spot Holly in the doorway. She looks serious and gestures for me to join her. Calista's noticed her too—she's already striding toward her.

I squeeze Levi's hand. "I'll be right back. My friends need me outside for a second."

Levi nods. "See you in a minute."

I step through the exit to gusting winds and heavy snow—it's a full-blown snowstorm out here. Holly and Calista are standing by Holly's car, and Janie's inside her car next to Denise, who's slumped over in the passenger seat.

"Are we leaving because of the weather?" I ask, brushing the wet snow out of my hair.

Holly grabs my arm and pulls me close to them. "It's Denise," she hisses. "I came outside, and she was sitting on the curb with her head in her hands and she kept repeating Farrah's name like she was in a trance. Then Janie saw me and convinced Denise to get into her car to talk to her. Denise is still hiding something."

"My parents are livid I'm not home and she's still keeping secrets?" Calista huffs, waving her hand around. "Unbelievable. I'm going to find out right now what her deal is. Right now." She storms over to Janie's car and raps on the window. Janie opens it a crack. "Let us in," Calista snaps. She tries the back door handle, but it's locked. "Now."

Janie makes a face, but she unlocks the car, and Calista and I slide into the back seat followed by Holly.

Denise is staring at her lap, struggling to catch her breath, and Janie's fidgeting with the rosary beads hanging from her rearview mirror. Is she praying? Yikes. This secret might be worse than I thought.

"What's going on?" Calista booms. "This is NOT the time for secrets anymore. All of our lives are in danger. You need to tell us everything."

Denise's breath quickens, and she stifles a sob.

"Give her a minute," Janie warns, resting her hand on Denise's thigh.

"YOU tell us then," Calista yells. "Someone needs to speak."

Janie cranes her neck to glare at her. "I don't know anything. She didn't tell me yet."

"Denise?" I say gently. "Denise, please just tell us."

Denise slowly twists around. Her eyes are puffy and bloodshot. "Farrah," she croaks.

"Why does she keep saying that?" Holly says, a hint of panic in her voice.

"What about Farrah?" I ask. "You can tell us."

Denise whimpers.

"What is it?" Calista yells, smacking the door in frustration.

"I killed her," Denise whispers.

"Fuck," Holly squeaks, frantically trying to open the locked car door. "Let me out!"

"No one's getting out right now," Janie says firmly. "We have to hear her out first."

"What do you mean you killed her?" Calista barks.

My hands tremble, and my heart pounds against my chest. "Did you push her off the cliff?"

Denise's back heaves with sobs.

"You pushed her off the cliff?" I repeat. "Why did you do that?"

"I didn't push her," Denise whispers. "But I killed her."

"How?" Calista asks.

"No one knew why she left her cabin in the middle of the night," Denise begins. "No one except me and Violet."

"Why then?" Holly says. "What did you do?"

"Violet hated Farrah. When Grayson was still around, Violet thought Farrah was practically throwing herself at him. She asked me to write a note like I was a guy who liked her, asking her to meet in the woods by the fence at one a.m. I did what she said. I thought Violet was right and it would be funny, but the next morning . . ." Denise breaks off and chokes on a sob. "The next morning, I heard sirens and I ran out of the cabin before any of you because I had a feeling in my gut that something went wrong. The police had surrounded the place. I just ran. I ran to the fence, but the police were already there, some had climbed over it and were staring down at the bottom talking on their radios. I saw her body . . . her legs and arms were bent in these broken angles. I heard the officers saying the words but I already knew it. She was dead. Because of me."

The car's silent. No one moves a muscle.

Calista clears her throat. "Why wouldn't you tell us this before?"

"I—I didn't want to go to jail," Denise stammers. "I basically killed her. If it wasn't for that note, Farrah would be alive." She puts her hands over her face and heaves with quiet sobs.

"You didn't tell her to climb the fence. You didn't push her. You didn't kill her," Janie says gently.

"The notes," Holly says. "The first one said something about the letter Denise sent and the second one mentioned Farrah by name. Someone knows one of us was involved."

"By the way Bradley was looking at me tonight, I know he knows." Denise takes a deep shuddery breath. "I think it's him. He got back at Violet, and now he wants to get back at me."

"But what about Damien?" I ask. "How does he fit into this?"

"Levi and Bradley both hated Damien," Calista says. She shakes her head and sighs. "Again, Denise, why didn't you tell us this before? We wouldn't have wasted our time being suspicious of Damien and Holly."

"Yeah, who can forget about that fun time?" Holly mutters.

Outside, the bar door swings open, and Mrs. Williams, Tom, Levi, and Bradley walk toward the parking lot, thick snow coming down on them. "Wait. Where are they going?" I lean across Holly to point out the window.

"We can't talk to Bradley," Denise cries, slumping down in her seat. "Don't go out there."

Calista bangs her fist on the car door. "Let us out, Janie."

Janie clicks the unlock button, and Calista jumps out of the car, and I step out behind her. "Mrs. Williams," she calls. "Are you leaving?"

Mrs. Williams staggers toward us with a giggle, with an unamused Tom on her right and a cheerful Levi and angry-looking Bradley on her left. "Tom invited me to his brother's for a party and I asked if I could bring my new friends along." She nudges Levi, who shoots me a lopsided grin.

"Yes, Tom said we were welcome to come along," Levi says. "Hey, Tom, do you mind if I bring these ladies?"

Tom nods gruffly, and his gaze rests on me. "You're the one I met in my office. A friend of Damien's?"

"No, no," I say, forcing a smile. "I'm a friend of Violet's."

He nods. "Fine. See you there." He gets into his black Cadillac Escalade and zips out of the parking lot.

Levi opens the door to a red Civic. "He didn't give us the address. Do you know the way, Tina?"

Mrs. Williams puts her hands on her hips and does a little wiggle. "Of course I know the way." She bats her eyelashes, and I want to jokingly-but-maybe-seriously tell her to back off, but then I glance at Bradley and my heart jumps into my throat. Denise might be right. He looks mad.

"We'll follow you guys then," Levi says. "This will be fun, eh, Bradley?"

Bradley grunts and gives me a long, cold look. "Yeah. Real fun," he mutters.

# 30
# Calista

FRIDAY, DECEMBER 31

It's 9:15 p.m. Nochevieja is going on without me. I can kiss my law internship goodbye. Right now, my entire family's eating lentil soup, vowing it will make them prosperous in the new year.

The only thing I want to be now is alive.

Mom texted:

> Your dad is so ashamed. Mr. Molina
> is here and is asking for you. You're
> grounded for three weeks now. In a
> few minutes it will be four.

The tension in the car is thick enough to slice through. We all want to talk about the bombshell Denise dropped but can't—not in front of Mrs. Williams.

The more I think about it, the more I know. The killer's Bradley. I'm certain it is.

"Holy snow," Holly mumbles. Her windshield wipers are shooting back and forth on their highest setting, but it's still hard to see the road through the blizzard. In the streetlight's glow, I catch a glint of Levi's red car, still following behind us.

I'm surprised Bradley hasn't had second thoughts and convinced Levi not to go. Soon they'll be walking into a house full of Violet's family members.

Wait until we tell them what he did.

"When do we turn?" Holly asks, and Mrs. Williams winds down her window and sticks her head out. "It's hard to tell. So much snow," she squeals, letting it cascade down on her before poking her snow-covered head back in the car. "Look. White hair." She giggles and shakes it off.

Wow. She's our navigator? We're getting lost for sure.

"Well?" I say. "Are we turning soon?"

"Right there." She points a wobbly finger at an open wrought-iron gate with intricate swirling details and crown finials.

"Kind of late notice." Holly brakes and skids to a stop then turns to drive over a mound of snow and down a path lined with tire tracks.

"They have an estate?" I ask. I can't see the house through the spruce trees yet, but judging by the endlessly long driveway, it's probably huge. I knew Violet's family was rich, but I didn't know they were this rich.

Mrs. Williams giggles. "Well, of course they have an estate. Multiple estates. They make my house look like it's meant for Barbie dolls."

Holly pulls up in a lot where at least fifteen cars are parked. She backs into a spot and Janie and Levi pull their cars in next to hers. We step outside into the snow squall, and I stare through the thick flakes at the three-story white mansion with floor-to-ceiling windows. It's every bit as impressive as I thought it would be. Guests are visible, chatting in groups, the heavy bass music booming.

Denise and Janie are still in the car, and Mrs. Williams has flung her arm around Levi. Bradley's turned away from us, facing the forest, his hands shoved into the back pockets of his jeans. He slowly spins around, his face contorted into a grotesque sneer.

Zoe starts toward Levi, and I grab her elbow and pull her close. Adrenaline edged with panic is coursing through my body, but Zoe's smiling serenely like she's on a date. "Be careful. He might be involved too," I whisper.

Zoe makes a face.

I give her arm a light squeeze. "You might think he's wonderful, but you need to watch out. He's best friends with a killer."

Holly leans into us. "What's the plan?"

"We need to rile Bradley up," I whisper. "We'll ask him questions, tell everyone what he did, and leave it to Violet's family to take care of him."

Zoe nods. "Okay, got it." She steps away from us and ambles over to Levi, who gives her a warm smile and takes her hand.

Mrs. Williams totters through the white carpet of snow in her tall stilettos, leading the way toward a black door with a large brass doorknob.

She pushes open the door and steps inside. No knocking for her. We all follow her into an expensively decorated foyer with the highest ceilings I've ever seen.

The conversation in the room seems to come to a halt. Everyone looks at Mrs. Williams as if she's carrying Violet's corpse in her arms.

"Tina," a man with curly brown hair calls from behind a glass railing on the second floor. I recognize him from the funeral as one of Violet's uncles. He slowly walks down the winding staircase. "So good of you all to make it. We were just about to play the video I made. Perfect timing. Let me get someone to take your coats." He gestures to a woman in a white collared shirt and black dress pants—one of his staff, I'm thinking. She steps forward and takes each of our jackets and hangs them in a closet.

The woman points us into the living room, where a man in the same uniform is starting a projector. Mrs. Williams plops down on a sofa close to the screen. "Violet Williams, a life gone too soon," appears on the wall, soft classical music starts playing, and we see images of Violet from her blond days, her smiling face illuminating the room just like when she was still here with us. Hector stands in front of the fireplace, his fist pressed up against his mouth. When Violet's image with her arms around him comes up on the screen, he covers his face with his hands.

I scan the crowd and see Tom on the opposite side of the room, talking to an attractive woman in a fur shawl. He catches my eye and nods.

Zoe and Levi sit on gold-and-black high-backed chairs near Mrs. Williams, and Denise and Janie beeline to the corner near the windows. Denise has her hands clutched together, and she looks around the room nervously. Janie's leaning into her, whispering something.

Holly stands close to me, and I don't think either of us is

interested in trying to get comfortable. We're both watching Bradley, who hovers beside an expansive built-in bookshelf, scowling.

The slideshow ends with one final photo of Violet, dark-haired and thin, probably taken not long before she passed. She stares into the camera almost defiantly. The room erupts in applause, and everyone clangs their glasses with each other, and there's a quiet moment before the dance music starts up again.

I check my watch. 9:35. "The night's speeding by and I really need this to be done," I whisper to Holly. "When do you think we should talk to Bradley?"

"Now," Holly mutters, her mouth set in a determined line. "What's he going to do to us here?" Before I can ask her what she's going to say, she links arms with me and jolts forward, dragging me along as she marches across the room toward him.

She stops directly in front of him and plants her hands on her hips.

Bradley rolls his eyes and glares at her hatefully. "What do you want, Holly?"

Her lips curl into a snarl. "We want to know the truth. We think you hated Violet. We also think you have a grudge. And we want to know why."

# 31
# Holly

Bradley snorts out a bitter laugh and clenches his fists at his sides, and his rage makes my heart race. "You think I have a grudge?" he repeats.

"Yeah, we do. What is it?" I say, my voice rising, cutting through other conversations in the room. Calista glances at me with admiration, and I catch a few people, including Hector, noticing my tone and looking at us curiously. Yeah, I may sound bold, but holy hell, are my legs ever shaking badly.

Bradley's cold eyes flash with anger, and he points toward the foyer. "Not here," he says in a low voice. "If you want to talk to me, come outside."

"Do you think we're stupid?" Calista snaps. "We're not going anywhere with you. We know how dangerous you are."

"Dangerous?" Bradley croaks, his mouth turned up in a snarl. "*You're* the dangerous ones."

Some guests nudge each other, and several move closer, likely sensing the tension and trying to hear what we're talking about. Then, there's an arm around my waist, and I jolt and turn in a panic to see Hector, his eyebrows lowered in concern.

"Is there a problem?" he asks.

"Yes." I step aside, out of Hector's gentle grip, and gesture at Bradley. "He's just about to tell me why he hated Violet and what he has against me and my friends. I think you'll be interested to hear what he has to say."

Bradley's face reddens, and he holds up a hand in protest. "No, no. I didn't hate Violet."

"Really?" Calista crosses her arms. "You're only saying that because her cousin's here."

Hector studies Bradley like he's trying to figure him out, then turns to me. "Let's go talk," he says and takes my arm, leading me across the room to an empty sofa near the fireplace. Bradley storms out of the room, but Calista's still standing where we were, looking at us like she's strongly considering joining us even though she wasn't invited.

Hector straightens his black tie and crosses his legs. He rests his elbow on his thigh and props up his chin with his hand. "You're so angry at him. Why?"

We all have to get home. We're running out of time. I have to say something and see what he thinks. I stare into his bright blue eyes. "We think someone might have . . . might have drowned Violet," I begin.

"You what?" Hector swivels around, probably checking if anyone is in earshot, but the nearest guests are lingering beside an hors d'oeuvre station, several yards away. "Please keep your voice down," he hisses. His brow furrows, and he uncrosses his legs and shifts closer to me. "You think someone killed her?" he whispers.

"My friends and I . . . we think Bradley did it. Violet was involved in a prank that went very wrong and we think Bradley knows about it and wanted to . . . get back at her, you know?"

Hector frowns and slowly shakes his head. "She was a good swimmer. Her drowning is hard to believe. I thought about it too," he says in a faraway voice. He runs his hand through his dark hair and sighs. "This is bad."

Calista's still standing across the room, watching me, and I give her a nod that I hope she can interpret as "I told him." She gives me a thumbs-up and steps toward us.

"Hold it," a male voice booms, and several workers in white collared shirts push through the crowd toward a commotion in the front foyer.

"Bradley!" I cry. "What's he doing?"

Hector springs to his feet.

A familiar voice shouts "Holly!" and my stomach clenches as I immediately place it, realizing whatever's happening is NOT about Bradley.

Hector freezes, looks down at me, and raises his eyebrows. "Isn't that you?" I don't remember telling him my name, but that's not the biggest issue on my radar right now.

"I'm just looking for my girlfriend," I hear Alex's voice yell. I'm stupid, so stupid for thinking he'd listen to me and go back home. I should have known that he'd stick around and track me. I knew it was fishy that he hasn't called or texted since he left Zoe's.

I sigh. Holy bad timing. I was finally getting somewhere.

"That's my stalker boyfriend. I'm sorry about this. I didn't think he'd just show up here. He's been tracking my phone."

Hector's face softens. "Do you want to talk to him?" he asks. "If you don't, I can help."

"No, I don't." I let out a long breath. "I told him I'd talk to him once I got back home, and I already said goodbye."

"Say no more." Hector texts something on his phone. "Let's go to my room while security handles it and we can talk further and get the facts straight about Bradley." He gestures to the staircase, and I start up the stairs.

When I reach the top, Hector steps ahead of me and opens the door to his room. It's like an executive suite at a hotel, with a spotless white carpet, smooth leather couches, and a shiny hardwood coffee table in a sitting area, and a long lamplit hallway leading to another room.

Hector sits on the couch and pats a place beside him. I perch on the edge, thinking of Bradley, hoping none of my friends have approached him on their own.

Hector crosses his legs and props his head up on one of his hands. I open my mouth to tell him we need eyes on Bradley. Who knows what he's going to do now that I confronted him?

"So, you're dating someone who tracks you?" Hector asks, his striking blue eyes looking at me curiously. He unfastens his tie and places it on the coffee table.

I spin my thumb ring and take a deep breath. "It's complicated. He watches out for me and is there for me when no one else is but sometimes it gets to be a little . . . much."

"He sounds extremely protective," Hector says softly and nods like he gets it. Yeah, Hector was protective of Violet, but I doubt he followed her from place to place.

I sniff. "I didn't expect him to come here. When security started yelling at him, I seriously thought Bradley was attacking someone."

Hector leans closer, his head hovering over my shoulder. His bright eyes widen. "Tell me truthfully, do you really think he killed Violet?"

I nod firmly. "I found something out tonight. He was livid with her about something huge. Something that's honestly unforgivable. And now he knows one of us was also involved. We've received threats."

"Which one of you was involved in this unforgivable thing with Violet?"

I blink quickly. There's no harm in telling him that much. That's all I'll say. "Denise," I reply.

"What did Denise and Violet do?" Hector asks. "If I'm going to tell my dad and my uncle about this, I'm going to need a little more information." He stares at me intently, his jaw set in a firm line, and something tells me that he's not going to take *I'm not telling you* for an answer.

# 32
# Denise

I can't believe I told them about Farrah. My mind's been swarming with nagging thoughts ever since.

*What goes around comes around, Denise. Maybe tonight Bradley will get his revenge.*

The room around me is spinning, and I'm so light-headed I feel like I'm going to pass out at any second. I lower myself onto the wide window ledge and run my hands along the smooth wood to ground myself. *You're okay. It's okay. There are security guards. You're safe here.*

"Are you feeling all right?" Janie asks. She crouches beside me, her eyes filling with concern. "You look really pale."

I gulp in a breath. I haven't seen Bradley since he ran out of the room a few minutes ago, looking furious, and it seems like shit's hitting the fan. What if he's coming back with a weapon? "I—I think we should leave," I stammer. "Being here is dangerous."

"If that's what you want," Janie murmurs, leaning forward to brush my bangs out of my eyes.

Calista strides across the room, her curly hair flying around her shoulders, Zoe on her heels. They stop in front of us, and Zoe nervously picks at the red nail polish on her fingernails. "Holly confronted Bradley and then told Hector she thinks Bradley did it," Calista whispers.

"Where are they now?" Janie asks. "Denise isn't feeling so good."

"Holly went upstairs with Hector when that whole Alex scene was happening a minute ago," Zoe says. "Bradley stormed away and Levi's talking to him in the foyer, trying to convince him not to leave."

"I guess it worked." Calista lifts her chin toward Levi and Bradley who slowly enter the room and walk toward a sofa near where Mrs. Williams stands, bleary-eyed and swaying in place, talking to an annoyed-looking Tom.

Bradley sits and stares straight ahead at the wall grimly. Levi leans over to say something to him then glances our way and starts walking over.

Levi wraps his arms around Zoe and stares at the hardwood floor for a few beats before he meets our eyes. "Why did Holly go off on Bradley like that?" he asks. "Bradley said she was yelling about him hating V and having a grudge against you girls? I think you've got it all wrong."

"Maybe there's stuff about Bradley you don't know," Calista says crisply. "Or maybe you're covering for him because he's your friend."

Levi frowns, his eyes on the floor again. "Bradley's an open book. He's been through a lot with his sister passing. This week's tough for him. Give him a break, will you? He's only bitter because your cabin stressed his mom out. People were always accusing V of stuff and he knew you girls were involved."

Calista raises her eyebrows. "With respect, I think it's more than that." She adjusts the collar of her blouse. "When Holly comes back, I think there's something we need to tell you. I need to talk to her first." She turns abruptly, beelines across the room, and stands with her arms crossed at the bottom of the staircase, looking to the top impatiently.

Levi shrugs and sighs, then heads back to Bradley.

"I'll talk to him," Zoe says softly. She trudges forward to stand in front of them, fidgeting nervously with the hem of her crop top.

I get up cautiously, my legs wobbly, my hand on the windowpane to steady myself. "I need some air."

"Sure. Let's go," Janie says, and we head toward the foyer, where Hector's dad is greeting two men in black pants and leather jackets whom I recognize from Mrs. Williams's party and Bennington's. We linger by a tall glass table to watch them, and Janie fidgets with a stack of red hardcover books.

"Ace, Vanworth, good to see you," Hector's dad says.

The two men shake Hector's dad's hand and then swivel around the room like they're looking for someone. The one wearing a black beanie and dark glasses looks nervous and out of place, and the one with his hair in a slicked-back ponytail looks tense, his eyes narrowed and his lips curved into an intimidating scowl.

"Where's Hector at?" he asks, holding up his phone and tapping it impatiently. "He's not answering my calls."

"I saw him go upstairs with a female friend. I'm sure he'll

be back down soon," Hector's dad answers with a sly smile. "In the meantime, help yourself to some refreshments."

The guys walk quickly past the long table of food toward the wall facing the staircase and the one with the ponytail types something on his phone.

"Oh my God," Janie gasps, dropping the book she was holding with a thud.

"What's wrong?" I cry.

"The guy with the ponytail. He looks like the guy I saw creeping around outside my house."

My heart thumps against my chest. I can't take much more of this—being wary of multiple people in one house. "We should tell the others." I look to where Calista paces at the bottom of the staircase. "Holly's been upstairs for a long time. Why do you think Hector isn't answering his phone?"

"What if Levi's right and Bradley really isn't involved? Maybe we're suspecting the wrong person?" Janie whispers.

If that's true, maybe Bradley doesn't know about the note I sent his sister. But if *he* doesn't know . . . someone else does.

The guy with the ponytail's jaw tenses, and he waves his hands around and says something to the guy with the hat, whose forehead crinkles in concern.

"But who are those guys to Violet?" I say. "I wish I knew what they were talking about. Whatever they want to tell Hector . . . it seems urgent."

Janie squints across the room at them. "Let's get closer so we can hear."

I nod, trying to ignore the nervousness fluttering in my stomach. "We could try. Let's get some appetizers and see if we can catch any of their conversation when we walk by."

Janie's face lights up. She seems to like all the missions we've been on lately. She takes my hand, and we slowly walk to one of the tables lined with large silver platters. She pops a sausage roll in her mouth and feeds me one. Although I'm sure it's been prepared by a star chef, it's like a mix of cardboard and rubber in my dry mouth. I steal a glance at the two men as we pass them. Their conversation halts immediately, and the guy with the ponytail glares in our direction. He pulls on the other guy's arm, and they head back out the front door.

"It might be easier to hide and eavesdrop if they keep talking out there. Let's go out another door so they don't see us." Janie weaves through the groups of people clustered in the living room, and I'm right behind her as she walks into the kitchen and steps toward the patio door.

Just as she rests her hand on the door handle, a man's voice from behind us asks, "Do you need something?"

I whirl around to face Violet's uncle Tom. He eyes us curiously, his gray hair gleaming in the light of the chandelier. "Just some air," Janie answers.

He squints at us suspiciously before sweeping his hand toward the patio. "Go ahead."

"Thanks," I squeak, and Janie opens the door. We step out into a cloud of smoke. A woman with a neat bun glances at us, takes a long drag of her cigarette, and goes back to her conversation with the blond woman beside her. We clutch the frozen railing as we make our way down the icy stairs. The heavy snow has stopped now, but the wind whips through the trees as we walk along the side of the house, hugging ourselves. I wish we had our coats. Across the lawn, the men huddle beside a black car close to Janie's.

"They've got their backs to us. Let's run over there and crouch down behind my car," Janie whispers eagerly.

I nod, panic flooding my body, trying to ignore the little voice in my head that's screaming, *You shouldn't do this. You're asking for trouble.*

We grip hands and crouch as we run toward Janie's car, where we kneel on the cold ground in front of the driver's-side door. Janie cups a hand around her ear, shivering violently. I wrap my arms around her and pull her into my chest, wondering if she can hear how fast my heart is beating.

All I can make out is a low rumble of conversation. No words.

I lean in so my mouth presses against Janie's ear. "We need to get closer," I whisper.

She nods and grabs my hand again. We scurry along the back of the cars, stopping at the car directly beside the two men. If they turn and walk in our direction, we're totally screwed.

The men's voices are hushed, but I can make out some words now that all that separates us is a single blue car. "Let's just go, Ace," says the one I assume is Vanworth.

"No. We need to tell Hector," Ace answers. "They should have left a long time ago. Not dug stuff up. They were warned."

I press my palm against my lips to stop myself from making a noise, gasping, yelping. There are a million things my body wants to do right now, and it's too dangerous to do any of them. Janie squeezes her eyes shut and grips my thigh.

"He's still not answering," Ace continues. "I'll try one more time, then I'm going upstairs."

"And if we run into one of those girls?" Vanworth asks.

"We kill them," Ace answers.

"They're kids," Vanworth says and makes a clicking noise with his throat. "They have to go home at some point. They'll stop poking around then. They won't tell anyone. We have stuff on them."

"Shut up," Ace growls, and there's a loud thwack like he's hit a car door. "It's too late for that." He crunches across the snow toward the front door, Vanworth following behind.

Janie sinks until she's sitting on the ground. "Kill us?" she repeats, her body shivering violently. "We need to get out of here. Now." She pulls her car keys out of her pocket. "Let's leave our stuff and go."

"I'm going back in for the others," I call, already halfway up the path. I fling open the door, the people around me fading into the background, scouring the room for my friends with panic-fueled tunnel vision. Janie rushes past me and links arms with Calista, steering her toward the door and whispering frantically in her ear, and Mrs. Williams stumbles along after them. I wildly gesture at Zoe, who leaves Levi talking to Bradley. "We're in trouble," I splutter. "Is Holly still upstairs?"

Zoe's forehead creases. "Yes. What's going on?"

I shake my head, every muscle in my body has clenched up, and I'm running on adrenaline. "I don't have time to explain. Go to the car. I'll go get Holly."

"No," Zoe says firmly. "I'll go get Holly. I watched her when she went up there with Hector and saw what room she went into. I'll tell Levi we're leaving."

"We don't have time for that," I cry. "You need to believe me. This is urgent."

Zoe's eyes widen, and she takes two clumsy steps backward, her hands shaking at her sides. "Okay, okay. I'll get her fast then."

"We'll be waiting by our cars," I say, my voice raspy. "You need to hurry."

# 33
# Zoe

"Do you really think the videos are good?" I ask eagerly. I want Violet to be so excited with my skills that she scoops me up in a giant hug. I miss my dad. It's been a while since I've had a good hug.

I'm thirteen, and Violet and I sit cross-legged on my bed. I just showed her a clip of Agnes and Clint smoking a joint in the woods, then making out. Agnes stripped down to her bra and panties and Clint was in his boxers, and it would have been rated R if the bullhorn didn't sound from back at camp, scaring their pants back on.

"They're not just good, they're amazing," Violet says with a laugh. "I love the way you zoom in on them. It looked like they were trying to eat each other's faces. If Clint ever threatens to tell on me about sneaking out to see Grayson, I'll march right into

Mrs. Felmont's office and show her that. Ha. That would show him not to mess with me." She pulls out two packages of sour gummy bears from her backpack. "You did so well, you get two packs of candy."

I giggle, take the candy, and put it in my drawer. "Thanks. Maybe I should go into film one day."

"Totally," Violet says. Her phone buzzes, and she looks at the screen eagerly. Her face falls.

"Who is it?" I ask.

Violet sighs. "It's just my cousin, Hector. He wants me to hang out with him on my day off."

"That sounds fun. I wish I had cousins," I say, and my voice sounds sadder and more wistful than I expected it to.

"Hector's great," Violet says, looking up at the ceiling. "We have so much fun together. He makes the best jokes, and he takes me to expensive restaurants, and we order loads of exotic food. Plus, he's a good listener and he'd do anything for me."

"So why did you seem upset he texted?" I ask.

"I wanted to spend my day off with Grayson," Violet says dreamily. "But Hector gets hurt feelings. If I tell him that, he'll be pissed. I haven't seen Hector in a few weeks. When I'm not here I see him almost every day."

"I wish I had someone who wanted to see me every day," I say softly. There's a pang in my stomach, and I bite my lip hard. If I cry right now, it'll be super embarrassing.

Violet wraps her arms around me in a tight hug, and I crumple in her embrace. She rests her lips on the top of my head. "You're awesome, Zoe. Don't forget that. Anyone would be lucky to see you every day."

I press my face against her shoulder and take a shuddery breath.

*Hopefully she can't feel my hot tears through her faded Camp Bell-*
*wood Lake T-shirt. "Thanks," I whisper.*

---

FRIDAY, DECEMBER 31

I charge toward the staircase. Hopefully no one will catch me
going up there and try to stop me. Denise is normally a little on
the anxious side, but this was different. She looked more terrified than she did when she found the note outside my house.
I'm a few yards away from the first step when I hear Levi's deep
voice behind me. "Why did your friends leave so suddenly? Are
they still mad at Bradley?"

"Long story," I say, trying to keep the panic out of my voice.
I give him my best attempt at a calm smile. I think Denise
would have told me if her scary news had anything to do with
Levi. "They think something bad's going to happen and they
want to leave."

"I'm pretty sure no one could get away with doing anything
wrong in this place." Levi laughs, which makes me think that what
Calista said about my expressions giving me away was wrong. If
it were true, Levi would know I'm completely freaking out right
now. "There are too many staff members here for something bad
to happen," he continues. "Including the three bouncers who
kicked your friend's stalker boyfriend out a few minutes ago."

"My friends can be paranoid sometimes, I guess," I say with
a strained laugh. "Anyway, I need to go and grab Holly. She left
her purse with her phone in it on the couch when she went upstairs, and I can't reach her."

"Okay. See you in a minute." He gives me his signature lopsided grin and heads back to Bradley, who's sipping on a glass of red wine and staring in my direction.

I creep up the stairs and stand in front of the door I saw Hector and Holly enter. I open it just a crack. Holly and Hector sit on a couch with their backs to me. Hector holds up his cell phone. "Sorry about that," he says softly. "I had to take that call. My friends just got here." Goose bumps travel up and down my arms. The friends he's talking about may be the reason Denise is freaking out. I need to do something. Fast. I can't just knock and ask Holly to join me. It's too late for that.

"Are you going to tell me yet?" Hector asks, and there's a sharp edge in his voice.

"It was a prank," Holly answers. "I don't want to betray my friends' trust by sharing all of the details." I need to make my move while they're talking and distracted.

I sneak into a half-open closet beside the bedroom door. I have a perfect view of them. Hector spins around as if he can sense my presence. He notices his bedroom door's open and mutters under his breath about guests looking for somewhere to bang. He steps closer to my hiding place, and my breath is coming out so hard that I think he hears it. He stops in his tracks and tilts his head, unblinking. My hand flies to my mouth and I breathe around my fingers as quietly as I can.

Hector snaps out of it, closes the door, and turns the lock. The click of it securing sends shivers down my spine.

Hector opens a small fridge and takes out a bottle of soda. "Would you like rum in your drink?" he asks, as he pours Coke into two tall glasses.

"No, thanks." Holly settles down on the couch and examines her nails. It's shocking that her guard isn't up more. Why is she so trusting of him? I'm supposedly the gullible one but I wouldn't have followed him upstairs in the first place. "I should probably be getting back to my friends now."

Hector fumbles with something on the counter, blocking my view of the drinks. Then he walks across the room and hands Holly a soda. I desperately want to yell out that she shouldn't trust him. She shouldn't take a sip.

"You know something?" he says. "I bet I know all about what Violet and Denise did. Violet used to tell me everything."

Does he know about Farrah? Or is he talking about something else? I'm helpless here. Observing them but not knowing if it's safe for me to intervene. Should I text Levi, tell him to come upstairs? Should I call the police? What if the bad thing Denise wanted to warn me about had nothing to do with Hector? I need to know what's going on before I can decide on my next move. I slip my phone out of my pocket to see a text from Denise:

WHERE ARE YOU? HURRY UP!

I write back:

In Hector's room. He's talking to
Holly. What should I do?

Then I remember there's one thing I've always been good at. I open my video app and tap Record.

# 34
# Calista

It's 10:28 p.m.

Zoe's been inside for fifteen minutes.

She should have been out here by now.

If she's safe in there, that is.

"What the heck is taking them so long?" I hiss to Denise, tapping my foot against the snow-covered concrete. We're huddled outside Janie's car, where Mrs. Williams is slumped over in the front seat beside Janie.

"The last text she sent was the one asking what she should do. I hope she's okay," Denise answers.

Janie rolls down her window, points beside her, and cringes. "This one won't stop repeating that she wants to go home."

"Take me home," Mrs. Williams wails, flailing her hands around wildly. "I want to go home now. Coming here was a mistake."

"What changed her mood?" I whisper. "We didn't even tell her what you overheard."

Janie shrugs. "All of a sudden, a switch flicked. She went from party-girl vibes to wasted and terrified."

"You should take her back to her house. She's making a scene. We'll meet you in a minute," Denise says. She bends forward and gives Janie a kiss. "Don't worry."

"We have Holly's purse and keys," I add. "I'll start her car now, so we'll be ready to leave as soon as they get out."

"Are you sure you guys will be okay?" Janie's eyes crinkle with concern, and creases form between her eyebrows. "If something happened to you, I'd never forgive myself for taking off on you."

"We'll be fine," Denise says. I know she's trying to sound soothing, but there's a tremor in her voice.

I nod and pat the side of her car to give her a hint that it's time to get going. "Denise is right. Plus, all of us hanging around outside by the cars looks suspicious."

Janie gives us one last worried look, then starts driving down the long driveway. Mrs. Williams sticks her head out the passenger-side window and regards us with hollow eyes. "Watch . . . watch out," she slurs.

I fling open Holly's car door and start the ignition. If Holly knew I was in the driver's seat of Red, she'd have a conniption. But all I want is for her to come out here and freak out on me because that will mean she's okay. I turn to see what's taking Denise so long when the back passenger-side door opens. "Why are you getting in the back?" I ask. "Sit up here with me."

Denise slides into the back seat with a ghostly white face. My eyes shift from her contorted expression to the gun pressed into her back. A guy wearing tinted glasses and a hat slides in next to her.

I freeze for a moment, torn between whether to scream or reason with him. He has a gun, and one stupid move could kill us. I snap out of it. "Do you want the car?" I cry, my heart accelerating. "We'll give you the car. Let us go. Please."

The driver's-side door is pulled open, and there's a second gun in my face. "Move over," a guy with a ponytail says in a low, menacing voice.

"But—but—" I stammer.

"Move over or I'll shoot you," he grunts, and his eyes are dark and reckless. I know he'd shoot Denise and me without a second thought, and I'm not going to try him.

"Ace . . ." the guy with the hat says.

"What?" Ace snaps, and his ponytail whips his neck as he swivels to glare at him.

The guy with the hat doesn't respond.

I gulp, my heart pounding, and slowly lift my body up and over the center console into the passenger side, trying to buy some time. Someone has to see us and help. "Where . . . where are you taking us?"

Denise sobs in the back seat. "Please let us go. Please let us go," she repeats, her voice rising.

"Both of you had better shut up," Ace says, turning away from the road to shoot us a warning look. "Or we'll shut you up ourselves."

I remember them now, from Mrs. Williams's house—I thought they were security guards. I don't know if they're connected to Violet and Damien or if this is about something else entirely. I stare out the window so I can keep track of where Ace is taking us. I recognize the cemetery, then the tree-lined streets of Zoe's neighborhood, and the wheels in my head spin frantically. There has to be some way that all of us will be okay. There has to be. I mentally run through the possibilities. 1) Maybe I can make some kind of scene, get their guns somehow. 2) Maybe Zoe or Holly saw the guys get into the car and called for help. 3) Maybe Zoe's dad felt bad and came home early.

Ace zips into Zoe's driveway, and I spot a familiar gray car. A surge of hope rushes up my spine. I doubt anyone's ever been as happy to see Holly's boyfriend as I am right now.

Alex gets out of his car and holds a hand over his eyes to block the glare of the headlights.

"Who the fuck is this?" Ace growls.

I stay silent.

"Tell me who the fuck this is," he repeats, his voice rising.

"My friend's boyfriend," I answer.

The guy with the hat throws open the car door and steps out with his gun trained on Alex. Alex raises his hands and takes a step backward. "Who are you?" he cries. "Where's Holly?"

Ace opens the door to the back seat and gestures for Denise to get out. He tapes her hands behind her back.

"No," she cries. "Please, let me go."

He snarls at her, puts a piece of tape across her lips, then yanks my door open. "Get out," he demands, his gun pointed at my chest. I step out of the car, and he walks behind me to the front door. His gun is still on my back as he picks the lock and pushes the door open. Bark rushes toward me, barking and growling at Ace. "Put that dog outside or I'll kill it," he says in a tone so calm it gives me chills.

I scoop an agitated Bark into my arms and let him out the

back door, desperately hoping that he barks so much out there that a neighbor hears and calls the cops.

"Downstairs," Ace yells, and he pushes the gun into the small of my back again. I trudge to the bottom of the stairs on shaky legs. He takes a roll of tape out of his pocket and tapes my wrists and my ankles together. He pushes me onto a chair and winds the tape around my body.

"Stop," I yell. "Please. Who are you? Why are you doing this?"

He leans into me so that his dark eyes lock on mine and a twisted smile tugs at the corners of his mouth. "You'll find out soon enough," he says and roughly slaps a piece of tape across my mouth.

He walks back up the stairs, and I can make out angry voices and the sounds of Bark in the backyard. "Where's Holly? Is she part of this?" Alex cries from upstairs.

"Shut him up, Vanworth," Ace says.

Alex stumbles down the stairs, tape on his mouth, his hands taped behind his back. Vanworth pulls out another chair, shoves Alex down roughly on it, and ties him up.

Ace rushes down the stairs, his eyes cold and hard. "How did you let the tall girl escape?"

Vanworth shoves Ace across the room, and he crashes into the coffee table with a loud thud. "How did *I* let the girl escape? It's your fault. I thought you were handling the girls while I handled this idiot," he points his gun at Alex.

Ace glowers at him. "The tall girl was your fault. Knowing you, you let her go on purpose. Remember what happened to the last guy who fucked up?"

"You better shut the hell up about that," Vanworth grunts. He adjusts his hat, and a muscle in his jaw twitches.

Hope bubbles in my chest. How did Denise manage to get away with her hands taped behind her back? Hopefully she'll find help.

Ace stands up, brushes back a strand of hair that fell loose from his ponytail and types something into his phone. "She won't make it far with her hands tied together and mouth taped. Our backup's on it."

# 35
# Holly

Hector hands me a soda, and I flash him a smile and take a mouthful. He types something on his phone, and I discreetly spit the drink out over the side of the couch. Because newsflash: I might look like an airhead, but I'm FAR from stupid. Yeah, I followed him to his room, but the alarm bells in my mind hadn't started going off at that point. They started going off when he began asking me questions. I'm obviously aware of the fact that there's a good chance he put something in my drink. And speaking of obvious? I saw a sliver of Zoe's teal phone case moving in the closet. I keep trying to distract Hector so he doesn't notice. Zoe isn't as smooth as she thinks she is. I quickly dump the rest of the drink out into a potted plant.

Hector looks up from his phone. "How are you feeling?" he asks. "You look a little tired."

I flop my head to the side and take a long blink. "I am feeling tired," I say. "Maybe I'll lie down for a minute."

Hector nods. "Absolutely," he says in an overly kind tone. "You can rest as long as you need to. I'll let your friends know you'll be back down in a little bit."

I nod. "Okay," I mumble.

"But first, you think Bradley killed Violet because of Farrah? Right?" Hector asks. "The note Denise wrote. I heard all about that."

My blood freezes. Shit. He does know. Which could mean . . . so many different things. I need to keep playing along. Find the right moment to escape. "Yeah . . ." I murmur, closing my eyes. "Do you think so too?"

"No," Hector says in a cold, distant voice. "I don't."

I lean my head back on the arm of the couch. "I feel so groggy," I whisper. "Maybe I ate too many hors d'oeuvres." Ha. Zoe's probably shitting her pants right now, thinking I've been roofied. I feel bad about that. She's the only one of them who had the foresight to know I might be in trouble.

I open my eyes just a crack to watch Hector pace from the couch to the door. When his back is to me, I raise one hand and wave it several times so Zoe will know I'm okay. Then, I focus on breathing deeply, calmly, so Hector will think I'm out cold. Meanwhile? Every muscle in my body has tensed up and adrenaline is coursing through my veins. What will Hector's next move be? Will Zoe and I manage to make it out of this situation alive?

Hector's phone rings, and he speaks into it. "Yeah, she's out cold. Have you got the others back at the girl's house?" He pauses. "What do you mean you only have one of them? I have one here so two are missing. Find them. I'll meet you there." My heart clenches, and I continue taking long, deep breaths even though I feel like hyperventilating. Which other girl is missing? Zoe's here. Who do they have?

I feel Hector close to me, his breath warm against my neck, then he hoists me up and over his shoulder. I try to keep my body limp as he carries me down the stairs. The dance music pulses, and I open my eyes a crack to see some party guests looking at us with curiosity. "She had too much to drink," Hector says, and honestly? If he didn't just try to drug me, I'd think he sounds compassionate. "I'm going to drive her home."

I consider yelling, screaming that I need help, but everyone at this party might be in on this with him. My mind is already busy making a plan that will work better.

The cold air wraps around me. Where's he taking me? I open my eyes just a slit as he opens the back door of his car and drops me onto the back seat. He turns the ignition and pulls onto the driveway. The timing needs to be perfect. I can't see from this angle whether other cars are on the road. There has to be. I'm desperate. I dig my nails into my palms. Waiting. Waiting. Then I suck in a breath and spring up. Before Hector can react, I slap my hands over his eyes.

"Shit!" he yells and swerves off the road and grinds to a stop. I frantically yank the door handle, but it's locked.

Hector gets out of the car and opens the back door. I'm ready for him, my leg shoots out, kicking him with all the strength I can muster. He staggers backward.

Where the hell is everybody? There are no cars on the road. No one to help. He rushes closer, pushes me down onto the road, and aims his gun at me. He pulls something out of his pocket, and it takes me a second to realize what it is: duct tape. He kneels down and tapes my wrists together. "Help!" I scream. He puts another strip of tape over my mouth and roughly hoists me back into his car.

# 36
# Denise

I sprint down Beech Grove Street past dim houses, moving as fast as I can with my hands taped behind my back. Just my luck that no cars are on the road. Zoe's neighborhood is deserted. My head moves wildly back and forth. I don't think those guys are following me. Not yet anyway.

There's a well-lit house on the other side of the street, and I can see a group of people in their twenties inside. The bass is so strong that the ground vibrates. I will myself to move faster as I shuffle up the driveway. I throw my body against the door with as much force as I can. No one notices. I sidestep to the window and slam into the glass. The music's so loud they don't even glance at me.

I choke back sobs as I run down the driveway and bolt toward the next house. It's only a matter of time until those guys find me.

"Denise?" a voice calls.

I look out to the road where a woman in a black BMW calls to me. It's April.

The tape stifles my words. "Thank God."

April rushes out and opens the door for me. I jump in. She gets back into the driver's seat and leans across the center console to pull the tape off my mouth.

I wince, and one of my taped hands twitch. "Call the police."

Her eyes search mine. "What's happening? What's going on?"

Tears pour down my face. "We need to get help. Call the police. Please. Tell them to go to Zoe's. The others are in trouble."

"Okay," April says and jumps out of the car. I crane my neck to see where she's going. Maybe she doesn't want to panic me by making a police call right next to me. She's trying to keep me calm.

"They're on their way," April assures me when she gets back in the car. "We should go there too."

"It's not safe. The guys will kill us," I cry. "Did you tell the 911 operator that the police need to hurry? They need to hurry."

"I told them," April says, and there's a strange tone in her voice that raises a sea of red flags. Suddenly, I don't trust her.

I shift in my seat with panic. "What's happening? April? Can you free my hands?"

April shakes her head. "I need something to cut the tape with." She turns at the end of the road and starts along Zoe's street.

"Go the other way. Or park here," I scream, struggling to get my hands loose. "Don't drive up there. I'm telling you. You can't. Please believe me."

April faces forward, and a cold, hard expression transforms her face.

"Why aren't you listening to me?" I scream. "Are you in on this sick, twisted shit too? You don't have to do this."

April continues driving until she's right in front of Zoe's bungalow. She leans forward and stretches the tape over my mouth again, and my heart sinks. She's given me my answer. As soon as she parks, Ace is at the passenger side. He flings the door open and carries me inside like I'm a sack of potatoes. I kick to free myself, but it's no use.

April's behind us. "I heard you're sticking your nose where it doesn't belong," she says. "Hector's not going to hurt you, he just wants to scare you. Let you know you're messing with the wrong people."

Ace chuckles like he thinks that's the funniest thing in the world.

"What are you laughing at?" April says, her hands on her hips. "Hector wants to scare her. What's funny about that?"

Ace grunts, opens the front door, and carries me downstairs. Holly, Calista, and Alex are all taped to chairs, duct tape over their mouths. They twist around, struggling to get loose.

Hector walks into the room. He runs a hand through his dark hair and gives each of us a long look. His face lights up when he sees Calista.

Calista turns her neck to face April. "H-help," she splutters, her voice muffled.

"You managed to nearly wear away the tape," Hector says with a laugh. He pulls the tape the rest of the way off her mouth. "Just for that, I'll let you speak."

I don't know how she managed to do that, but I wiggle my lips and try to wet the tape with my saliva. My pulse throbs in my neck.

Calista turns to April. "Help us. You're not like him. You need to help us."

April struts forward and stops in front of Calista. "Hector told me that you were interfering with his operations. He wants to scare you. Me and the guys are going to find Zoe."

"They're not trying to scare us, they're going to kill us," Calista shrieks. "Get help."

April's laugh rings out and sounds menacing in this tense room. "Hector wouldn't hurt you. Anyway, I'm leaving."

"See you later," Hector says, planting a kiss on April's cheek.

"No!" Calista yells. "Don't believe him."

April shakes her head. "I tried to warn you. Hector asked me to leave you notes to get you to back off. If you listened, none of this would have happened."

"How did you know all of our friends' and family members' names? Where we live?" Calista asks.

April shrugs. "Instagram. You guys post all of your business on there. Holly's the most private on that site by the way. I didn't learn a lot from following her."

"You left the note for Violet too," Calista cries. "You knew she was murdered the whole time? You were involved?"

"No," April cries. "Don't be ridiculous. I warned her to back off, just like Hector asked me to. Her death was an accident. A coincidence."

"The police," Calista says. "Are they really corrupt like you said?"

"One of them is. Not sure about the rest. By the way, who's Farrah? Hector thought her name might scare some sense into you."

"She's got nothing to do with this," Calista says, her face twisted in fear.

April shrugs and walks toward the staircase.

"You can't leave us," Calista says in a hoarse voice. "Please."

April rolls her eyes and storms upstairs. Vanworth and Ace trail behind her, leaving us alone with Hector.

Hector paces around the room and laughs. "April, April, April. That bitch doesn't know the half of it. If only Violet could see you now. Her little protégés, so close to meeting the same fate. Who would have guessed?"

# 37

# Zoe

"Where is she?" says a male voice outside of Hector's room. I rush back into the closet just as the door bursts open, and my breath quickens as a guy with a hat hastily checks under the bed, behind the couch, then steps toward my hiding place. Alarm courses through my veins. I hit Record on my phone again, shove it into my pocket, crouch down, and grit my teeth. Ready.

The guy takes a step closer.

I inhale a shaky breath.

*Keep it together, Zoe. You have to keep it together.*

The guy pushes the sliding door open, and my fists fly straight into his testicles. He lurches backward into a shelf with a low groan.

I take the opportunity to sprint out of the room toward the staircase. A guy with a scraggly ponytail lunges forward and grabs me. I yelp and thrash around, trying to free myself. He pulls a gun out of his waistband and presses it into my side. "Make another noise, and I'll shoot," he whispers. "We're moving toward the door. Act like we're together and everything's normal. Got it?"

"Y-yep," I whisper. What other choice do I have at this point?

We step down the staircase, and with every second, I'm painfully aware of the barrel of his gun digging into my hip. My pulse races, and my mouth is bone dry. Several guests are gathered at the bottom of the stairs, speaking in loud voices above the blaring pop music. I scan the room for Levi and Bradley. They're in the kitchen. If I yelled their names, they'd look up. They'd see me. But I'd be shot. I don't make a noise, but I let myself look as terrified as I feel. Hopefully someone notices that—or the fact that a teenager is leaving a party with a man who looks at least twenty-eight—and realizes I'm in trouble. But they don't.

The guy leads me down the hallway and out the front door into the bitter wind. My body shakes—partly from the cold and partly because I've never been more terrified. He opens the door of a black car. "Get in," he grunts. I climb into the back seat, and he slides in next to me and takes out a roll of duct tape and a pair of snips. He roughly tapes my wrists together. I remember my video recording—which hopefully I'll stay alive long enough to share. "Why are you doing this? Where are you taking me?" I ask.

"You're going to have to wait and see," he says in a sarcastic tone. He snips off a piece of tape and pulls it across my lips.

The guy with the hat gets into the driver's seat, mumbling under his breath. "She punched me in the nuts," he growls, shooting me a menacing look in the rearview mirror that makes my insides clench up.

The guy with the ponytail snorts. "Hector will get her back. And then some."

We pass rows of houses, the cemetery, then we're in my neighborhood. They're taking me home. My stomach twists in knots. Who knows what kind of bad situation is waiting for me? Hopefully one of the others managed to get help.

Hat Guy pulls onto my driveway and parks between a Range Rover that must belong to Hector and a gray car I immediately recognize as Alex's. How did Alex get involved in this? Bark's yipping in the backyard, and my heart soars into my throat. Thank God he's alive. Hopefully everyone else is. Ponytail opens the car door and hoists me out. Hat Guy hurls the front door open, and Ponytail carries me inside and down into the basement. I scan the room in a panic. Calista, Holly, Denise, and Alex sit taped to my old wooden chairs, writhing around.

Ponytail drops me onto a chair, and Hector strides toward us. "Go help April with Janie and Tina," he barks at the two guys. "Wait for my instructions about what to do with them."

April? She's involved in this too? I should have known.

The two men nod and rush upstairs. I quickly swing around, looking for something to cut the tape with, but nothing. There has to be a way out of this. There has to be.

Hector paces the room. The smile on his face is giving me the creeps. He takes the prayer card from the funeral out of his pocket and kisses Violet's photo.

Denise squirms until she falls over, splayed out on the floor, the tape still loosely around her middle. She narrows her eyes.

Hector glares at her. "Do you have something to say?"

Denise nods her head wildly.

Hector whips the tape off her mouth and she grimaces. "Go ahead. What is it?"

"You kill Violet, then you kiss her picture?"

"So what if I kiss her?" Hector barks. "She wasn't even my actual cousin. Her mom cheated on her dad. There's no blood relationship. I showed her proof. Took care of everyone who was bad for her. I tried to tell her how perfect we'd be together, but she didn't get it." He sighs and his lip twitches like it's about to give way to a smile. "And now? Now she's dead."

Denise shakes her head at him. "How could you?"

Hector laughs coldly. "You're just as bad. You wrote the note that led Farrah to me. Violet hated her, and I took care of her. You and me are quite a team."

Denise lets out a sob and wraps her arms around herself, rocking back and forth.

I swallow hard. That's what he meant by all the people he thought were bad for her. He killed Farrah, Grayson, Damien, and Violet herself when she rejected him. How could anyone be so sick? What a monster.

"Let us go!" Denise yells.

Hector smirks, pacing from the stairs to the far wall and back, passing the roll of duct tape from hand to hand. "You did this to yourself. You couldn't just leave everything alone? You needed to hunt and investigate, involve people."

"Did Violet kill people too?" Denise croaks.

Hector's jaw clenches. "No. She just made them wish they were dead."

Alex moves back and forth in a panic. "Mmh. Mmh," his muffled voice grunts.

Hector rips off his tape and grins as Alex flinches in pain. "I'd like to hear what the stalker boy thinks about all of this. I bet you're impressed."

"Let us go," Alex shouts, his dark hair sweaty and slick against his forehead. "If you do, I swear on my life I won't say anything."

"No deal," Hector says with a laugh. "Good try though."

"What if you just let *me* go then?" Alex says, his eyes bulging so much they look like they'll shoot out of his face. "I didn't do anything wrong. I just got here."

"Did anyone ever tell you you're a real winner?" Hector smirks. "Soon you'll be a dead winner."

Alex glares at Holly, a vein in his neck pulsing. "See, you should have listened to me. You should have stayed home. You got entangled with the wrong people here, just like I told you." What the hell, buddy? Bad timing on the insults. Terrible timing, really.

Hector pulls off Holly's tape. "What do you have to say about that, Barbie?"

Holly whips around to face Alex. "My friends are not the wrong people. We don't deserve to be connected with these murderers."

She turns to Hector. "The guy with the hat. I thought I recognized him. Violet got me to talk to him in the bar a few weeks ago. I asked him about Grayson."

"Oh, I know," Hector says. "Violet was trying every tactic she could think of."

"You were involved in this a few weeks ago as well?" Alex cries. "You left me twice for *this*?" His nostrils flare. "And where's the necklace I gave you? You're not wearing it anymore?"

Holly's cheeks redden, and she lets out a loud rush of breath. "What. The. Fuck? We're going to be murdered and you're asking me about a stupid necklace? Unbelievable."

Hector raises his eyebrows. "I'll be glad to shut those two up again." He pulls my tape off. "Do you have any last words?"

"Don't . . . don't do this," I say, and my voice sounds small and squeaky, trembling with fear. I think of the phone in my pocket, recording every second of this conversation. "The bones in the woods. Are they Grayson's?"

Hector rubs his chin, and one corner of his mouth climbs upward. "Maybe. Maybe not."

Holly clears her throat. "What do you mean by that?"

"I mean I'm not telling you," Hector snaps, and there's a coldness in his eyes that looks too evil to be human. So evil that he killed four people. Now he wants to kill us too. There's a way out of this. There has to be a way out of this. "That's enough questions," Hector growls. "Time for this to end."

# 38
# Calista

FRIDAY, DECEMBER 31

My eyes skip around the room to rest on the clock above the TV.

11:37 p.m. I swallow a sob. A few hours ago, I was freaking out about getting home for a party, and now I don't think I'll ever go home again at all.

How are the police not here yet? Mrs. Williams and Janie must have realized we're taking too long and called them. If they couldn't find us at Violet's relatives' house, the obvious next place to look is here.

Hector's bounding up the basement stairs. God knows what he's planning.

"Wait," Denise cries.

Hector sighs and turns to look at her. "What do you want?"

Denise gives him a small smile. "She wouldn't want you to do this," she says softly. "Violet cared about you. She used to talk about you all the time. We knew Violet well. We can tell you everything you want to know about how much she loved you."

I perk up. She's trying to buy us more time. Smart. "Yeah," I add, unable to keep the trembling out of my voice. "Before you kill us you should hear us out."

Hector inches closer to Denise with a faraway look in his eyes. His upper lip twitches as he runs a hand across her cheek and through her hair. She flinches. Ew. My skin's crawling just watching that.

"What do you have to say?" Hector asks.

"She'd look forward to your phone calls," Denise begins. "Every time you'd call, she'd be so excited, she'd light up . . ." She continues talking, and I concentrate on making a plan. Violet's pocketknife is still in my purse. If I can only move across the room to where I dropped it, I can cut the tape.

"And she wouldn't want you to do this to us," Denise repeats soothingly. "She cared about us."

"Wrong," Hector shouts. "She only cared about herself." He bolts up the stairs, and the front door slams.

"Where's he going?" Zoe cries. "Do you think he's leaving?"

"I doubt it," I say. "But we don't have much time." I heave in a breath and lunge my chair forward. The tape's looser with all the moving I've done. I take a deep breath and topple my chair. I land sideways on the carpet with a thud. Pain shoots through my side, and I wince.

But there's no time for crying.

"Calista, what can I do?" Holly asks. She jumps her chair closer to me.

I crane my neck to look behind me. "Slide my purse over."

Holly moves forward and pushes my bag toward me with

her boot. Behind my back, I feel around in my purse, touching my wallet, my phone, and then Violet's pocketknife.

"Careful! Don't cut yourself," Holly cries.

I open the blade.

"Tilt it up," Holly instructs.

I carefully angle it upward.

"You're getting it. You're getting it," she gasps.

I hear the front door open and a cupboard door slam.

I carefully saw the tape binding my wrists. When it comes loose, I spread my arms apart in one violent movement, clutching the knife for dear life. My hand shakes as I slice the tape around my body and between my ankles. It breaks open. I'm free. "Yes," I croak. My heart's in my throat as I sprint around the room, cutting through the others' tape. "Don't get up," I bark, adrenaline charging through me. "Hold the tape around your body from the back like you're still stuck."

Hector's heavy footsteps pound against the ceiling. He'll be back down at any second.

Denise's eyes meet mine, her face paper white. "What's the plan?"

"Wait until I tell you to get up," I say. If they don't listen, we're all goners.

Alex glares at me, and his nostrils flare. "Hell no. I'm getting out of here. Forget the plan."

"Trust her," Holly snaps. "If you don't, you'll die. Believe me."

Alex frowns, but he sits on the chair holding the tape around him anyway.

The door creaks open. I dive back onto my chair, pull the tape across my stomach, and grip the ends behind my back. Hector runs down the stairs holding a large bottle of rum. His hateful glare pierces through us. "Here's the story. Some girls get together for their camp counselor's funeral. They stay at one of the girls' houses and no parents are home. They drink a lot." Hector splatters the bottle of amber liquid until it's pooling on the carpet. "They smoke a lot." He takes a cigarette package out of his pocket, opens the window, and tosses it outside. "And then they get so drunk that they accidentally set the house on fire. All of them gone. Poof."

Zoe shudders. "Don't you think the police will think it's suspicious? All of these so-called accidental deaths?"

"Violet was known to have reckless friends. You've met some of them. An out-of-control party on New Year's Eve is totally believable." Hector holds up a box of matches and smirks. "All set."

"You don't have to do this," Holly says in a smooth voice. "Let's figure something else out."

"You all should have minded your own business," Hector growls. He nods his head at Holly. "Especially you." He strikes a match and tosses it in the puddle of rum. Flames climb higher and higher.

We need to get out of here. Fast.

"That's the basement taken care of. Now, for the rest of the house." Hector turns toward the staircase and calmly ambles upstairs. The door swings closed behind him.

"Go," I shout, and we all spring to our feet, rushing upstairs as everything—boxes, sleeping bags, and suitcases—catch on fire. "Where's your extinguisher?" I yell at Zoe.

"In the kitchen," she cries.

We open the basement door to see Hector by the front door with his back to us, pouring more rum on the carpet. He lights a match, tosses it, and red-and-orange flames blaze.

Zoe sprints into the kitchen and comes out spraying, Holly on one side of her and Denise and I on the other. Alex crouches behind the couch like a coward. Hector lunges at Zoe, and Holly kicks his thigh, sending him stumbling. Zoe holds the extinguisher up and bashes it down on his head.

"You bitch," he yells. His hands fly to cover his face.

"No, you bitch," she shouts, bringing the extinguisher back down on his head with a crack. His eyes roll back and close, and he drops to his knees.

I reach into his back pocket for the duct tape and quickly bind his wrists and ankles together while he's still out cold.

Alex jumps up and sprints through the flames and out the front door without looking back. Seriously? Holly sure knows how to pick them.

The blare of a siren sounds in the distance. I'm not about to wait around. I grab the extinguisher from Zoe and spray the living room, then I open the basement door, stand on the top stair, and spray below. The fire's not out, but it isn't as bad.

The front door swings open, and at first I think it's Alex, back to tell us to get out. But it's not. Ace and Vanworth barge inside. "Hell no," Holly yells and sprints into the kitchen.

The guys see Hector on the ground tied up, dark smoke rising around him. Ace reaches in his waistband for his gun. Holly runs up behind him and brings a large brass pot down on his head. He falls forward. Zoe throws herself down onto his back and snatches his gun. "Get off me," he shouts.

She presses the gun into his spine. "Move and I'll shoot," she breathes. "Sound familiar?"

Vanworth reaches for his gun, but before he can draw it, I spray his face with a blast of the extinguisher's white foam. He yelps, and his hands fly to his eyes. Holly cracks the pot down over his head. Denise grabs the extinguisher from me and shoots him in the face again; then she crashes it down on his head.

Wow. I didn't think she had that in her.

Once he's down, I bind each of their ankles and wrists together. The three men lie face down on the carpet.

"We did it," Denise says. She drops the extinguisher on the floor with a clunk and drapes her arms around Holly and Zoe, and Zoe pulls me into the group hug—all of us jumping up and down. "We did it," Denise says again. "On our own."

The door opens again, and a group of firefighters steps into the foyer. They gaze around the room with bewildered expressions.

Zoe points at Hector and his guys, still unconscious on the carpet. "They killed people. Are there cops here? They need to be arrested."

The firefighters spring into action. Some of them spray the smoldering flames, several hoist the men toward the door, and the others barge downstairs. "What are you still doing in here?" one firefighter yells. "There's too much smoke. Get out." His hand's on my back, shoving me outside. The others hurtle through the doorway behind me, coughing.

# 39
# Holly

Zoe's front yard is a chaotic zoo with a fire truck on her driveway, two ambulances at the end of it, and police cars blocking the street. A crowd of people gathers on the edge of the lawn, gawking at us. They move to let the paramedics get through with their stretchers.

"We're taking you to the hospital," a paramedic with short curly hair tells us. She presses her hand against my forearm. "Lie down. We need to check your vitals."

Janie runs down the driveway, tears streaming down her face, and she pulls Denise into a tight hug. "I'm so glad you're okay."

An officer opens the back gate, and Bark bounds out of the backyard, sprinting toward Zoe, his tongue hanging out. She scoops him up in her arms, and he licks her dirty face. She gives the paramedic trying to get her to lie on a stretcher a determined look. "I'm not going to the hospital. I have to stay with him."

"I'll bring him back to my house," Janie says soothingly, dabbing her tears with the back of her hand. "Come over as soon as you're released."

The paramedics push my stretcher up the ramp, into the ambulance, followed by Zoe's. Calista and Denise are put into the other one, Calista mumbling about how she's fine and really just needs to get home. The siren wails as it lurches forward with a jolt, and Zoe yelps. The paramedic rests her hand against Zoe's forehead. "You're going to be okay."

"I have footage. I recorded stuff on my phone. Stuff—stuff Hector said," she stammers. Her eyes are red, and her face is covered with black soot. She looks rough, but I'm sure I look just as terrible.

"I'll let the police know and they'll take your phone for evidence once we get you to the hospital. You can rest now."

I stare at the roof of the ambulance, and honestly? I have to blink back the tears. I could have been dead. We all could have.

"It's time for the countdown." The paramedic beside me points at her watch and gives the paramedic with Zoe a small smile. I expected to ring in the new year with Alex, probably watching a movie, my mom working as usual. I never expected to be driving in the back of an ambulance with a camp friend I didn't think I'd see again. But full disclosure: After all we've been through this week, the girls feel like so much more than camp friends.

"I'm sure this isn't the New Year's celebration you wanted," the paramedic says as though she can hear my thoughts. She hovers over me and rests her hand on my forearm. She holds her other arm close to her face and stares at her watch. "Ten, nine, eight, seven, six, five," she chants along with the other paramedic.

"Four, three, two, one," we say in unison. The paramedic

smiles down at me. "Happy New Year." She gives the other paramedic a quick hug and then pats my arm.

---

We've got the all clear, only minor bruises, and we're on our way out of the hospital, ready to head to the police station. Our parents have been called and will have arrived by the time we get there, probably all panicking and completely losing their shit. We're walking through the waiting room when the news show playing on the TV says a name that makes us stop in our tracks.

We huddle together to hear the story.

A female reporter wearing a red pantsuit stands on the sidewalk in front of a small brick bungalow and stares into the camera. And then she says the name again, sending chills running up my spine.

"Grayson Dante, who has been missing for the last four years and presumed dead, has been discovered. Police searched the premises of Hector Williams, Alvin 'Ace' Burski, and John Vanworth following their arrests in connection to the deaths of Hector's cousin, Violet Williams, and of Damien Terrance, the aforementioned victim's boyfriend. The police discovered an underground bunker on Vanworth's property, where Grayson has been held captive for the last four years. Williams and Burski were allegedly unaware of this and assumed Dante was dead. Vanworth stated that kidnapping and holding Dante captive was to protect him and that he'd 'never wanted to get in so deep' and had 'no intention of hurting Dante.' Police investigations are still proceeding, and anyone with additional information is urged to come forward."

I rub my temples. The headache I've had since the fire just set into overdrive. My mind's been completely blown.

"I knew Vanworth was the nicer one," Denise breathes. "I'm pretty sure he let me escape on purpose."

I make a face. "None of those sickos were nice."

Zoe's arms are crossed tightly around her body. "I can't believe this. After all of this time, Grayson's . . . alive?"

We whirl around to look at each other, our eyes bugging out of our heads. To say that we have questions is the understatement of the century.

# 40

# Denise

*I'm thirteen years old. I rest my head on Violet's lap, and she combs her fingers through my hair rhythmically. The other girls are at the campfire. I slipped away thinking no one noticed, but Violet did. She followed me back to the cabin. "Grayson used to do this for me, every time I was sad," she says. "What's bugging you?"*

*"Summer's almost over," I whisper, turning my head slightly to look up at her. "I'm going to miss you."*

*"Oh, Denise," Violet murmurs. "Sit up for a second."*

*I rise obediently, and she cups my chin in her palm and stares into my eyes. "You don't need to miss me because I'll always be around. Our cabin's connected now. Through all of our secrets. Like a family."*

*"Really?" I ask, blinking quickly because there's a tingle in my eyes and this doesn't feel like the right time to cry.*

*"You know who else is around?" Violet's blue eyes harden with a surge of intensity. "Grayson's around."*

*"I know," I whisper. "And he's okay."*

*"We have a bond I cannot even explain to you in words, Denise." Violet's wavering voice rises and cracks. "Even if I tried. And I know he's alive. I can feel it. Whoever took him . . . if they killed him, I'd feel it. Here." She jabs me in the chest, then cradles her hand against her abdomen, her chin trembling. "And the only thing I feel is pissed off. Very pissed off."*

*I nod. Violet's face is contorted in anger. She frightens me when she's mad like this.*

*"Are you going to help me find him, Denise?"*

*I nod again. "I will," I say firmly. "I'll do whatever I can."*

*"You'd better," Violet says, her eyes widening as her anger gives way to desperation. "I'm counting on you."*

———

SATURDAY, JULY 9

"And this is my favorite part," Grayson says, gesturing at the long cedar dock over the sparkling water.

The girls and I have just arrived at Grayson's new trailer, across the lake from Camp Bellwood, and it might not be the oceanfront home of Violet's dreams, but there's no doubt about the fact that it's nice.

Grayson stares back at it. It's cream-colored and pretty new, surrounded by trees and purple flowers—Violet's favorite. He passes each of us a beige folding chair and brushes his wavy brown hair out of his eyes. "What do you think?" he asks, looking at us hopefully.

I open the chair and sit facing the calm water. "It's great."

"Yeah," Zoe agrees. She's wearing a Metallica T-shirt and jean cutoffs, and her bare arms and legs are already slightly sunburned.

Grayson grins. "You really think so?"

"Absolutely. It's so peaceful," Holly says, and she's right. The sky is a cloudless blue, and there are no sounds besides the chirp of a bird or two every so often. It reminds me of quiet mornings at Camp Bellwood Lake before Grayson disappeared and when Violet was still happy. Holly tucks a strand of blond hair behind her ear and picks at a thread hanging from the bottom of her jean capris. She's wearing a white T-shirt and light makeup—back to looking like the girl next door—her style has definitely changed since our last meeting. She peers down at the lake, then sits on the dock, slips her sandals off, and dips her feet in the water for just a second before she flinches and pulls them back. "Shit. It's colder than I remember."

"Violet would love it here," Calista adds, straightening the straps of her blue pleated sundress.

Grayson makes a little sound in his throat like he wanted to say something but stopped himself. "Yeah," he finally whispers, a look of sadness flitting across his face. In the few times I've seen him over the last months, I've noticed he mainly looks this way, but sometimes there's fury in his eyes, and if I'm being honest, I get the feeling that the next stage will be anger. Hector killed the woman he loved. I wouldn't be surprised if one day Grayson wants revenge.

Regardless, I can't get over how much healthier he looks compared to how he appeared in the news interviews after he was discovered—thin, pale, and disheveled. He's got his ruddy, outdoorsy complexion back now, looking tanned in his white golf shirt and khaki shorts. He lets out a small sigh and skips a rock across the water. "Violet would have loved that we're all together." His voice cracks, and I reach across Zoe to pat his hand. "I'll be back in a sec," he murmurs, then turns and heads toward the trailer.

He's told us everything. How many times he tried to escape during those four years. How many times Vanworth tried to convince him that it was for his own good. The story is that Hector asked Vanworth to drown Grayson in the lake, but Vanworth couldn't bring himself to do it—the same way he couldn't bring himself to carry me downstairs to Hector. Vanworth is not a killer like the other two. He kept Grayson alive all these years because he knew Hector would kill both of them if he found out. Police confirmed that the person buried at camp was one of Hector's guys who supposedly failed a job. During questioning, Vanworth told the police about Farrah. Thankfully, and honestly very strangely, none of them mentioned my note. Hector, Vanworth, and Ace are in jail. Hopefully for a long time.

Now, as hard as it is to move on after our worlds were completely blown up because of them, we have to.

I look back at my orange car parked on the dirt road by the trailer and shiver excitedly. *That's mine. That's what progress looks like for me.* Zoe catches me and smiles.

"It's awesome you're driving now. I thought you didn't want your license because of what happened to . . ." She trails off.

I shake my head. "I need my license now that I'm seeing Janie. I didn't want her to always have to do the driving." My face is hot, and I pat it with the back of my hand. Talking about Janie still does that to me.

"That's awesome," Holly says and makes another short attempt to dip her feet in the lake. "Ugh, that's way too cold to be enjoyable. It's July. You'd think the sun would have warmed it up by now."

"How's stuff with you?" I ask, really hoping she hasn't gotten back with Alex since we last talked.

Holly shoots me a sparkling white smile. "I'm taking some time out from relationships to be my own boss. It's going well."

"Nice," Calista answers and taps her foot, looking like she's eager to share her news as well. I open my mouth to ask how she's doing, but she starts talking before I have the chance. "Well, I'm still busy interning at the law office. Mr. Molina— Mateo—is amazing. I'm learning so much from him. I know now more than ever this is what I want to do. Hopefully they hire me full-time after I'm finished with school."

"I take it your parents are over you missing Nochevieja?" Holly asks dryly.

Calista raises her eyebrows. "Are you kidding me? They think we're crime-solving stars. They're so proud." She turns to look at each of us. "What about everyone else? Excited for college?" She glances at Zoe and flinches. "Or whatever else you have planned that's not an overly expensive waste of time?"

"Well . . . I left this piece of news until we met in person," Zoe says dramatically. She leans forward and taps her fingers against the dock like a drumroll, her entire face lighting up. "I'm going to college too. Turns out Dad was setting aside some money for me, and I've been working at Rise and Shine to earn the rest." She pauses and tugs on one of her hoop earrings, happily taking in Calista's growing smile. "I'm majoring in film at the community college here. We had this awkward conversation after you talked to me about the loan options. He was all shy about it and he was like, 'I had the money just in case. I didn't think you wanted to go, and I didn't want to make you feel like I expected you to.'"

"That's amazing," Calista gushes, beaming like this is the best news she's heard in weeks. Zoe's finally Team Higher Education.

"What about Levi?" Holly asks. "Last I heard you were still talking. Are you still a thing?"

"We are." Zoe waggles her eyebrows in her usual silly way. "We'll see what happens. You'll see him later. Bradley too."

"Oh, really?" I frown. *That doesn't sound like my idea of fun.* Holly apologized to Bradley for yelling at him, and we learned from asking a few pointed questions that he doesn't seem to know about the note. The girls convinced me to stop feeling guilty about it. My intention was for Farrah to go to the woods and be scared, not for her to die. I'm not the sicko who murdered her. Telling anyone won't bring her back, Janie's been telling me. It would only bring more bad feelings to people who've finally found their closure.

Zoe gets up and walks over to the rocky section at the start of the dock. She leans down to pick up a stone and tosses it into the lake. Instead of skipping across the water, it immediately sinks. "Since the trial ended, Bradley's been a lot . . . nicer. I was going to surprise you guys, but after we leave here, he wants to show us what he's done so far at Camp Bellwood Lake. He took out a loan and has started renovating it. He said Farrah always loved it there and one day he's going to reopen it in her honor."

Calista cringes. "Seriously? Isn't that a bad idea? Don't you think parents of prospective campers will be kind of turned off, knowing a girl was killed there and someone else was buried?"

"Maybe." Zoe's lips stretch into a thin line. "He says he's going to hold off opening it until the attention dies down."

Grayson comes up from behind us, sits on his chair, and holds out a package of sparklers. "I was thinking we could light these, share some memories of Violet."

The others nod in agreement.

I want to tell them how I've developed a slight fear of fire, but this is supposed to be a bonding moment so I suck it up and let Grayson hand us each a lit sparkler. The girls and I wave them around. I write Janie's name in the air as it sizzles to a stop.

Grayson clears his throat, and his brow knits together. "I still can't get over that this happened to her. She would never hurt a soul. Besides trusting her evil cousin, she never made a mistake in her life."

I feel my cheeks redden and sneak a peek at the others. Holly chews on her lip, Calista twists her charm bracelet around her wrist, and Zoe's eye twitches. We're probably all thinking the same thing. Let Grayson remember Violet the way he does. She deeply screwed up each of our lives, but knowing that won't help him deal with her loss.

Later this afternoon we'll be back at the place we first met, a full-circle moment. And with Hector behind bars, it will be a beautiful place again, the way it was when we first started going there—not the deadly place it became.

———

I drive us there, pausing to look at the new Camp Bellwood Lake sign before turning down the path—it's larger, with black cursive letters. "Fancy, fancy," Holly says.

The Felmonts' house has been renovated, with a new gate and a metal roof. We park in the driveway beside Levi's Civic, and a few seconds later, Levi and Bradley step out from the backyard. The first thing I notice is that Bradley's clean-shaven and looks relaxed for a change. Like a new man. Levi's wearing a tank top and jeans, and Zoe's eyes light up when they rest on his tanned biceps. After he greets her with a kiss, she turns to shoot us a goofy grin and mouths the words *hubba, hubba*. Calista shakes her head, and I stifle a laugh.

Bradley steps forward, and we exchange shocked looks as he gives each of us a hug—I'm last. After he lets go, he lingers in front of me, and even though he's smiling, goose bumps rise up and down my arms. "Good to see you. You're not looking scared of me like you were the last time I saw you," he says, meeting my gaze with a glint in his eyes. "I've got so much to show you. The water's warm today. Farrah would have loved it. It's a beautiful day for a swim."

# Acknowledgments

One night in January 2021, I turned to my husband and said, "This is my year. I'm going to write something and get a book deal. Mark my words." The next morning, I woke up to discover that Brendan Deneen, who was then the president of literary and IP development at Assemble Media, had followed me on Twitter. My agent, Emmy Nordstrom Higdon, had sent him some of my short stories a few months prior. Emmy emailed me an hour later and told me that Brendan wanted to set up a meeting with me.

After several conversations, Brendan approached me with a concept: a novel about four friends who drifted apart after years of going to summer camp together. They are reunited at their former counselor's funeral, suspect her so-called accidental death was murder, and decide to investigate. As a huge fan of thrillers, I knew this plot was right up my alley. Brendan and Assemble Media hired me to write the first fifty pages.

Several months later, when Brendan moved to Blackstone Publishing as director of media, TV, and film, he acquired the book, and my authorly dreams came true: I got to write the rest of it.

I'd recently moved to a small town, and the world was in the midst of the COVID-19 pandemic. Diving into Zoe, Calista, Holly, and Denise's story on a daily basis was an exciting escape, and the gratitude I felt was overwhelming.

I would like to sincerely thank my agent, Emmy Nordstrom Higdon, for choosing to represent me, for believing in me, and for giving me so many awesome opportunities.

Thank you, Brendan Deneen, for being such a phenomenal editor, mentor, and person. Our collaboration, emailing back and forth about all the plot points, was an incredible creative experience. You changed everything for me, and I'll be eternally grateful.

Thank you to Assemble Media's founder, director, and producer, Jack Heller, along with Caitlin de Lisser-Ellen, Madison Wolk, and Steven Salpeter, for your expertise throughout this project. I feel so fortunate that you chose me for this opportunity.

Thank you to everyone at Blackstone Publishing for guiding this book through the editorial and production process, including Caitlin Vander Meulen, Megan Bixler, Ananda Finwall, Stephanie Stanton, and Josie Woodbridge. Thank you to the talented Sarah Riedlinger for designing the most perfect cover I could imagine. It's everything I could want and more.

Thank you to Bronwyn Clark and Lacee Little for choosing

to mentor me in Pitch Wars. That experience taught me so much about writing and opened so many doors for me.

Many thanks to Leah Rose Kessler, who was there for me right from the day I first began writing this. Thank you for your wisdom, advice, words of encouragement, and attention to detail. I am truly grateful for you.

To the Mid-May Writers: our group has always kept me motivated, and I care about you all and wish you happiness and success.

To Melinda Chaves: thank you for reading this and for all your advice, encouragement, and support.

To Marta, my elementary school partner in crime: thank you for reading my work, giving me tips, and letting me bounce ideas off you.

Thank you to Erica Kenny, Cristina Spizzirri, Michelle Wallace, Luke Vandermeer, and Sarah Newton for being early readers, and for your feedback, and to Heather Vandermeer for taking my author photo.

Thank you to all the teachers who encouraged me over the years, including Peter Yan, my ninth-grade English teacher, who was one of the first people to see me as a writer.

To my grade 8 and grade 7/8 students at St. Stephen: thank you for your encouragement while I wrote this, and to Abby, Emily, and Kate for being early beta readers.

Thank you to my supportive friends and family, including James Hoy and Jenn Woyce, my awesome brother and sister-in-law—thank you for always pumping me up and being there to give me advice.

Thank you to my mother, Dianne Hoy, for your love and guidance, and for being my biggest supporter, talking to me about all things books on a daily basis. Thank you to my father, James Hoy, for being so caring and encouraging. You are the most incredible parents.

And to my children, Liona and Everett, and husband, Jimmy Kenny: thank you for being proud of me and for inspiring me every day.